Untouchable

Brenda Adcock

Yellow Rose Books
by Regal Crest

Tennessee

ISBN 978-1-61929-210-9

First Printing 2016

9 8 7 6 5 4 3 2 1

Cover design by AcornGraphics

Published by:

Regal Crest Enterprises
1042 Mount Lebanon Road
Maryville, TN 37804

Find us on the World Wide Web at
http://www.regalcrest.biz

Published in the United States of America

Acknowledgments

The past couple of years have been difficult for me as I adjust to my new reality. Continuing to write keeps me on a relatively even keel, but I feel like a beginner again. I am grateful for those who continue to encourage me and lift my spirits on a regular basis. I will always cherish that gift.

My editor, Patty Schramm, is my hero. Her patience, even when dealing with her own personal problems, has been consistent and unwavering. There will never be a way to thank her for everything she does for me. My publisher, Cathy Bryerose, is so much more than that. She is a friend, who was willing to take a chance on my first book, and continues to be supportive.

I have to also thank my friend, Devi Powers, someone who lifts me up virtually every day even though she may not realize how much she does. And, of course, there is my partner, Cheryl. She has seen me at my worst and, after almost twenty years together, is still here. She is a phenomenal woman who still loves me, flaws and all.

Lastly, I have to thank my readers. I would be nothing without you and your support. I hope to continue to improve and write stories you will enjoy reading. I owe you that for everything you've given me over the years. It was more than I ever envisioned. Thank you.

Dedication

For Cheryl, for always. I love you.

Chapter One

September, 1989
Overland University, Middleton, Ohio

RAMIE SUNDERLUND PAUSED on the second floor landing of her dormitory, once again wishing she had enough money to afford a dorm with an elevator. She readjusted her grip on the old IBM Selectric typewriter her parents had given her when she started university, then grunted trying to get her hands in a more comfortable position. The damn thing must weigh a hundred frickin' pounds. She rested the back of the monster machine against the railing and used one hand to quickly brush strands of her curly blonde hair off her face.

"Ramie!" Leslie Maddsen's, voice, echoed down the stairwell. "Phone call! It's a gu-uy!"

"Take a number and I'll call whoever it is back!"

The sound of footsteps pounding up the bare wooden steps of the old dorm made Ramie tighten her grip on the old typewriter.

"What's up, Ramie?" a cheerful voice asked.

Ramie looked up in time to see the powerful legs of Donna Westin, who lived down the hall from her and was a member of the women's wrestling team, nimbly run up the stairs.

"Hey Donna! I'll pay you to carry this thing to my room," Ramie said.

"Sure. No problem," Donna agreed, turning around to bounce down the steps again.

A few minutes later the cheerful brunette breezed through the doorway, carrying the monster as if it were a feather and deposited it on the desk Leslie shared with Ramie. A minute later Ramie stopped and leaned against the door frame, gasping for breath. Loose strands of curly hair fell over her forehead again and she blew them out of the way. At only twenty she felt like she was ancient. At least thirty. "Thanks, Donna," she panted. She turned her attention to Leslie. "Remind me again why I ever agreed to move into Quasimoto's bell tower with you." She rummaged around the desktop. "God! I need a cigarette."

"You're here because you love me...and we don't have to share a bathroom with forty other girls, most of whom not even you are desperate enough to want to see naked," Leslie answered as she threw her arm around Ramie's neck and kissed her sloppily on the temple. She pulled a cigarette from her pocket and handed it to her.

"Yuck!" Ramie squawked, wiping her temple with the palm of her hand.

"Hey! You guys together now?" Donna asked with a grin.

"No!" they answered in unison.

Ramie looked around the assorted stacks that covered the bottom bunk, part of the floor, and the top of the desk and shook her head. "Who knew we had so much crap? Glad I have the top bunk." She climbed up to her bunk and collapsed onto the thin mattress, sucking in a lungful of smoke and exhaling contentedly. "Who called?" she mumbled.

Leslie shrugged. "Some guy who said he needed to speak to you like *muy* pronto."

"About what?"

"Didn't say. His number's on the wall next to the phone."

Donna left a few minutes later to get ready for wrestling practice and Ramie finally worked up the energy to slither over the side of her bunk. She went to the phone and stared at the wall. "Which number? There's twenty numbers here," she frowned.

Leslie joined her and ran a finger over the numbers. She finally tapped one. "This one. I think."

"You think?"

"It looks newer than the others." Leslie shrugged.

"I hope your mother sent her usual back-to-school gift," Ramie said. "I could definitely use a drink about now."

Leslie closed and locked the door to their room and ducked into the bathroom. Emerging a moment later with a fifth of Jack Daniels she held it up triumphantly.

"You have the coolest mother," Ramie declared with a huge smile as she dialed the number on the black wall phone and slid down the wall to sit as the number rang.

"Caffey," a man's voice answered

"Oh, Dr. Caffey. This is Laramie Sunderlund. My roommate said you called," Ramie said, sitting up straighter.

"I need to see you immediately, Miss Sunderlund," her academic advisor broke in. "How soon can you be in my office?"

"Twenty minutes," she answered.

"It'll have to do, I suppose. Is there some reason you failed to answer the letter I mailed to your home?"

"I didn't get a letter. When did you send it?"

"About a week or ten days ago."

"It must have been delivered after I left to return to school."

"I knew I should have sent it certified. Hopefully, it's not too late. I'll see you in twenty and don't be late."

A dial tone greeted Ramie's ear and she looked at Leslie and shrugged. "Hold that drink for me," she said as she crushed out her cigarette. "I should be back in less than an hour and will probably need it."

MORE FRICKIN' STEPS, Ramie mentally groaned as she looked up the wide stairs leading to the second floor offices of the Fine Arts Building. Why were all her classes located in buildings constructed before the invention of the elevator, she wondered. It wasn't like she was middle-aged or anything, but she definitely needed to consider exercising more. She lifted a leg and forced her body upward. Dr. Caffey's office was located at the far rear of the building and she forced her legs to move faster. She collapsed against the door and turned the knob, coming to an abrupt halt and leaning against his office assistant's desk. "I...I'm supposed to see Dr. Caffey," she said breathlessly. She glanced at the clock on the wall. "In one minute exactly," she finished, wishing Overland was a smaller campus.

"Name?" the young assistant asked.

"Sunderlund."

"He's expecting you. Go on in."

Ramie swallowed and nodded. "Thanks." She adjusted her clothes and knocked on the door to his office. She peeked in and saw Dr. Caffey slumped behind a loose stack of paperwork.

He looked up when the door opened. "Sunderlund?" he asked.

"Yes, sir."

"You'll be glad to know that I think I've solved your problem."

"I didn't know I had a problem, Dr. Caffey," she said as she made her way to a scarred wooden chair in front of his desk.

"When I was going over your transcript, I discovered you were three credits short of the number required for graduation," he said, scratching the side of his bearded face.

"That can't be right. I've always taken more than the number of hours I needed every semester," she protested.

"But not in the right courses. I show you with only nine credit hours of English and your degree in Art Education requires twelve. Classes begin Monday morning and unless another student dropped dead over the weekend, there simply were no vacancies for you." When Ramie opened her mouth to say something, he continued. "However, I have found a graduate level course that has *no* prerequisites and is still available for students."

Ramie smiled. "Great!"

He looked at her over the top of his glasses and said, "Yes. Anyway the course is in Twentieth Century American Literature."

"Well, that's a relief," Ramie said. "I hate reading that old British stuff."

Dr. Caffey reached across his cluttered desk and handed Ramie a punched card that would admit her to the class. "How is your portfolio coming along?"

"I think I'm a little ahead."

He picked up a folder and flipped through it. "I see you're planning a sculpture for your final project. Very ambitious."

"I like sculpting, especially in stone, revealing the piece hidden inside," she said enthusiastically. "I've already begun the clay model and plan to begin the actual piece before the final semester begins."

"Well, let me know how everything goes. I'm sure it will be an excellent project. I'll be anxious to see it when it's completed."

"Thank you, Dr. Caffey. I appreciate you finding a course for my final English hours. I should have kept up with that myself. I know how busy you are," Ramie said as she stood to leave the office.

"Have a good senior year," he muttered as he picked up another folder and began dialing a number.

"OKAY, HAND OVER my much needed drink," Ramie panted when she entered her dorm room after climbing once again up three flights of stairs. "I'll be twenty-one in less than two months and plan to start celebrating that milestone today."

"What was the problem?" Leslie asked as she pulled a bottle of Coke from an ice chest in the bathroom. "Here. Drink some out of this," she said as she handed the frosty bottle to her. When Ramie handed it back, Leslie poured in enough Jack Daniels to refill the bottle. She placed her thumb over the mouth and inverted it slowly, allowing the whiskey to mix with the soda. She turned it back over and handed the bottle to Ramie, licking the liquid from her thumb.

Ramie took a long drink and swished it around in her mouth before swallowing. "Ah, perfect," she sighed.

"I invited Donna and Suz up later for cards. You up for it? I thought we could order a couple of pizzas to go with the drinks."

"You have enough Jack for everyone?"

"My mother decided that since I won't be home until Thanksgiving I might need more than one bottle so she stocked me up. At a dollar a shot I should be able to save enough money to buy Christmas presents."

"Must be why you're a business major," Ramie chuckled as she swallowed another gulp.

"No more freebies except for you after tonight. Cheers!"

The first to arrive at the pre-class celebration was Susanna Culpepper, better known as just Suz. She was a studious girl who had gradually loosened up since they all first met as freshmen. Although rather plain-looking with mousy brown hair and thick, oversized glasses that magnified her hazel eyes, and slightly bucked-teeth, she had a fun personality and a fabulously dry sense of humor. She was an English major with plans to one day teach at the university level. She was the resident genius when it came to writing term papers and only charged a small fee to correct everyone's spelling and grammar. She did Ramie's for free in exchange for using the monster for her own papers. Fortunately, Ramie didn't have to write many papers for her art classes after the first couple of years of introductory courses. Everything she did in her junior year was hands-on and now she was looking forward to working on bigger projects.

While Leslie prepared a drink for her, Suz helped Ramie clear everything from the large double desk that was perfect for playing cards. Suz picked up a stack of paperwork and squatted down to set it in the corner of the room. After she stood, she bent back over and picked up a punch card. "Whose is this?" she asked.

Ramie looked up and said, "Oh, that's mine. My advisor discovered I needed an extra three hours of lit and was able to get me into that class."

"Does he hate you?"

"Dr. Caffey? No. He's doing me a favor so I can graduate. Why?"

Suz looked at her and frowned. "I won't even sign up for a course with this professor. She's got the highest failure rate on campus. The student government tried to get her fired last year because of it, but the administration refused."

"How bad is she?" Ramie asked.

"She never passes more than twenty per cent, max. It's a graduate level course. I can't believe they let you in it."

"Caffey said there are no pre-reqs so they can't keep an undergrad out."

"Believe me, Ramie, Rothenberg won't feel sorry for you because you're an undergrad in a graduate course or because you were stuck taking it."

"I may be spending a lot of time in your room this semester then."

"I'll help you if I can, but am not sure how much that'll be." Suz shrugged. "The good news is that if you fail, you can still pick up something else in the spring."

"There's no room in my spring schedule for another course. It's full up with senior art projects and I have to work on my final sculpture project to have it ready by May."

"I know a couple of grad students in English. I'll see what I can do to help you at least pass."

"I don't care if it's a D minus minus." From the look on Suz's face even that didn't seem like a possibility.

A series of rhythmic taps at the door got their attention. "What's that?" Suz asked. "The secret knock?"

Leslie handed Suz her drink and said, "It has to be Donna. She's so melodramatic." She went to the door and said, "What's the secret password?"

"I got my dollar," came through the door.

Leslie shrugged. "Close enough." She opened the door just far enough for Donna to squeeze through sideways. The girl was a jock, but clueless.

Donna took her bottle into the bathroom. She looked over her shoulder at Leslie. "I can fix it," she said as she picked up the bottle of Jack and poured a healthy amount into her half empty soda bottle.

"Okay," Leslie said. "Just don't sh–"

The beginning of the warning came too late as Donna stuck her thumb over the mouth of the soda bottle and shook it vigorously. The second she removed her thumb Coke and Jack sprayed all over the walls and sink before dripping down to cover the floor. Leslie slammed the bathroom door shut to keep the liquid from getting into the main room. A few moments later she opened the door and took in the mess in their bathroom. Small dark foamy drops fell from the ceiling.

"A total waste of perfectly good Jack," Suz said.

"Our room smells like a distillery," Ramie moaned. "How long will it take to get the smell out?"

"Days, weeks, maybe months," Leslie said.

"Oh, come on guys," Donna said. "It's not that bad. Just keep the bathroom door closed."

"And what about when the dorm director comes in for her weekly inspection?" Leslie snapped.

Donna frowned and then her face brightened. "If one of you is in the shower or on the can, she won't come in, right?"

"Right," Ramie said, drawing the word out. She looked at Leslie. "She always comes around the same time every Wednesday." She shrugged. "Guess we could take turns missing a class."

Leslie frowned. "Until the pizza arrives, we're scrubbing." She shoved a sponge at Donna. "You first, genius."

After giving the girls across the hall a little bribe money, generously donated by Donna, Leslie and Ramie left their door and window open virtually around the clock, as did their neighbors. With the aid of a fan blowing from the doorway across the hall and another sitting in their own window and acting as an exhaust fan, the odor eventually faded to a tolerable level in about a week. One thing for sure, they definitely had the cleanest bathroom on campus. And Donna was never allowed to mix her own drinks again...ever.

Chapter Two

RAMIE MOPED AROUND her dorm room for the next two days, contemplating slitting her wrists, and setting a new all-time low on the overall depression meter. Her senior level courses in art would require an enormous amount of her time. That, added to her job as a student assistant in the university library, wouldn't leave much time to delve into the inner mindset of Twentieth Century American authors. She was wallowing in self-pity when the door to the room popped open and Leslie strode in.

"Get dressed, girlfriend. You're in some serious need of fresh air and sunshine on our last day of freedom!" Leslie announced.

"With the black cloud hanging over my head right now, Les, the sun would never reach my face," Ramie said, attempting a brave smile.

"That's pure unadulterated bullshit! Now get your walking shoes on and let's truck on outta here. Everyone is waiting in the bus."

"Who's everyone?"

"Just some gals I rounded up for a little wilderness adventure. If you're lucky maybe a bear will maul you to death and you won't have to face Rothenberg tomorrow."

"I've never been very lucky."

"Of course you have. You got me as a roommate, didn't ya? Now come on. I'll get you through Rothenbitch's class with no sweat."

"You had her class and passed?" Ramie asked hopefully.

"Do I look like a total moron? Because only a total moron would sign up for her course in the first place."

"Thanks," Ramie mumbled. "I feel *so* much better now."

Seeing the crestfallen look on her friend's face, Leslie smiled. "You were tricked into it by an advisor who is obviously related to the Marquis de Sade, but not in a good way. Fortunately for you, however, I'm dating a guy who actually passed her class last year. He's a doofus, but I'm willing to go out with him if it helps you, my best friend. It will be a serious sacrifice on my part, but I can keep him hanging around long enough to get you through this momentary crisis."

"He must be cute because I know you wouldn't go out with a mutt. Now my entire future rests in the hands of Little Miss Love 'em and Leave 'em."

Twenty minutes later Ramie climbed over Donna, Suz, and a third girl she didn't know and into the back seat of Leslie's Volkswagen bus. Leslie jumped into the driver's seat and started the vehicle. Before she pulled out of the dormitory parking lot she glanced over her shoulder at her van full of passengers. "Everyone got their water and a snack? I've got bug spray."

Donna and Suz looked at each other before saying, "Yes, Ranger Rick!"

"Where the hell are you kidnapping us to anyway, Leslie?" the perky blonde in the middle seat asked.

"I found a cool waterfall a few miles outside of town near the lake while I was taking a couple of classes over the summer"

"You mean re-taking, don't you?" Suz said with a smirk.

"So I'm not a genius in anthropology. But the instructor was cute as hell, so sue me," Leslie said as she stuck her tongue out at her friend. "Anyway ladies, there's a fabulous waterfall that empties into a pool of clear water. It would be a great place to cool off with a little dip."

"You didn't tell us to bring something to swim in," several voices said in unison.

"What? You never heard of skinny dippin'?"

"Not with a bunch of other girls," the blonde complained.

"Well, sweetie, you've got the same equipment as the rest of us and we've all enjoyed the communal showers in phys ed at one time or another, so there's no need to get all shy." Leslie caught Ramie's eyes in the rearview mirror and smiled.

"You're right," the blonde said with a laugh. "It's not like we're a bunch of lesbos or anything."

Ramie saw Leslie's eyes staring at her through the rearview mirror again and shrank back into her seat, looking at the campus buildings passing by. She had dated a few guys since she left Vermont, but had only done it to keep the others from questioning her sexuality. She had even deigned to allow a couple of her dates to kiss her, but no fireworks or bells and whistles went off with any of them. Not even a sputter. She would never forgive Leslie for arranging a blind date with some guy who thought her breast was a ripe cantaloupe. She had a future all mapped out and it certainly didn't include romantic entanglements that would leave her barefoot and pregnant while she slaved over a hot stove. She shuddered involuntarily at the thought.

"You cold, Ramie?" Donna asked. "You can borrow my jacket."

"No thanks," Ramie smiled. "Just one of those shivers that seem to come out of nowhere."

"You mean like someone walking over your grave?" Suz asked.

Ramie blinked at her friend, wondering where that idea had come from and smiled. "I guess." Probably a predictor of her own very near future.

IT DIDN'T TAKE the girls long to lose their inhibitions after they trudged through a heavily forested area and found the refreshing-looking pool of sparkling blue water Leslie had promised. They had all worked up a mild sweat and didn't waste much time shedding their clothing and wading, giggling, into the cool water. Leslie spread out two blankets on the grass and they all plopped down to dry off naturally. Ramie enjoyed the vision of the girls naked, but none of them captured her attention. She already had a mental list of the physical attributes she was interested in and none of these girls filled the bill. Maybe it was because they, except for the little blonde Leslie had dragged along, were her friends. Judy, the blonde, did have the small breasts Ramie preferred. However, the lack of a nicely rounded ass was a definite turn-off. Although she did wonder about Donna, who had a wrestler's physique and the rippling back muscles you only read about in magazines, all of Ramie's friends were straight. Donna was cute, and obviously unashamed of her body, but if Ramie was wrong and put the moves on her, she figured Donna knew at least one wrestling hold guaranteed to break her neck.

After everyone untangled their clothing and redressed, Leslie took a different path back to her bus. They'd walked for half an hour when Ramie noticed her sneaker had come untied.

"You go ahead," she said to the others as she stopped and squatted down to re-tie it. "I'll catch up with you."

Ramie sat down on a nearby log and took her sneakers off. Dirt from around the waterhole had gotten into her shoes and made walking uncomfortable. She stuck her hand inside each shoe and wiped out any debris that might have found its way inside before slipping her feet back into them. As she was tying the last shoestring she heard a noise. It sounded like people talking and laughing and seemed to come from someplace nearby. Following the sound of the voices, she made her way as quietly as possible toward it. When she got near the edge of a clearing she saw a small log cabin. It looked like a postcard picture and Ramie could see a sliver of the lake not far beyond the cabin. Who would be living this far from town, virtually in the middle of nowhere, surrounded by a forest and a lake?

She no longer heard the voices and turned to walk away. She glanced back over her shoulder in time to see two women, one chasing the other. Both women were dressed in Capri pants and sleeveless blouses and wore white sneakers. Ramie ducked behind a tree where she wouldn't be seen and watched the game of tag. The women were older than her, but she couldn't tell how much older. One of them was tall and slender and seemed to be physically fit, running gracefully through the grass in pursuit of a slightly shorter woman. The taller woman had short, layered cinnamon hair that lay close to her head and wore gold wire-rimmed glasses. Ramie was fascinated by the way her hair bounced as she ran. The woman being pursued had medium length dark hair that blew around her face as she continued looking behind at her pursuer, laughing as she did.

The woman who seemed to be doing the chasing increased her speed slightly and overtook the second woman near the edge of the tree line. She held the other woman's hands, laughing and breathing heavily. As Ramie watched, the redhead pressed her body against the brunette and smiled as she brushed hair away from her face. They were speaking, but Ramie couldn't hear what they were saying. Slowly the redhead took the brunette's face between her hands, her thumbs tenderly skimming over the shorter woman's cheeks, before lowering her head toward the brunette, who was running her hands through the redhead's hair. Ramie gasped and covered her mouth as the women's lips met. The brunette broke the kiss with a smile, bringing her hand up to remove the other woman's glasses before draping her arm over her companion's shoulder and returning to the kiss, letting the glasses dangle loosely from her fingertips. Ramie couldn't tear her eyes away as the kiss, which began tenderly, grew steadily into a passionate, full-mouthed kiss. No one, not even the gropers, had kissed her that way. Skin became partially exposed as clothing was pulled away and buttons were undone. Ramie's abdomen clenched as the women's hands explored one another. She felt her body flush at the unbridled passion between them. She felt a burst of heat begin on her neck and move steadily onto her face as the redhead's hand moved smoothly up her companion's body and cupped her breast as her thigh pressed between the brunette's legs. The brunette pressed her body closer and deepened the kiss in response. What must it feel like to be touched so intimately by someone whose touch you wanted, Ramie thought. Several minutes passed before the redhead took the brunette's hand and led her toward the cabin, stopping periodically to steal another kiss. As the women moved out of sight, Ramie turned away to locate her companions.

RAMIE DIDN'T TELL her friends about the intimate scene she had encountered, but it never left her mind. She dreamed about it that night. She was always one of the women, but each time, just as her lips were almost touching those of another woman, the dream ended abruptly, leaving her frustrated and irritable. By Monday morning she found her erotic dream being interrupted by visions of an unknown nightmare named Dr. Emma Rothenberg. She had been quite old in Ramie's dream and vaguely resembled the Wicked Witch of the West from the *Wizard of Oz*.

The first day of classes was usually an exciting time of discovery, especially now that Ramie was in her senior level classes. She knew most of the students in her courses as well as the professors and instructors. They had formed a close-knit family within their own department and helped one another through the occasional tough time. So far none of her friends were able to offer a single word of encouragement about her English class, especially when they heard the name Rothenberg. They all mentioned the possibility of summer school.

Students swarmed around Ramie that afternoon as she trudged up the staircase leading to the classroom on the third floor of Donlevy Hall. She didn't want to be late the first day and hadn't taken the time to change her clothing. The evidence of two hours of shaping and molding clay lingered on her old jeans and yellow peasant blouse. The reddish tint of the clay clung around her cuticles and stained her hands. A seat in the rear of the classroom seemed her safest possibility. She lingered near the restroom and water fountain, killing as much time as possible before entering the room of doom. To her surprise there were about twenty students in the small classroom and all but a few seats in the first two or three rows were occupied. A hand-written sign attached to the podium instructed them to move to the front of the room. None of the students seemed to be any more overjoyed about the idea of facing Dr. Rothenberg than Ramie was. The thought strangely comforted her as she took a desk on the aisle of the third row and pulled out her notebook and pen. Her mouth was dry and she took a bottle of water she'd filled from a fountain in the hall from her shoulder satchel and sucked it down greedily.

The side door into the room opened. A tall woman wearing a light gray pinstriped suit, gold wire-rimmed glasses, and sensible gray flats stepped into the room. Short, slightly wind-blown cinnamon hair casually framed her face. She strode forward and set her briefcase on a chair next to the podium. Without a smile or introduction, she handed a sheaf of papers to a young man who had accompanied her. The woman looked up at the class, adjusting her wire-rimmed glasses as her eyes scanned the students' faces briefly, nodding to a few she apparently already knew.

Ramie knew she was gaping at the woman. The calm, cool female in front of her was a far cry from the one she had seen passionately kissing the brunette less than twenty-four hours earlier. She certainly wasn't the Wicked Witch of the West or any other direction. Flashes of exposed skin and sure, tapered fingers moving over the brunette's inviting body sped through Ramie's mind. Dr. Rothenberg looked like a totally different person than the one who'd been laughing and playful only the day before. Her skin was lightly tanned and a smattering of freckles flowed across her nose. Her voice was soothing, but commanded attention. Ramie smiled, wondering what happened between the two women after she left them to their privacy. A momentary image of nude, toned and tanned bodies entwined around one another on pure white, cool sheets was interrupted by a voice speaking.

"Twentieth Century American authors have stretched the boundaries of literature in ways not anticipated a mere twenty years earlier," Dr. Rothenberg intoned in a clear, strong voice without introduction. She stepped away from the podium and stood in front of it, speaking without the assistance of notes. Ramie frowned, considering that alone a bad omen. It meant Rothenberg knew everything and everything she said would be important. Information poured from her virtually non-stop for almost an hour. Ramie glanced at the clock on the wall behind the podium. Her hand ached from the continuous writing and she shook it for a second.

Near the end of the designated class period Dr. Rothenberg stopped talking after assigning a list of readings for the next meeting and walked around the podium again. She picked up a card and said, "Laramie Sunderlund. Please meet with me in my office at the end of this class." Ramie jumped when she heard her name. Almost as abruptly as she appeared, Dr. Rothenberg dropped her papers into the briefcase, snapped it shut, and pushed through the side door of the auditorium. The students around Ramie began packing notebooks and pens away, standing to chat briefly among themselves.

"Excuse me," Ramie asked a nearby young woman. "Was that Dr. Rothenberg?"

"Of course," the student huffed. She stared at Ramie for a

moment, wrinkling her nose as she scanned her dirty jeans and blouse. "You're not an English Lit major are you?" she asked.

"No," Ramie answered with a frown.

"Then what are you doing in here? It's not too late to drop the course, you know."

"I need the credits to graduate and this was the only class available."

"Well, honey, your timing sucks. This is an upper-level course. If you're Sunderlund, that's probably why Rothie wants to speak to you."

"I'm enrolled so we're stuck with each other now," Ramie said with a shrug.

"Rothie will have you dropped by the next time we meet. She doesn't feel the need to suffer idiots in her class."

"I'm not an idiot!"

"Maybe not, but she'll make you feel like one in less than a minute." The young woman nodded to another student and joined him in the aisle.

Ramie draped the satchel's woven strap over her neck and made her way into the hallway, unsure where Rothenberg's office was. She walked until she found a door emblazoned with the name *Emma J. Rothenberg, Ph.D. English Department*. Ramie looked down at her clothing. Cheap woven sandals she'd found at an international bazaar on campus the previous spring adorned her feet. Overall, she was comfortable with her rather Bohemian look, even if it was slightly dirty at the moment. She took a deep breath, and knocked on the wooden door facing.

"Come," a voice called out.

Ramie sucked in a deep breath, brushed her curly shoulder-length blonde hair away from her face, and opened the office door. She stepped inside and quietly closed the door behind her. She turned around and the woman seated behind the office desk looked up at her. She had removed her glasses and the jacket to her suit hung neatly on the back of her desk chair. Clear hazel eyes met hers and Ramie suddenly didn't believe she would be able to breathe again. She had never seen such beautiful, expressive eyes. The light greenish-brown in the center radiated toward darker outer edges. As much as she knew she should, Ramie couldn't tear her eyes away from the alluring eyes that were beckoning to her, drinking her in as they pierced her soul.

"I assume you are Laramie Sunderlund," Dr. Rothenberg finally said as she leaned back in her chair and entwined her fingers in front of her, breaking the uncomfortable silence.

Ramie forced her eyes away from the eyes that had entrapped hers to drift down to thin, perfect lips. Lips that had joined another woman's twenty-four hours before. The memory made Ramie nervously lick her own lips. She was startled as she watched one corner of Dr. Rothenberg's mouth lift slightly.

"Everyone calls me Ramie," she answered. God that sounded so lame. What a wonderful way to impress such a sophisticated-looking woman. And Emma Rothenberg was definitely a woman, not a girl. She carried herself with studied confidence Ramie admired. She had never been with a real woman before, only girls who dreamed of the day they would become women.

"Are you from Wyoming?" Dr. Rothenberg asked benignly.

Finally, Ramie's brain slammed into gear and she smiled. "Everyone thinks that, but actually my parents are Larry and Amie, with an i-e, Sunderlund. They combined the two in sort of a pre-hippie moment. Guess they forgot to remember a state had already claimed that name for a city." She stopped speaking and gazed at the floor. "Sorry, you probably didn't need to know all that. I'm from Vermont."

"A lovely story and another beautiful state. Do you have any idea why I wanted to speak to you?"

Ramie shrugged. "Probably because you think I don't belong in your class."

"Do you think you belong in my class?"

"I don't have a choice, Dr. Rothenberg. My advisor and I miscounted my credits and I didn't know until I returned to campus that I was three credits short in English. All of the other classes were full and yours was the only course left that didn't have a pre-req. I can't afford to stay and graduate at the end of next summer."

Rothenberg took a deep breath and exhaled slowly. "Being enrolled in the course is far from a guarantee that you will pass it. It's possible, perhaps even probable, you won't pass the curriculum and will still be looking at a summer course."

"I won't fail," Ramie insisted.

"What is your major area of study?"

"I have a scholarship in Art Education, but am planning to be an artist. I sculpt."

"That's a very difficult medium."

"I enjoy creating something out of nothing except what I see in my mind."

Dr. Rothenberg stood and walked around her desk, stopping in front of Ramie, who found herself suddenly fascinated with the intricate lace that highlighted the bodice of Dr. Rothenberg's blouse. It was beautiful and delicate in an amazingly seductive way, revealing no more than a hint of the lightly freckled skin beneath and joined by delicate pearl buttons. Extremely classy.

"May I see your hands?" Dr. Rothenberg asked, her voice soft and intimate.

Ramie hesitated before holding her hands out for her professor's inspection. She took Ramie's hands, examining them carefully, turning them over, and lightly running her thumbs across the palms. Ramie closed her eyes and took a deep breath in an attempt to ignore the tingle traveling from her palms through her fingers. She had never felt such a sensuous touch before. The impulse to fold her fingers around Dr. Rothenberg's hands was almost overpowering.

"You have the hands of a sculptress," she said with a slight smile. "Strong hands with long, delicate fingers."

"Thank you. It's hard to keep my skin hydrated when I work with clay, but I love the way it feels." She looked up and met Dr. Rothenberg's eyes. "There's something sensuous about the feel of my hands slipping over and into it."

"They're perfect." Dr. Rothenberg blinked once, hard, and quickly released Ramie's hands. Was it possible she had felt the same tingle, Ramie wondered. "I won't request that you be removed from my course," she said as she cleared her throat and returned to her chair. "However, if you fall behind in the reading assignments, I can assure your future will not be a bright one. I strongly suggest you read at least the first third of the first assignment before the next class meeting. Unfortunately for you, I now know your name and you can expect to be called upon. Unless you have any questions, I need to prepare for my next lecture."

"I understand, Dr. Rothenberg," Ramie said. Her hands felt cooler after Rothenberg released them and they shook slightly. Ramie stuck them in the pockets of her jeans. "Thank you for giving me this chance."

"I'll see you Wednesday then, Miss Sunderlund," she said, dismissing Ramie as she slipped her glasses on and turned her attention back to the papers on her desk.

AS SOON AS her office door closed Emma expelled a sigh of relief. She rubbed her fingers together, the feel of Ramie's strong fingers still in her thoughts. The flow of energy from Ramie's hands had been powerful and palpable. She shook her head and thought this semester might be the longest of her career. You're being ridiculous, she thought. That girl is half your age. But she looked eerily like Frances. Emma took a deep breath and closed her eyes as she exhaled in an attempt to flush the memory of Fran from her mind, hoping it would not return every time she saw

Ramie Sunderlund.

The telephone on Emma's desk rang and she was glad for the interruption. She removed her glasses and placed them on the papers in front of her. "Emma Rothenberg," she said pleasantly as she placed the receiver to her ear.

"Are you terribly busy, darling," a low, husky voice asked.

"Never too busy for you, Millie," Emma answered. The weekend she'd just spent with Millie Carver quickly replaced her unwarranted thoughts about Ramie Sunderlund. "What can I do for you?"

"You don't really want me to answer that question, do you?" Millie responded with a throaty laugh.

"I know what I'd enjoy doing with you right now," Emma said. "But I'm sure that's not why you called." Emma knew her affair with Millicent Carver was ill-advised, but she hadn't been able to resist the southern charms of the attractive brunette. Their liaison would never develop into a permanent relationship and they both knew it. They had set sensible rules for their relationship, both agreeing that when it ended it would simply be over and they would go their separate ways with no ill or bruised feelings. But Emma knew the longer it continued, the harder a separation would be.

"I was hoping you would agree to be my partner for the student-faculty tennis tournament this year," Millie said. "I had to agree to play, but I don't know many other women my age I'd be willing to have as my doubles partner. Please say yes, darling."

"You know I will, Millie, as long as it doesn't interfere with my teaching schedule."

"Unless you teach on Saturdays now, it shouldn't, darling. I'll let the committee know. It's a month from now, October sixth. We'll have to find time to practice before then of course."

Emma wrote the date on her calendar.

"Have lunch with me today," Millie said.

"That might not be a good idea considering we just spent the weekend together."

"But we're the only ones who know that, Emma. Meet me at the Faculty Club at one."

"Will Stanton be joining us?" Emma asked, referring to Millie's husband.

"Not if I can avoid it," Millie answered with a laugh.

"I'll see you there. I have some work I need to finish first."

Emma placed the receiver back on its cradle. She was being foolhardy by engaging in an affair with the wife of the Dean of the School of Arts and Sciences. What had she been thinking?

They met near the end of the previous term and became physically involved not long afterward. Dean Carver was away most of the summer at conferences, leaving his wife home, but not unattended. Emma's greatest fear was that she might fall in love with Millie Carver, even though she knew Millie would never leave the security her marriage provided. Their relationship had already lasted longer than any of Emma's previous liaisons except possibly one which had been the result of a youthful indiscretion and ended poorly, leaving Emma emotionally crushed. She rubbed her fingers under her glasses and over her eyes to erase a memory long buried.

"HOW WAS YOUR first day in Rothenberg's class?" Leslie asked when Ramie finally returned to their dorm room.

"She's letting me stay in the course, so I guess it's okay for now," Ramie said with a shrug as she dropped her books on the desk. "I have a shitload of reading to do before Wednesday though and she assured me she would be asking me, personally, questions on the material."

"Was she threatening you?"

"I don't think so. More like a warning to be prepared. She cares about her subject."

"It's always lethal when they know you by name. What are you reading?"

Ramie picked up a book and looked at the cover. "*The Fountainhead*," she said. She glanced at the syllabus, which was stuck inside the book. "The first unit is called 'The Tragic Hero in American Literature'. Apparently the opening volley for the unit."

"Sounds fascinating," Leslie said sarcastically.

"Have you read it?"

"I'm a business major, sweetie. I took English for football players. Maybe there's a Cliff's Notes for it."

"There's not. I already checked at the bookstore after class," Ramie said.

THE WEEKEND DIDN'T arrive soon enough for Ramie. She had spent the week as jumpy as a cat trapped in a kennel with growling, snapping dogs on either side. She kept pace with her reading assignments for Dr. Rothenberg's class, but couldn't shake the feeling that her answers to her professor's questions were inadequate, devoid of any evidence of deep thought. Ramie couldn't remember the last time anyone had made her feel so stupid. And she knew it was being reflected in her art. She had accumulated a trash can full of crumpled paper from her numerous attempts to sketch a still life in her Art IV class. It was an assignment she would have been able to complete easily just the previous semester.

She had to find a way to flush Rothenberg from her mind. She woke from a dream about watching Dr. Rothenberg kissing the brunette the week before classes began and found her hand cupping her own crotch. She jerked it away and went into the bathroom to splash cold water on her face, wondering if she had ever done that before.

This was ridiculous, she thought. Leslie was still buried under a mountain of covers, sleeping off too many alcoholic beverages, and Ramie didn't have the heart to wake her. Instead, she slipped on a pair of sweat pants and a long-sleeve thermal top and sneaked out of their room with her sketchpad under her arm. Her mind cleared as soon as she stepped out the side door of the dorm. The sky was a clear light blue, but there was a cool nip in the early morning air, suggesting that fall was not far away. She sucked in a deep breath and shoved her hands into the pockets of her sweats to warm them. By noon the cool air would dissipate and sunshine would drive the temperature into the pleasant mid-seventies. She walked across the dewy grass surrounding the dorm and cut across a parking lot. She trotted across the street that ran in front of the football stadium and off campus.

She turned down a nearby residential street. There were a number of fraternity and sorority houses that lined it and she studied the architecture of each as she walked. Architectural renderings weren't her favorite thing, but she could always use them for her senior portfolio. It would be more impressive than drawings of a bowl of fruit. She cut down a side street and admired several residences that were probably the homes of university professors. Someday, if her future unfolded as she hoped, she might live in a similar home and invite her students to join her from time to time.

Several blocks down the next tree-lined street she could see cars traveling on the main thoroughfare through town and she turned down the next street to make her way back toward the campus.

Like a picture postcard from an earlier era, the thick branches of decades-old trees canopied over the streets, their leaves beginning their subtle annual transformation to vibrant reds, oranges, and yellows. Ramie didn't believe the fall changes were as dramatic as the ones she had grown up with in Vermont, but it was a sight she still enjoyed. The area would make an impressive addition to her portfolio. She stopped to examine the contours of an interesting looking knothole that was eye level on a tree whose roots had begun buckling a section of the sidewalk. She stood on her tiptoes to peek into the hole.

"I wouldn't disturb his nest if I were you," a voice said. "He's been working quite diligently to fill it before winter arrives."

Ramie stepped away from the tree guiltily to find Dr. Rothenberg ambling toward her. She looked comfortable in tan thin-wale corduroy slacks and a lightweight forest green sweater. Slightly ahead of her was the largest Bassett hound Ramie had ever seen. She smiled at the long ears that nearly dragged the ground. Ramie knelt down and greeted the animal that approached her with curious, sad-looking eyes. She held her hand out and was met with a thorough sniff, followed by a generous lick of her fingers.

"He's beautiful," Ramie said as she stroked the dog's head and ran her fingers down his silky feeling ears. "What's his name?"

"Louie," Emma said.

"You're a big boy, Louie," Ramie said as she cradled the dog's large head along her forearm and stroked the length of his body.

"He hasn't missed many meals since I got him," Dr. Rothenberg said.

"How long have you had him?"

"About four years now. I think he's stopped growing for the most part. I had no idea a Bassett could grow so large."

Ramie stood up and brushed off her knees. "Well, I have to get back to the dorm," she said. "I have some reading I need to finish before tomorrow."

"Enjoy it," Dr. Rothenberg said with a smile as she lightly tugged Louie's leash and stepped around Ramie to continue her walk.

The crispness of the early morning air had given Dr. Rothenberg's cheeks a warm, rosy glow. Ramie opened her sketchpad and sat on the curb, using her knees and thighs as a platform. She spent a few minutes roughly sketching the knothole and Louie's soulful face. She grinned as she used the side of her pinkie to shadow in a few areas. These would definitely be better than bowls of fruit.

Chapter Three

NEAR THE FIRST of October, a bleary-eyed Ramie trudged up the stairs in Donlevy Hall. The assignments for her upper-level art courses were daunting. She had meticulously planned her schedule to get everything done. It allowed enough time for everything except eating and sleeping. And socializing was out of the question. The heart of her work would be her portfolio, a collection of her best works, which would be judged by a committee of faculty members. While her emphasis had always been sculpting, her portfolio would have to include examples of her competence in other media, including painting, photography, and pencil drawing. Each medium had to include both still life or abstracts and the use of models. Ramie had spent hours going through the extensive list.

She'd spent most of the previous night reading the next one hundred pages of the culminating assignment for the first unit in English. It was an interesting story of individualism and the steps one man was willing to take in order to maintain his individuality. So far she managed to keep her nose above water in a course that was way over her head. With two and a half months remaining in the semester, Ramie wasn't sure how much longer she could tread water.

She slipped into her usual seat on the third row and pulled the built-in desktop over her lap. She took a spiral notebook from her satchel and dug out a pen. With five minutes left before class began she closed her eyes and rested her cheek on her hand.

"Miss Sunderlund," a sharp voice said.

The students sitting around Ramie snickered as her eyes were startled open and she ran her hand across her mouth. When her vision focused she found herself staring into the stormy hazel eyes of an angry-looking Emma Rothenberg.

"Am I *boring* you, Miss Sunderlund?"

Ramie straightened in her seat. "N...no, of course not, Dr. Rothenberg." Her voice was raspy and she cleared her throat to avoid sounding like a frightened fourth grader. "I'm sorry, ma'am."

"If you have any hope of being successful in this class, you'll have to do better than that."

"Yes, ma'am." Ramie watched Dr. Rothenberg return to the lectern at the front of the room. She shook her head and stared down at her notebook. She knew she was blushing from the sight of her professor's firm, perfectly rounded ass and muscular calves moving as she retreated down the steps to the front. Ramie was certain she would need a second part-time job to pay for summer school. There was no way in hell she would pass Rothenberg's class after today, no matter how hard she tried. She glanced at the student next at her and swallowed when the girl drew a finger across her neck as if cutting her throat. Ramie thought about going to Rothenberg's office to apologize again, but dismissed the idea as a sign of fear and weakness. She needed this course, but refused to grovel...yet.

EMMA FACED THE class again and continued with her lecture, stopping occasionally to field a question or ask one, purposely avoiding eye contact with Ramie Sunderlund. There was something distracting about the young woman's eyes. She looked adorable with her head propped on her hand as she slept, a thin, glistening thread of drool poised at the corner of her full, pouty lips. Ramie was definitely a fish out of water in the advanced literature class. Emma lobbied unsuccessfully for the past three or four years to establish a pre-requisite for enrollment. She'd taken her argument all the way to the dean, but Stanton Carver had not agreed, calling her an elitist snob where literature was concerned. A barely perceivable smile crossed Emma's thin lips. It was during her discussion with Dean Carver that she met his wife, Millicent. In Emma's mind, her battle to establish pre-reqs had not been without its victories.

Emma observed the other students in her class and it hadn't escaped her attention that Ramie Sunderlund was separated from them in more ways than one. Obviously English literature was not the young woman's forte, but Emma had to give her credit for her efforts to grasp the occasionally deep underlying themes of the books and short stories they were reading. Ramie's clothing also set her apart, with her rather Bohemian wardrobe. She was the personification of everything the word artist brought to mind. Personally, Emma found her attire quite alluring. She blinked hard, bringing her attention back to a student's response to her last question.

When Emma dismissed the class and gathered her notes, she couldn't help but seek a glimpse of Ramie Sunderlund as she prepared to leave. She knew she had embarrassed her and that Ramie would not look her way. However, there was something enticing about the way Ramie's body moved as she made her way up the steps toward the auditorium exit. Something youthful and exciting in the way her hips swayed hypnotically from side to side. Something…so longingly familiar.

"I CAN'T GO!" Ramie insisted as Leslie grabbed her by the wrist and dragged her toward the door of their room.

"We're only a month into the first semester, Ramie, and you're going to burn out before the Thanksgiving break," Leslie said.

"I don't have time for a date. I'm behind in everything, especially English. After Rothenberg caught me napping in class Wednesday I might be dead anyway."

"Just take today off to recharge." Leslie's face brightened. "Gloria's an English major. Maybe she can help you, physically and mentally. You're going to explode if you don't get lucky…soon," Leslie pleaded. Changing her tactic, she added, "She's cuuute and just your type."

"What type is that?"

"The friendly, willing, and eager type. Now let's go."

Ramie knew there was no arguing with Leslie. She walked into the bathroom to brush her teeth and attempt to do something with her unruly curls. "You don't mind if I pee before this afternoon of fun and frolic, do you?"

"Just as long as you make it a quick pee. We're already late. I'll call down to let them know we'll be there soon."

Leslie was right. Gloria Sumner was the friendly, eager type. And reasonably cute. A freshman with softly frosted light brown hair and a lithe, young body, but Gloria was apparently enamored with the idea of dating an upper-classman, a senior no less. In addition, she was Ramie's least favorite type, a chronic toucher. Not that Ramie didn't like to be touched, especially by an attractive young woman, but Gloria proved to be incapable of talking without touching. From her limited experiences, Ramie had discovered she preferred the kind of touching that wasn't accompanied by talking.

She shot daggers at Leslie throughout the early part of the afternoon. Leslie gave up on the English doofus after a couple of dates. Her date that weekend was a handsome poli-sci graduate student who also happened to be Gloria's brother. He promised to spend the day with Leslie, but also promised to include his younger sister. By arranging the double date, Leslie solved that minor problem. She offered Ramie up as a sacrificial lamb in order to be with Ted.

Ted suggested they all take in the student-faculty tennis tournament that afternoon and they agreed. Ramie agreed for her own protection. Ted drove a claustrophobically small car and even when she sat smashed against one door in the back seat and Gloria sat against the other one, they were still sitting hip-to-hip, a position that Gloria quickly changed to hand-to-thigh when the opportunity presented itself.

Ramie blushed furiously when she saw the disapproving look in Ted's eyes in the rearview mirror. Out from beneath her parents' thumb, Gloria was eager to expand her boundaries. Based on the way she acted, Ramie seriously doubted Gloria had much, if any, experience. Even when Ramie tried to relax and get into the spirit of the "date" by allowing Gloria to kiss her it was completely devoid of emotion. Gloria was a sweet kid, but it just wasn't happening. Their date had barely begun and Ramie knew it was a mistake. Ramie managed to rest her hand on the seat when Ted pulled into a parking space. Unexpectedly Gloria slid her hand between Ramie's thighs as Ramie fought to release her seat belt. She jumped, banging her head on the roof of the vehicle. She blinked back the stars that floated before her eyes and slid out of the car to re-arrange the crotch of her jeans.

"Don't you like it?" Gloria asked when she joined Ramie and ran her hand ran over Ramie's buttocks. "You've got a nice ass. You should show it off more."

"I barely know you," Ramie hissed, looking around. "So give it a rest, okay. I don't enjoy being pawed, by anyone."

"Wow!" Gloria said. "A prude."

"I'm not a prude," Ramie insisted. "But I know enough to be cautious." After the love, sex and rock and roll that had dominated the Sixties, life in the late Eighties was mellower, but Ramie knew blatant homosexuality was still unacceptable and seriously frowned upon. Apparently Gloria hadn't learned that hard lesson yet.

Once they finally located seats at the campus tennis courts, Ramie and Leslie left to hit the refreshment stand. Gloria insisted on holding Ramie's hand and it took Ramie a moment to free it.

"So how's it going, Ramie?" Leslie asked. "I think Gloria likes you."

"She'd like anyone with two hands and a mouth," Ramie snorted, flexing her fingers. "Ted doesn't look too thrilled about his sister attempting to get friendly with another girl in the back seat of that postage stamp he calls a car."

"Relax," Leslie said, waving her hand dismissively. "Ted's a liberal Kennedy Democrat. He'll get over it and you'll score."

"I don't want to score! The girl's an octopus. It...it's embarrassing, for God's sake!"

"When did you start objecting to that? She's just being friendly."

"Friendly my ass," Ramie breathed. "After this, take me back to the dorm. I don't feel like being anyone's social experiment today. I have work to do."

"Then I won't score," Leslie whined.

"Not my problem, girlfriend."

"I thought Gloria could help you with English," Leslie pouted.

"She's a fucking freshman and doesn't even know who Rothenberg is. Look, I can pass the course by myself. I only have to *pass* with the lowest possible grade to earn the credits. I'll have to forget I ever had such a thing as a social life until the end of this semester so don't do me any more favors."

"Water, please," a familiar voice in the line next to Ramie said.

Ramie scrunched her eyes shut and hoped against all hope that the voice didn't belong to who she thought it did. She tried to look nonchalant when she opened her eyes and rotated them to her left. Emma Rothenberg took the bottle of water and handed the student worker behind the counter one crisp dollar bill. As she turned to leave, she glanced at Ramie and quirked her mouth into what could have been described as a smile, if one were optimistic or on really good drugs. Ramie nodded to acknowledge Emma's presence, but refused to meet her eyes. She waited a few seconds after Emma walked away before glancing over her shoulder at the retreating figure. Now those are lips that know how a woman should be kissed, Ramie thought. Her brain screamed Teach me! Teach me!

"Who's that?" Leslie asked.

"Rothenberg," Ramie said, her mouth feeling as if it were filled with sand.

"She's cute, for a mature woman. Do you think she heard us?" Leslie asked.

"Probably has hearing like a Mexican fruit bat. And since you never heard of the word whisper, I'm dead," Ramie said as she stared at Emma's back. Her tennis shorts hugged her hips and ass. This was the second time she had seen those beautiful, long, muscular legs. She shook her head to drive the image from her mind and stepped up to the counter to place her order.

After two or three relatively boring matches, Ramie was sure she would resemble a boiled Maine lobster by the next day. No one had thought to bring suntan lotion and the stands where they were seated had no shelter. She was ready to demand they leave when the final match was announced. Two senior members of the women's tennis team would be facing Millicent Carver, wife of the Dean of the School of Arts and Sciences and her partner, Dr.

Emma Rothenberg of the English Department. Suddenly, Ramie completely forgot about her growing sunburn discomfort and the still roaming hands of Gloria Sumner as Emma and the dean's wife trotted to the net to shake hands with their much younger opponents. Emma looked amazing. She apparently remembered to slather her exposed limbs with sunscreen and her body gleamed like a bronzed goddess in the glaring sunlight. The sun glittered off her reddish hair.

For a moment Ramie was so entranced by the sight of Emma Rothenberg that she almost didn't notice her tennis partner, Millicent Carver. "Oh my God," she breathed.

"What, baby?" Gloria asked, running her hand up Ramie's thigh and toward her crotch as she nuzzled against Ramie's neck, ignoring the disgusted looks of the spectators near them.

"What?" Ramie asked, jerking her head away and looking at Gloria.

"You said 'oh my God'. What was that for?"

"Oh, nothing. I just thought of something I need to do later." Millicent Carver was the wife of the dean. Emma Rothenberg was having an affair with her boss's wife!

Mrs. Carver was a striking-looking woman about a head shorter than Emma and without the athletic build. But there was no doubt she was the woman Ramie saw passionately kissing, and no doubt tonguing, Dr. Rothenberg the weekend before classes started. A moment of jealousy jolted Ramie's brain. Why would she be jealous of these two women? She watched as Dean Carver gave his wife a chaste good luck kiss on the cheek and wondered if he had a clue. Ramie shivered at the thought of her tongue slipping between Dr. Rothenberg's shapely, parted, full lips. For an instant, blackmail crossed Ramie's mind as a way to a D minus. She rejected the idea just as quickly.

In a way, knowing that Dr. Rothenberg enjoyed the company of women made Ramie feel closer to her. An interest in women was something they shared, even though Emma Rothenberg would never know it. Ramie would never be able to look at her professor the same way again. Or think of her the same way either.

As she watched the match, her eyes became fixated on droplets of perspiration slowly sliding down the side of Dr. Rothenberg's face and trickling along her neck before disappearing beneath her white polo shirt. Ramie fantasized about licking the droplets away and groaned. Her eyes shifted to Emma's legs. She licked her lips, watching the hypnotic movement of muscles in Emma's calves and thighs beneath tanned skin as she swayed from side-to-side awaiting a serve. The definition of tendons stretching and relaxing along the bend of Emma's knees made Ramie's mouth water as she wondered how they would feel under her fingers or beneath her lips as she licked and sucked the sensitive area. Ramie's stomach clenched at the thought and she licked her lips. Gloria moved to sit on the bleacher in front of Ramie and leaned back between her thighs. Unconsciously, Ramie brought her hands up and began kneading the girl's shoulders, pretending she was touching someone else.

Surprisingly, and to the shock of the younger players, Emma and Mrs. Carver were able to eke out a victory, thanks in part to Emma's brilliant returns. Ramie watched as they were each presented with small trophies and acknowledged the applause of the audience. Emma's gaze landed on Ramie the same moment Gloria decided to become more adventurous, causing her to jump. By the time Ramie extracted herself from Gloria's clutches, the moment had passed.

ON THE WAY out of the tennis complex, Gloria insisted on holding Ramie's hand and leaning slightly against her. Ramie was so damned turned on from watching Emma she was sure her tight grip was sending Gloria the wrong message. All Ramie could think about were Emma's long legs, the way her body stretched as she reached for the ball, and, God, the way lines of sweat traveled smoothly over her neck and bronzed shoulders. Ramie had been pawed to distraction and allowed her mind to combine Gloria's clumsy touches with the images in her imagination. At the exit into the parking lot, Ramie lost her battle to control her mind. She grabbed Gloria's hand and dragged her into a niche in the wall surrounding the complex.

It wasn't her finest hour as she pressed her against the wall and crushed her mouth with hungry, needy lips and a probing tongue as her hands groped the girl's young, supple body, all the while fantasizing it was Emma's. Her thigh moved between the younger woman's legs and insinuated itself firmly into her crotch. Gloria pushed against Ramie's chest and separated their bodies, leaving Ramie breathing heavily. Ramie saw the look in the girl's eyes and stepped away, embarrassed by what she'd done. She was certain the handsy freshman had never been groped by another woman and was embarrassed that she had allowed her imagination to overwhelm her normally cautious behavior. Ramie stuck her hands in her pockets and mumbled, "I'm sorry."

Ramie was surprised when she felt the sting of Gloria's hand against her cheek. "You're an animal," Gloria said as she shoved past Ramie to rejoin Ted and Leslie. Ted embraced his distraught sister as he glared at Ramie.

Ramie leaned against the wall and shook her head, ashamed at her lack of control. She looked up when a shadow blocked the late afternoon sunlight. A preppy-looking young man stood in front of her. He looked familiar, but she couldn't place him. He was about five-eleven and wore dress slacks topped by a long-sleeve shirt and a pullover sweater vest. He was wearing glasses that added to his attractiveness, in a studious kind of way.

"Aren't you Laramie Sunderlund?" he asked with a smile that reminded her of a used car salesman.

"Yeah," Ramie answered, squinting at him.

"Travis Whitman," he said, offering his hand. "Dr. Rothenberg's graduate assistant. I've been hoping to speak to you and now that your girlfriend seems to have left this seems as good a time as any," he said glancing around to make sure they were alone.

"She's not my girlfriend," Ramie corrected him after clearing her throat. "What did you want to speak to me about?"

He turned and leaned against the wall next to Ramie, his demeanor shifting to serious. "I know you're struggling in Rothenberg's class. I might be able to help you."

Ramie barked out a harsh laugh. "You gonna shoot me and put me out of my misery?"

He smiled as his eyes moved down her body and back up to meet her eyes. "I know you have to pass her course. I wouldn't make this offer to just anyone, but..." he said with a shrug of his shoulders as his eyes tracked down Ramie's body.

She saw the look in his eyes and moved away from the wall to glare at him. "But in my case, you'll make an exception."

"What's it worth to you?"

"I don't have a spare dime to bribe you with."

"What makes you think I expect anything in return?"

"Because I'm not as stupid as everyone in that damn class thinks."

"We might be able to come to some...other arrangement."

Ramie laughed. "I don't have anything you'd want."

"You just told me you weren't stupid. Don't start now," he said, his face suddenly serious.

Ramie smiled and squinted one eye as she tilted her face up at Whitman. "I'm not fucking you either."

"Let me make your life easier." He shrugged. "It's no big deal."

"I can make it without your help, Mr. Whitman."

"I'm simply offering you a chance to concentrate on your art without worrying about this course."

"How do you know I'm an artist?"

"I asked around," Whitman answered with another shrug.

"I could report you to the dean."

"No one would believe you and it would only be your word against mine." His lips turned pouty as he whined, "A poor, desperate little undergrad willing to do anything to pass a course."

Ramie looked at him and smiled. "I'm not desperate enough to sleep with you. There's not enough alcohol on the planet," she said. "As you may have noticed, you're not exactly my type."

"Think about it," he said as he turned away. Then he stopped and gazed back at her, smiling. "You do know, of course, that part of my job includes grading exams. The closer we get to the end, the better my offer might look."

She scowled and muttered, "Yeah, but you'll still be disgusting." Her eyes briefly scanned him from head to toe before she began walking away.

EMMA ROTHENBERG FINISHED her shower and exchanged her tennis outfit for comfortable Capri pants and a sleeveless shirt. She slipped her feet into well-worn Keds and picked up her tennis racket. Her last shot was an accident that curved slightly to bounce inside their opponent's line. She looked at the trophy and almost laughed. Hopefully they had raised enough money for the scholarship fund to make a difference. She was distracted more than once by the presence of Ramie Sunderlund. She saw her at the refreshment stand and then caught glimpses of her in the stands a few times. She frowned thinking about the young woman sitting with Ramie and wondered about their possible relationship. She looked like a child and had trouble keeping her hands off Ramie. She wasn't sure why, but was glad Ramie appeared to be annoyed by the young woman's attention.

Emma dug her keys from her duffle bag as she walked toward her car. She opened the trunk of her older model Chevrolet and tossed her racket and duffle inside. When she slammed the trunk closed, she glanced back at the tennis complex. She squinted when she saw Ramie leaning against the wall, chatting with Emma's graduate assistant, Travis Whitman. It was the height of impropriety. Ramie walked away before Emma could do anything and Travis watched her for a moment before walking in the opposite direction and joining some friends.

Emma opened her car door and sat there for a few minutes until Ramie was almost out of sight. Then she started her vehicle and drove slowly away. She watched as Ramie turned off the main sidewalk through campus and walked toward the Fine Arts Building. Emma would need to speak to Travis Monday morning. It was possible that the conversation between him and Ramie had been nothing. Innocent small talk.

Chapter Four

TRAVIS LEANED BACK in the old wooden chair in the office he shared with three other graduate assistants. The room was as small as a rabbit warren and afforded absolutely no privacy. The only time he could study in peace was early in the morning. He pulled a lower drawer out and propped his feet on it, reading from the text in his lap. He lit a cigarette and sipped cold coffee while he read. He was startled when the intercom on his desk buzzed loudly. He sat up and pushed the button.

"Whitman," he answered.

"Come into my office for a moment, please, Mr. Whitman," Dr. Rothenberg's voice crackled.

"Be there in a moment, Dr. Rothenberg."

He released the button and threw his textbook on the desk as he stood. What could that fuckin' bitch want at seven in the morning, he thought as he took one last drag before stubbing out the cigarette. He took a deep breath to calm himself and left his office.

Emma's office was on the same floor of Donlevy Hall, but in what the graduate students referred to as the high rent section. The inhabitants could actually turn around in their offices. Bookcases lined the walls. The whole area smelled like the stacks in the library, the scent of serious academia. Travis stopped at a water fountain near the restrooms and took a drink to get the taste of coffee out of his mouth. He reached in his pant pocket and popped a breath mint into his mouth as he rapped on Emma's door.

"Enter," her voice called out.

Travis opened the door and cast a bright smile in Emma's direction. He took a seat in front of her desk and waited until she finished writing on the paper in front of her. She took her glasses off and placed the cap back on her fountain pen before readjusting her body and resting her elbows on the desk.

"I saw you at the tennis tournament over the weekend," Emma started.

"Congratulations on your victory, by the way," Travis interrupted.

"Lucky shot," she acknowledged. "When I was leaving I happened to see you talking with Miss Sunderlund, a student in my Twentieth Century American Author class."

"Sunderlund?" Travis asked.

Emma watched him as he pretended to think. Finally, he said, "The blonde, right?"

"Yes," Emma said.

Travis wiggled slightly in the chair.

"It's completely improper and a violation of university rules of ethics for you to interact socially with any student in my classes while you are acting as my assistant, Mr. Whitman."

He exhaled a deep breath before speaking. "I told her that, Dr. Rothenberg. I didn't want to get her in trouble. The truth is, and it's a little embarrassing, she approached me about altering her grade."

"What led her to believe you would agree to such a thing?"

Travis cleared his throat and leaned closer. "I have no idea, but she...uh...she offered to...uh...have sex with me if I agreed."

"I gather you didn't find that offer...tempting."

"No. I mean, she's a pretty girl and all, Dr. Rothenberg, but not really my type. And she's a little young. I would never risk such a thing."

She gave him an ingenuous smile. "That was all I wanted to know, Mr. Whitman. Thank you."

Travis stood and turned to go. His hand had barely touched the door to her office when she said, "Oh, before I forget." He stopped and looked back at her. "I'm caught up with my paperwork and would like to grade Friday's exams personally. I'll collect them myself and take them home over the weekend. Thank you," she said, shoving her glasses back on and uncapping her pen again.

"I don't mind reading them, Dr. Rothenberg," Travis offered.

"I need to get a feel for my students' level of comprehension. Take the weekend off." She looked up at him. "I insist."

"THE TRAGIC HERO in American literature is a character whose origins can be traced back through history. He can be seen easily in the character of Oedipus and certainly in numerous Shakespearian works such as *Othello*," Emma said near the end of class the following Wednesday afternoon. "Are there any questions or comments?"

Ramie raised her hand tentatively. When Emma noticed, she nodded. "Miss Sunderlund?"

"I don't agree that Othello should be included in a list of tragic heroes," Ramie said. "In fact, I wouldn't describe him as a hero at all, tragic or otherwise."

"Really," Emma responded drolly, resting an elbow on the lectern.

Ramie heard a flurry of subdued muttering around her, but persisted with the discussion. "Othello was nothing more than an insecure coward, hardly worthy of being called any kind of hero. He may have been tragic, but far from a hero."

Ramie was shocked when Emma strode from the elevated stage and was suddenly standing over her, her eyes sharp and as menacing as storm clouds. "You don't have the expertise to dispute decades of study in literature, Miss Sunderlund."

"No, I don't, Dr. Rothenberg. However, Othello was a man who was eaten up by unfounded jealousy and distrust."

"Eaten up? A very erudite phrase," Emma chuckled.

"But accurate nonetheless," Ramie pressed on, although she was certain she was blushing, hoping not to make a total ass of herself. "Othello professed to love Desdemona and apparently they enjoyed an active and pleasurable private life." She watched Emma's brow rise and continued. "Despite that, he distrusted her enough to accept the unfounded word of another that she had cheated on him. Rather than confront her with his suspicions, his jealousy drove him to murder her without learning her side of the story. When he discovered he'd killed an innocent woman, he committed suicide rather than face judgment for his crime. That makes him a coward in my eyes. A true hero would have faced whatever punishment his actions dictated."

The longer Ramie spoke the closer Dr. Rothenberg came to her. She was so close that Ramie detected a delightful musky lavender and vanilla fragrance wafting off her body. "Assuming there is any merit whatsoever to what you say, how would you compare him to Roark in *The Fountainhead*?"

"Well, I can see Roark as a heroic character and I can see him as a tragic figure, but hesitate to put the two ideas together to call him a tragic hero. To me a tragic hero is a man, or woman, who achieves at least a partial victory against great odds, knowing they cannot survive the fight without facing some form of punishment. They sacrifice themselves for a greater good. Roark knew the risks and the rules. He took the risk, which was illegal, and deserved whatever punishment the law allowed. Sometimes breaking the rules can be a good thing, but not when it serves no greater good. Rosa Parks' refusal to sit at the back of the bus served a greater good because it affected many people. When Roark destroyed the building he had designed because he thought his ideas had been compromised, he was only concerned about himself. In the process he destroyed property that had been bought and paid for by others and could have served as homes for others. In essence, he deprived the owners of their property and others of a place to live."

"So individuality should be sold as a commodity?"

Ramie re-arranged her body and shrugged. "That's the way it is. I'm a sculptor. If a consumer commissions a piece from me, but they want it done in a manner and style that is offensive to me personally, my choices are to turn down the commission or take the money. If I accept it, but hate what I've created, that's the price I have to pay to earn the money I want. I might refuse to put my name to the work though," Ramie finished with a smile.

"Please see me in my office after class," Emma said in a low voice before turning away.

"I thought you needed this credit for graduation?" a young woman behind Ramie whispered.

"I do, but it's not illegal to think or have an opinion."

"Good luck with that argument, honey. No one disagrees with Rothenberg and lives to talk about it."

RAMIE STRAIGHTENED HER clothing and tapped at the door to Dr. Rothenberg's office.

"Come," Emma's voice said loudly.

Ramie closed the door behind her. "You wanted to see me, Dr. Rothenberg?"

Emma leaned back in her chair and removed her glasses. "That was a very interesting discussion today, Miss Sunderlund."

"It's only my opinion."

"Please. Have a seat." Emma waited until Ramie sat in the chair facing her desk. "I have to confess that you surprised me today."

"Why?"

"I don't know exactly. You're usually very quiet."

"Perhaps you think I really don't have anything of importance to contribute."

"I wouldn't go that far."

Ramie felt oddly emboldened and relaxed into her chair before speaking again. "I would. You know why I'm in this course. Literature is not my thing, but even I am capable of forming coherent thoughts about what I've read. And, in the long run, isn't that why this, or any other book or play is written? To encourage the reader to think and form their *own* opinion about what the author is saying, as well as how it is presented. This book expresses the author's opinion and she was hoping to convince her readers to agree with her opinion through the story."

"That's true. Virtually every fictional story is based on the author's opinion, belief or personal experiences. Do you like this author, Miss Sunderlund?"

"More than I thought I would. As an artist I understand Roark and I sympathize with his plight. However, I don't agree with the method he used to express his unhappiness."

"You would never destroy something you created because you don't like how it's being used?"

Ramie looked down at her hands and flexed her fingers. "Right now I don't believe I would, but there's always the possibility I might change my mind as I mature and gain more experience," she said with a smile.

Emma leaned her head back and stared at the ceiling for a few moments. The next time she looked at Ramie she said, "It wasn't my intention to insult you, Miss Sunderlund. I have given the same lecture on the tragic hero for several years now. Every year I deliberately say the same things, hoping to stimulate a discussion of what makes a tragic hero. Until today, my students have taken my words as Gospel and never challenged what I said."

"I think they lack confidence in their own knowledge level," Ramie said. She hesitated a moment before continuing. "It doesn't help that they're, well, afraid of you. I'm sorry, Dr. Rothenberg."

"Don't apologize, my dear. You're the first student in a long time with enough guts to express your opinion and then defend it rationally. A teacher cannot ask for more than that." Emma shrugged. "If I intimidate students in the process, there isn't much I can do about that. You seem to have recovered."

Ramie didn't know exactly what to say. "Well, thank you, I guess."

"Never be afraid to express a well-thought out opinion, Ms. Sunderlund. I would be the ogre my students believe I am if I discouraged freethinking. I am considered an expert in my field, but that doesn't mean everything I say is accurate or even intended to be."

"Yes, ma'am."

"That is all I wanted to say." Emma picked up her glasses and slid them on. "Don't forget we will start a new unit next week after the exam."

Ramie slung her satchel over her shoulder and left Emma's office.

RAMIE MADE HER way down the quiet corridor, her conversation with Emma running through her mind. Emma had surprised her. Instead of being angry because Ramie had challenged her, she seemed almost grateful for their verbal sparring. Away from the lecture setting, Emma Rothenberg's voice had a rich quality that Ramie found attractive. And the way her eyes seemed alive as they penetrated Ramie's took her breath away. Damn! The sound of her own footsteps brought Ramie's attention back to what she was doing. Unlike the bustling and often boisterous hallways of the art department, the English department hallways seemed as quiet as a tomb. Ramie shuddered at the thought, knowing she couldn't tolerate working daily in such a sterile environment.

An office door opened as she passed by and a hand grabbed her upper arm. She was startled and jerked away.

"What were you doing in Rothenberg's office?" Travis hissed as he shoved her roughly into the wall. The back of her head struck the wall and she pushed against him.

"It didn't involve you or your friendly offer," Ramie said.

"Then why is she insisting on grading the next exam herself?" he asked as he pressed his body closer.

"I'm not a freakin' mind reader. She might have heard about your little scheme from someone else, but it wasn't me," she insisted.

"It better not have been or you'll regret it."

"Don't threaten me," she growled as she lowered her shoulder and pushed him away.

Chapter Five

FRIDAY AFTER LUNCH Ramie hurried up the steps of Donlevy Hall. She had been up all night studying for the unit final in Dr. Rothenberg's class. As soon as her butt hit her customary seat on row three, she pulled a pen and a blue book from her backpack and was ready to begin, hopefully before she forgot everything she had crammed into her brain overnight. She watched Travis Whitman enter the lecture hall and begin counting out the number of test papers for each row. The exam consisted, as usual, of a single sheet of paper. She refused to look at him as he stepped up to her row. She took the top exam and passed the remaining papers to her right as she glanced over the five essay questions on the single sheet. Obviously, Rothenberg had never heard of the words "multiple-choice".

Ramie smiled, confidant she could adequately answer at least four of the questions in front of her. The final question wasn't really a question. It was more of an interpretation statement. In other words, it required an opinion. Since Ramie didn't believe an individual's opinion could be wrong, she felt certain she could posit an answer and back it up with enough factual information to get at least partial credit. She settled into her seat and began writing, quickly regurgitating what she knew concerning *The Fountainhead* and its themes.

Ramie was so intent on getting everything she knew or thought on paper that she didn't pay attention to Emma as she entered the room. Emma spoke briefly to Travis and walked slowly around the auditorium after he left. As Emma passed Ramie's seat, she paused for a moment. Ramie caught a wisp of a familiar scent she would recognize anywhere and smiled as it calmed her. She was momentarily distracted by the movement of Emma's hips as they swayed beneath the fabric of her slacks. She was so engrossed in observing the muscles moving against the fabric that she was startled when she heard, "Stop writing and insert your exam into your blue book before passing them toward the center aisle." Ramie finished a sentence and placed her materials on top of the stack as it reached her. Before Emma took the stack from her, she said softly, "Name?"

Ramie looked at the front of her blue book and saw it was blank. She grabbed the book and scribbled her name on it. When she handed it back she said quietly, "Thank you."

When Emma dismissed the class, Ramie felt light-headed as she stood to leave. Perhaps her brain was lighter now that she had purged it of the information it held before the test began. She hoisted her satchel over her head and picked up her portfolio.

She quickly rounded the railing on the third floor and started down the stairs. At the second floor landing she saw Travis Whitman, chatting with another graduate assistant. They parted company and Travis rested against the landing wall, waiting as Ramie made her way toward him.

"So how do you think you did on the exam, Sunderlund?" Travis asked.

"Good enough," Ramie said as she tried to continue down the stairs without stopping.

Travis stepped in front of her and momentarily blocked her descent. He grabbed her arm and pressed her against the landing wall.

EMMA LEFT HER office and locked it behind her. She glanced at her wristwatch. She still had twenty minutes to make it to a meeting in Dean Carver's office. He was a blowhard and his monotone voice was boring enough to put a zombie back to sleep. I don't know how Millie endures it, she thought with a smile. She'd decided she needed caffeine to stay awake for the next couple of hours and was planning to stop at the Student Union for an extra-large cup of coffee. She reached the top of the staircase and was pulling her overcoat over her shoulders when she heard angry-sounding voices coming from lower on the staircase. When she peeked around the corner she saw her assistant in a heated discussion with Ramie Sunderlund.

"You're making a serious mistake, Sunderlund," Travis hissed bringing his face closer to Ramie's and jabbing his fingers into her shoulder. "There's no way in hell you'll pass Rothenberg's class without my assistance. I'll see to that!"

"Get out of my way before I have to hurt you!" Ramie demanded, her voice as hard as steel.

Ramie attempted to shove past Travis, but his hands grabbed the neck of her jacket and pulled her face closer to his. "Don't mess with me, you little bitch," he warned.

Ramie brought her knee up solidly into his crotch. She managed to push him away when he doubled over and released her. "You remember that and don't threaten me again, you prick!" she said loudly before hurrying down the remaining steps while flipping him the bird.

Then Whitman straightened, and took a few moments in an

attempt to re-establish his dignity and self-control. After taking a deep breath and re-arranging his slacks he turned to climb up the final flight of steps. "Bitch," he muttered. "I'll fix you."

Emma backed away and returned quickly to her office. She picked up the phone on her desk and dialed. From her office window she watched as Ramie walked purposefully across the grassy mall toward the Fine Arts Building.

RAMIE WAS STILL angry when she entered a studio on the first floor of the art department. She slammed the door shut and threw her satchel. She would pass Rothenberg's class, dammit, and then concentrate all her energy on completing her portfolio. She yanked away the sheet covering the slab of marble she had purchased for her final sculpture. She stared at it a few moments, letting her hands skim over the smooth stone until she could feel it warming under her touch. She placed both hands on the marble and stood stock still, taking deep breaths until her mind cleared and relaxed. Then she examined the clay model she'd made for the larger piece. She planned to entitle the piece "Untouchable" and smiled as the image of the finished piece came to her mind. No one would ever know the identity of her imaginary model, but even the title seemed to describe Emma Rothenberg. Like Emma, the stone seemed cold and unfeeling, hiding what lay beneath. It was a highly stylized piece and the face should match that perspective. She worked on various angles and finally made the decision to sculpt a hand that would cover the face to obstruct a complete view of a face in ecstasy.

THE TELEPHONE IN Ramie's room was ringing when she returned to her dorm later that evening. She unlocked the door and stepped inside. Leslie was sound asleep and buried beneath her usual mound of covers. Ramie grabbed the phone and whispered, "Hello."

"Miss Sunderlund? This is Dr. Rothenberg."

"Stop kiddin' around, Donna. Leslie's asleep, for cryin' out loud."

"Miss Sunderlund," the voice repeated. "I can assure you that I am not...Donna, was it? Do you have, by any chance, the previous exams you've taken in my course?"

"Probably, but it would take me a while to locate them."

"When you do, would you bring them to my office before the Thanksgiving break?"

"Need a laugh to cheer you up?" Ramie quipped.

"I need to see them."

"Will I get them back for my memory book?"

Emma chuckled, a sound that strangely warmed Ramie's ear. "Absolutely."

"I'll see what I can do before the class meets again. If you prefer, I work as a student assistant at the university library tomorrow from one until six. I can take them to work with me."

"I...I appreciate that, Miss Sunderlund. Have a pleasant evening." Emma said before she disconnected.

"I...will," Ramie said to a dead phone line. She leaned against the wall and hung up. She'd never noticed how breathy—how intimate Dr. Rothenberg's voice was before. Maybe it was only because she was standing in a virtually dark room. Or perhaps it was because she herself was whispering to avoid waking Leslie. Whatever it was, it aroused Ramie and made her weak in the knees.

EMMA LEANED BACK in her chair behind the desk in her home office and took one last puff from the cigarette between her fingers before crushing it in an ashtray. She had chosen to only smoke when alone at home and never had more than two or three cigarettes over the course of an evening. The room was dark except for the banker's lamp her father had given her years earlier. She had been trying for hours to contact Ramie Sunderland. She placed her elbows on the desk and gazed at her grade book. How could anyone do so consistently poorly on written exams and still make valuable contributions during a class discussion? She had been strangely disappointed, especially after Ramie had shown a bright mind on a subject she didn't really care about. Perhaps Emma should begin to care about more than literature. There was probably much an artist like Ramie Sunderlund could teach her...about art. Emma cleared her throat and stood to organize her desk. She had spent part of the evening reading the answers to the latest exam Ramie had taken. The answers had been astute and concise. The examples provided were beyond the scope of what had been discussed in class. Without seeing Ramie's previous exams there wasn't much she could do in the middle of the night. She flipped the desk light off and made her way upstairs to her bedroom with the memory of Ramie's whispered voice in her mind.

THE FOLLOWING AFTERNOON, Ramie grabbed the two previous exams she had taken in Rothenberg's class and stuffed them into her shoulder satchel. She hoped it would be a slow shift at the library. She needed to survey the information in several books to compile an annotated bibliography of Renaissance artists as part of an assignment for her History of Renaissance Art class. It was boring and something of a no-brainer, but had to be done. She gnawed on an apple as she walked across campus. Leaves were beginning to desert trees as the fall weather grew cooler. She was assigned to work in Special Collections that afternoon and didn't really expect many to be using the collections for research on a Thursday. She finished her apple by the time she started up the broad steps toward the building's main doors. She waved at the student worker behind the main desk and made her way to the employee break room to stash her snack for later in the day in the refrigerator. She pulled her library identification from her satchel and clipped it to the front of her clothing. After chatting with the student worker who had the morning shift, she shoved her satchel into a legal-size file cabinet and sat behind the Special Collections desk.

She stayed surprisingly busy for the first half of her shift. Non-university individuals doing private research took a great deal of her time as she explained how to locate items and made sure they knew they were to wear white cotton gloves and use nothing other than a pencil to make a paper request. Many of their documents were quite old and had to be handled carefully. No one was allowed to have more than one box of materials at a time and those were delivered to them by a collections worker.

Ramie was pushing a library cart with a large container of maps for a gentleman working on a project involving early Ohio cartography when she saw Dr. Rothenberg enter the Special Collections area. Ramie dropped the requested materials off at a table and repeated the rules for handling the maps. If he needed copies made, he would have to make a written request.

Ramie strolled slowly back toward the desk area giving herself a chance to take in Emma's casual clothing. She smiled as she stepped behind the desk. "Welcome to Special Collections, Dr. Rothenberg."

"Thank you, Miss Sunderlund. Were you able to locate your exams?"

"Yes," Ramie said as she reached beneath the counter and opened the drawer of the file cabinet that held her shoulder satchel. She reached inside and pulled the two blue books from the satchel and placed them on the desk.

"May I use one of the private carrels?"

"Of course. It's a slow day so pick one."

EMMA SELECTED A private room to go over Ramie's exams, as well as several others she suspected may have been incorrectly graded by Travis Whitman. She spent a considerable amount of time spot-checking the exams based on what Travis Whitman had recorded and found a number of discrepancies, most involving young women. Other than Ramie's, Emma found several grades had been raised and she didn't want to think about the implications of that. She discovered that even though Ramie Sunderlund had not earned higher than a C average, she was not failing the course. Others who should have failed the exams were given higher grades. She was prepared to acknowledge the discrepancies with the students involved. She would need to turn in a written statement to the Dean's Office. Travis Whitman had already been dismissed for what she perceived as ethical violations and her statement would merely seal those actions. She stretched and packed up the suspect exams. She opened the door to the small room, but when she glanced at the clock on the wall, it was after six. Ramie would be gone. Emma had already made the grade changes in her grade record and would inform the students involved after they returned from the up-coming Thanksgiving break. As she left the library, she was proud of herself for discovering and proving Whitman's illegal sideline.

Chapter Six

RAMIE WAVED AS Leslie's VW bus turned out of the parking lot of their dormitory at dusk. She took a deep breath as she spun around to re-enter the old brick building. She'd spoken to her mother a few days earlier and pled her case for not taking the bus home for Thanksgiving. She had a week off and would spend four days in a cramped seat, surrounded by holiday travelers, including small, screaming children. She would have much more time at home to visit and rest if she waited for the nearly month-long Christmas break. Although Ramie knew her mother was probably crying on the other end of the line, she knew it was for the best. She'd already made arrangements to stay in the dorm, along with a few other girls from out-of-state, and the dorm director was preparing a Thanksgiving meal for them. Ramie had also spoken to the head of the art department and been given a key to the studio area. The only class she would have to worry about was Rothenberg's English course and now she would have the time to finish her reading assignments in peace. She looked up at the overcast sky and deeply inhaled the cool, crisp fall air. A light dusting of snow from earlier in the day covered everything. The blades of grass crunched under her feet as she made her way up the steps into the dorm.

Just a few more months and she would begin a new life. If her plans fell into place, next fall she would be a graduate instructor in studio art. Her dream was to teach others to love art, especially sculpture. Eventually she would find a way to produce her own works and hopefully sell them to supplement her income. She wrapped her arms around her body as she moved down the abnormally quiet hall.

After climbing the three flights of stairs to her room, Ramie stuffed a few things into her satchel and grabbed her portfolio. She would spend part of the evening going over each item and compiling a list of what she still needed to produce to complete the senior portfolio required for graduation.

"Don't stay out too late, Ramie," the dorm director said as Ramie came down the stairs and into the main lobby.

"I won't, Miss DeMaris. What time will you lock the doors tonight?"

"About nine. Are you still having turkey and the fixings with us on Thursday?"

Ramie smiled at the friendly older woman. "I wouldn't miss it," she said.

The woman leaned forward slightly. "If you come in late tonight, just ring the bell. I'll be up later than usual reading. Be careful."

"I will." Ramie pushed the front door open and began her walk across campus to the Fine Arts Building. She tightened her coat belt and stuffed her hands in her coat pockets. She hated working with cold hands. The marble she worked with never felt right with cold hands.

SNOW BEGAN FALLING early in the evening, marking the beginning of a long season of snow and ice. Emma loved the sight of new-fallen snow before people and animals trampled it into a brown slushy mess. She had been surprised to receive a phone call from Millie at her home earlier that evening. Ordinarily Emma would still be in her office, but had decided to leave early due to the holiday. Millie needed to speak to Emma as soon as possible, but preferred to speak to her in person.

"Let's go, Louie," Emma called lightly as she removed the Bassett's leash and harness from the closet near the front door of her home. The animal, his ears dragging slightly, stretched as he left his warm comfortable bed next to Emma's favorite chair. His ears lifted slightly as he spun in a circle in front of her. He then sat patiently as she slipped his harness on and opened the front door.

Twenty minutes later, after several short stops to allow Louie to investigate an interesting scent, she waited in a small copse of evergreens near the perimeter of the campus. Emma thought back to the brief conversation with Millie. It was unusual for Millie to call her, especially at home in the evening. Millie had sounded upset. The wind from the previous day had died down and Emma's calf-length lambskin coat, which was belted over her cream turtleneck and black slacks, was enough to keep her body warm inside the shelter of the thick trees.

She saw Millie and waved to her as she came closer, while Louie picked up the familiar scent, which caused his tail to wag furiously. The fur-lined hood of Millie's thigh-length winter parka partially shielded her face, but Emma didn't see her familiar smile as she approached. She knelt down to acknowledge Louie's eager greeting. She pulled a rawhide treat from her pocket and offered it to him. He accepted the gift and found a clear spot beneath a nearby tree and plopped down, holding the rawhide between his front paws as he began to gnaw contentedly.

Emma wrapped Millie in a warm embrace after Millie joined her in the small sheltered alcove of evergreens.

"What was so urgent, darling?" Emma asked after she kissed Millie lightly.

"Stanton has accepted the chancellor's position at Pitt," Millie said. "I wanted you to hear it from me first."

"You're leaving?" Emma asked with a frown.

"He's staying until the end of the semester."

"That's only a month away."

They stood together silently for several minutes before Millie said, "He wants me to leave after Thanksgiving to get the house ready before he arrives."

"Do you think he suspects?"

"I don't think he really cares," Millie snorted "But it's a wonderful opportunity for him."

Emma saw tears forming in Millie's eyes. "Please don't, Millie," she said as she took her lover in her arms and hugged her. "We knew it would happen."

"But not so damn soon," Millie mumbled against Emma's shoulder. "I'll miss you, darling."

"I'll miss you, too."

"Just hold me, Emma. I promise not to embarrass either of us." She searched Emma's face. "Will there be a time for us to be together one last time?" she asked.

"We'll make time," Emma assured her with a gentle smile.

RAMIE WANDERED SLOWLY across the deserted quadrangle that separated the engineering buildings near the edge of the campus, enjoying the invigorating cold air accompanying the light snowfall that had begun before she left the dorm. The gray clouds overhead promised more snow that night. A smile crossed her lips as she stopped and removed her satchel. Setting her portfolio down, she fell onto her back in an undisturbed patch of snow and raised and lowered her arms while her legs spread back and forth, creating a snow angel.

Ramie carefully stood and looked at her creation while brushing snow from her legs and arms. She felt like a child again and, in spite of everything, was happy. As she shrugged her satchel back on, she saw movement not far away near a small stand of evergreens. She watched as a figure stepped from behind the trees and was joined by a slightly smaller figure. They embraced briefly and Ramie saw it was two women. One removed her glove before reaching up and caressing the taller woman's face tenderly. Ramie looked around to be sure no one would see her before creeping closer. She was shocked when she peeked through the trees in time to catch a glimpse of Dr. Rothenberg's face as she brought Millicent Carver's hand to her lips and kissed it tenderly. Emma stepped a half step closer and pulled Mrs. Carver into an embrace as their lips met in a lingering kiss. Ramie closed her eyes, embarrassed at observing such an intimate moment. When she cracked her eyes open again, the women had separated, now linked only by a single hand. Millicent Carver released Rothenberg's hand and turned away slowly, walking from within the trees. Emma watched her departure, her hands jammed into the pockets of her coat for several moments before turning and moving in the opposite direction with Louie in tow. Sure she hadn't been seen, Ramie backed away. She felt sadness and a little pity for Dr. Rothenberg, having to secretly meet a woman she obviously cared about, but was unable to really be with, unable to acknowledge her feelings openly to anyone. However, Emma Rothenberg was a grown woman and knew there were consequences to every decision.

Chapter Seven

RAMIE OPENED THE front glass door of the Fine Arts Building and smiled up at the old glass and steel building. She made her way to a group of rooms that formed a semi-circle along the back wall. A bronze fountain sat in the center of the semi-circle and water tumbled from below the feet of a huntsman standing over a frightened fawn lying beside the still body of its mother. The fountain sculpture had been created by another student a few years earlier and even though it had been beautifully rendered in great detail, Ramie hated it. She didn't like the subject and the huntsman's face revealed little emotion. Maybe that was the point. The huntsman's face showed no remorse about what he'd done. The fate of the fawn would forever be in doubt.

Ramie took the key to studio room five from her jean pocket and opened the door. She reached inside and flipped on the bright overhead lights and carried her portfolio to the large worktable. She shrugged her coat off and hung it on the back of the studio door. She dragged a stool up to the worktable and unzipped her portfolio. She slipped headphones over her head and inserted a cassette into her portable player. Once the soothing music started, she carefully examined each piece from her portfolio and re-read the process descriptions she had prepared to accompany each one. There were a total of twenty projects which demonstrated her understanding and level of mastery in each medium as well as the variations of each medium. She examined each piece under a variety of light sources set up around the small room and made notes of any differences in texture she found. Photography wasn't her strongest medium, but she was generally pleased by her effort.

Eventually she felt the strain in her eyes and decided to take a break before turning her attention to the large, pink-hued marble slab that sat on a smaller turntable behind her. She plucked an apple from her satchel, along with a bottle of water. She swiveled her stool and visually examined the stone. It would be a slow process finding the hidden figure inside the rock. In her mind's eye she could see how the finished project should look. Thus far she had only found the time to roughly free the figure. As soon as the fall semester ended, she'd be able to devote much more time to the piece. The final step would be the polishing.

Then it would gleam.

She smiled as she chewed then slipped off the stool. She ran a hand over the roughed out figure waiting to be brought to life. She hummed and moved her feet in rhythm to the music, shutting out everything else. It was the tradition of the art department to donate the senior sculptures to the city to adorn the parks throughout the town unless they were purchased by private collectors. She wasn't sure she wanted others staring at her fantasy.

She finished her apple and tossed the core into a nearby garbage can and picked up her hammer and chisel to further coax the figure from the stone. She clipped the cassette player onto the waist of her jeans and increased the volume before she began working.

Suddenly the light was extinguished, leaving her in total darkness in the windowless room. She had been preparing to strike the marble, but managed to stop the hammer's downward movement before it hit the chisel. A moment later she was blinded by a bright light. A gloved hand covered her mouth from behind. Ramie attempted to strike the person with the hammer. She missed, but managed to stab something solid with the pointed chisel.

"Bitch!" a man's voice hissed, releasing her.

Ramie took the opportunity to make a break for the door. She found the knob, but was grabbed from behind again and torn away from the door. She ran into the marble and wrapped her arms around it to prevent it from falling from the worktable. While she stabilized it, a fist struck the side of her head and dazed her, knocking her headphones off. Before she could clear her mind, a hand grabbed her sweatshirt and jerked her forward. She opened her mouth to scream, but a blow to her abdomen knocked the breath from her body and doubled her over. The hand released her and she fell to her knees, her arms wrapping around her abdomen as she fought to catch her breath. She was trying to push her body up when she was shoved over and kicked in the ribs. To protect her head, she brought her hands up to cover it. A hand grabbed her arm and moved it to deliver another blow to her face, splitting her bottom lip. She groaned and didn't fight back when she was forced onto her back. A heavy body sat across her lower abdomen to hold her down.

"Grab her other arm," the man ordered.

Fingers wrapped tightly around her left wrist and pulled her arm out shoulder-height away from her body. Her right wrist was pressed against the cold floor. Ramie jerked at a prick of pain in the center of her right hand. Her eyes widened as they followed the beam of the headlamp.

"No!" she screamed, twisting her body in an attempt to

escape before the hand covered her mouth again.

"You should've just gone along," a voice rasped as the body straddling hers leaned forward.

The hand over her mouth was making it difficult to breathe. She could do no more than watch as the rock hammer fell forcefully, driving the chisel through the tender palm of her right hand. Unbearably excruciating pain shot through her hand and radiated out into her fingers. Her body bucked to dislodge the man holding her down and tears blurred her vision as she struggled against the pain until the hammer struck the chisel again. She heard the snap of bone as the chisel was driven through soft flesh, pinning her hand to the hardwood floor. Her final scream died as she passed out.

RAMIE BLINKED AS indescribable pain brought back the memory of the assault. She tried to move, but searing pain stopped her. My hands! her mind screamed. She struggled to draw a deep breath. It was black in the studio and she didn't know what time it was. Was it even the same night? Something was very wrong. She couldn't move either arm without blinding pain. Something was in her mouth! Panic began to creep in. Would her assailants return? Her mind was fuzzy and battling the throbbing surges of pain being sent from both hands.

It's unbearable! Don't think about it. Block it out so you can get help! No! It hurts too much to block out. You have to protect your hands! Too late. You can't even move them! Someone will come. Who, you idiot? It's Thanksgiving break. You're here alone and helpless. You're never helpless! Think of something. Please, it hurts so much!

Despite the disjointed conversation in her head, Ramie felt disoriented. Every time she woke up it was dark. The studio lights were turned off. She was hungry and, God, she was so thirsty. Her hands were numb, but still pulsed in unison with her heartbeat. Had she been lying on the cold floor minutes, hours, or days? Tears burned her eyes, but she couldn't blink them away. Her left eye was swollen shut and whatever was stuffed into her mouth prevented saliva from forming. Breathing was a little difficult and she wondered if her nose was broken. She caught a faint scent of something burned, but couldn't identify it. Was she going to die alone in the studio? When the helplessness became too much to bear she allowed her body to give in to what she hoped became an endless sleep.

"CAREFUL, CAREFUL. WATCH her hands," someone said.

Ramie wanted to open her eyes as she dreamed her body was moving. She felt something being pulled away from her cheeks and then something else sliding from her mouth. It was so dry. Jolts of pain struck her as someone gripped her wrists. Something soft and spongy now enclosed her hands, but the pain of a thousand needles punctured them. She moaned like a wounded animal as the chisels, meant to create beauty, were slowly pulled away. She tried, despite the pain, to bring her arms closer to her body and cradle her mangled hands against her chest.

Bright light blinded her and she shook her head. "No," she begged. "No more." Sobs racked her body.

"We won't hurt you, honey. Let us help you," a voice whispered calmly. "Get that gurney in here!"

Ramie managed to open her right eye and saw she was surrounded by people she didn't know. "How...long?" she rasped out.

"You're gonna be fine," a man starting an IV said.

"How long?" Ramie asked again, pouring all the strength she had into her voice.

The man looked startled and glanced at her. "A few hours," he finally answered.

"Can't feel my hands," she whispered as tears fell down the side of her bruised and bloodied face. She finally looked at the man working on her and asked, "Why?"

He shook his head. "I don't know, sweetie. Wish I did."

"Was I..." she wanted to ask, but couldn't bring herself to finish the question.

Suddenly she was lifted and rolled away. All she saw was a glimpse of the destruction around her. The beautiful marble slab had been shattered and her precious portfolio had been burned and the blackened remnants scattered haphazardly around the studio.

THREE DAYS AFTER the students returned from the Thanksgiving break, Emma was more than prepared to acknowledge the grading errors she had found. However, Ramie Sunderlund had been absent from class on Monday. She had been absent again today.

A bold rap on Emma's office door broke her concentration. "Enter," she called out.

A young women Emma didn't know opened the door and poked her head around it. Emma was certain she wasn't one of her students.

"Dr. Rothenberg?"

"Yes. Can I help you?"

"Um, my name is Leslie Maddsen. I'm Ramie Sunderlund's roommate."

Emma leaned back in her chair and looked at the nervous young woman. "Why are you here?" she asked pointedly.

"Ramie hasn't been to your class in a couple of days."

"Where is she?"

"Actually, she's in the hospital."

"Did she have an accident while she was home for Thanksgiving?"

"Oh, she didn't go home for Thanksgiving, Dr. Rothenberg. She stayed here to try to get ahead on her class work. Mostly on her portfolio." Leslie frowned and tears came to her eyes. "Someone assaulted her while she was working in her studio." Leslie swallowed and pulled a tissue from her pocket. "She was hurt pretty bad and her portfolio was destroyed."

"Badly. She was hurt pretty badly, Miss Maddsen," Emma said tightly, unsure why the grammatical error seemed even remotely important.

"Of course," Leslie mumbled as she blew her nose. Afterward she cleared her throat. "She asked me to find out what work she'd be missing. She doesn't know yet how long it will take her to recover. A few weeks at least. She's worried about her English grade."

Emma frowned before asking, "Is she in the local hospital?"

"Yeah, room 220."

Emma stood up and went around the desk. "I'll gather whatever I have available and see that she receives it. Please tell her it's important that she try to keep up with the reading assignments. Thank you for letting me know."

"No prob," Leslie said, glancing at her wristwatch. "I have to contact her other professors before it gets any later." She backed toward the door and grabbed the handle. She pulled the door open and nodded toward Emma as she left.

Emma slumped back against her desk and covered her face with a hand. She took a steadying breath, walked around her desk, leaning down to open a bottom drawer and picked up her purse, slinging it over her shoulder. Without bothering to tidy up the papers on her desk as she usually did, Emma turned off her office lights and locked the door before she hurried out of the building and toward her vehicle. Ordinarily she would have walked to school, but the weather that morning had been nasty enough that she decided to drive instead. Walking was excellent exercise and saved gasoline, but now she felt the need to hurry.

EMMA TAPPED ON the closed door of room 220 in the four-story hospital that served the area around the university. Even though it was the height of visiting hours, there were no lights on in Ramie Sunderlund's room.

"Can I help you, ma'am?" a nurse asked as she wheeled her drug cart out of the room next door. "Are you here to see Ramie?"

"Yes."

"Are you her mom?"

Emma raised her chin and glared at the nurse. "No. I am one of her professors. I just found out she'd been injured and came to check on her."

"I'm sorry, ma'am. We thought one of her parents might be here by now."

"Can she have visitors?"

"She's had quite a few friends drop by, but she stays pretty loopy from the pain killers right now."

"Perhaps I should come back when she's feeling better," Emma said and started to turn away.

"That will probably be quite a while," the nurse said. "After her surgery."

"Surgery! For what? I was told she'd been assaulted."

"More like she had the snot beat out of her. And her poor hands! I don't know if she'll ever be able to use them again."

The nurse's statement hit Emma like a bucket of cold water. She turned and pushed open the door to Ramie's room. She must be devastated, Emma thought as she stood frozen in the semi-dark room, staring at the figure lying on the bed. Her arms were elevated slightly and held in place by a traction bar. Thick gauze bandages encased both hands. Emma felt the beginning of tears prickle behind her eyes.

"Leslie?" a weak voice asked through the darkness.

Emma stepped forward, closer to the bed. "No," she answered softly. "It's Dr. Rothenberg. Leslie told me you were injured."

"Light," Ramie croaked.

Emma moved next to the bed and leaned over Ramie to find the switch for the lights. She fumbled with the switch as she glanced down. The fading light seeping through the shades highlighted Ramie's face. Her eyes glistened. Despite her injuries, Ramie's eyes held volumes of things unsaid. Emma closed her eyes and took a steadying breath.

"Cover your eyes in case this is the wrong switch," Emma said.

"Can't."

Emma lowered her right hand and held it slightly above

Ramie's face. The low, indirect light hummed a moment before it flickered on above the metal headboard. Emma slowly removed her hand and drew it into a tight fist as she gazed down at Ramie. Her delicate features were marred by bruises, deep and purple. Her eyes were bloodshot and her lips were split.

"Oh, my God," Emma breathed. "Who did this?

"Don't know," Ramie answered. "I'm a mess," she said softly. She tried to readjust her body on the bed and sucked in a sharp breath as the apparatus holding her arms moved. Around the bandages, Emma could see dark purple or blackened fingertips protruding from beneath.

"Will you be all right, Miss Sunderlund?"

"Oh yeah," she said, forcing a smile that died before it was fully formed.

"Is there anything I can get for you?"

Ramie blinked up at Emma and suddenly her face softened. Despite the cuts and bruises she was still alluring. Ramie moved her lips to say something, but nothing came out. Instead she slowly shook her head and her eyes sparkled with unshed tears.

Emma cleared her throat and placed her hand lightly on Ramie's shoulder. "When is your surgery?"

"To...tomorrow m...m...morning," Ramie stuttered. "I...I'm scared." Tears swelled in her eyes and overflowed down the sides of her head, disappearing into curly blonde ringlets. "What...what if I can't scul...sculpt again?" Although she tried to stop it, a sob broke loose.

Emma wiped away the tears and laid her hand across Ramie's cheek. "You will," she said as soon as Ramie looked at her. "You have to believe you will. I do. For now don't worry about anything except getting well again."

Emma stayed until Ramie fell asleep. She couldn't give an answer to why anyone would do such a horrible thing to the young woman. She drove home slowly, thinking. She would never admit that Ramie had gotten under her skin or that she cared what happened to her. She pulled into her garage and entered her house through the back door, stopping long enough to set her tea kettle on the stove to heat some water. A cup of tea would taste good right now. As she passed the clock in the downstairs hallway she was surprised at how long she'd stayed at the hospital. She called to Louie and let him into the back yard. He was a patient animal and she smiled as she watched him explore the areas he had already investigated many times before. She went into her home office and picked up the handset of the phone. She waited as the phone rang on the other end.

"Hello?" a woman's voice finally answered.

"Margaret, this is Dr. Rothenberg. Something has come up and I won't be in tomorrow. Would it be possible for you to cover my classes for the day?"

"Sure, Dr. Rothenberg. Anything special you want me to discuss in class?"

"There are notes on my desk you can use to guide you through the next lecture. They'll probably be glad to see someone besides me."

"Are you all right, Dr. Rothenberg?"

Emma rubbed her forehead with her thumb and forefinger. "Yes, I'm fine. Just a little tired."

"Don't worry about a thing," the cheerful voice of her new assistant said. "I'll leave the paperwork on your desk after the last class. Enjoy a long weekend."

"Thank you. I will. Good night, Margaret."

Emma returned the receiver to its cradle and walked back to the kitchen, catching the tea pot as it started to whistle. She filled Louie's food bowl and replenished his water, then pushed the back door open. He trotted inside, heading for the food that awaited him. She reached into the cabinet next to the sink and placed a tea bag in a cup, then poured hot water over it and dunked the tea bag a few times. She stirred in a spoonful of sugar before carrying the cup upstairs to her bedroom. She changed her clothes and slumped on her bed. She couldn't imagine anyone doing to another human being what had been done to Ramie Sunderlund. Someone, obviously a sadist, had tried very hard to destroy who the young woman was.

EARLY THE NEXT morning Emma returned to the hospital. She went to the second floor and hoped someone would tell her when Ramie's surgery would be. She stood at the nurse's desk and waited for the busy woman to acknowledge her.

"Can I help you?" the nurse finally asked as she stood to carry an armload of binders back to a shelf.

"Can you tell me when Miss Sunderlund's surgery will be today?"

The nurse glanced at the clock on the wall. "Should be here for her any time now. She's already been partially sedated. I think a nurse is removing her bandages now."

"I know it isn't visiting hours, but may I see her for a few moments so she knows she's not alone?" Emma asked.

"Are you a relative?"

Emma paused for a moment before answering. "Her aunt," she said.

"You can go in so she knows you're here, but don't get in the way, please."

"Thank you," Emma said. She walked to Ramie's room and took a deep breath before she pushed the door open.

Ramie was biting her lower lip and staring at the ceiling. Why the hell weren't Ramie's parents here to support her, Emma wondered. Surely they would know how frightened their daughter was. A nurse stood on the right side of the bed, carefully unwrapping the thick bandages. The more exposed parts of Ramie's hand Emma saw the queasier she felt. She braced herself and moved to the left side of the bed, nodding at the nurse and catching Ramie's eyes which looked a little unfocused.

"Dr. Rosencranz," Ramie slurred as she blinked to clear her vision. "Whatcha doin' here?"

"Making sure you'll be all right," Emma said softly.

"Ahhh, you care," Ramie said with a lop-sided grin. "That's sweet."

"I didn't think you should be alone, my dear."

Ramie flopped her head toward the nurse. "Did you hear that? She called me dear."

"I heard." The nurse looked at Emma and smiled. "She's a little out there from the first sedation to relax her."

"So it would seem," Emma nodded with a smile.

"This might be a little uncomfortable, Ramie. We're on the final layer. I'll work as quickly as I can and try not to hurt you," the nurse said.

"You're a good nurse." Ramie nodded at her vigorously. A portion of the gauze stuck to an area where bloody drainage had dried. Ramie sucked a breath in quickly and blinked her eyes rapidly.

Emma reached down and took Ramie's arm, squeezing it tightly. Ramie's head flopped to her left and she fought to keep her eyes on Emma's. Emma leaned down and whispered in Ramie's ear in an attempt to keep her calm as the nurse worked. Periodically Emma saw the extent of the damage that had been done to Ramie's hands. The delicate bones across the backs of her hands had been shattered and the skin torn, exposing swollen tendons. Emma felt her stomach rebel, but fought it off. As the nurse worked, Emma could see lines of small stitches that temporarily held the skin in place. Ramie squeezed her eyes shut and breathed quickly through her mouth.

"Please...don't leave me," Ramie said through gritted teeth. Then her eyes took in the injuries to her hands and tears ran from the corners of her eyes in a steady stream. "I'll never sculpt again," she whispered.

"You will," Emma said. 'You were born to sculpt."

Suddenly rage filled Ramie's voice. "You can't say that! You don't know what it's like to have your future ripped away without even knowing why."

"You're right," Emma conceded. "Tell me how to help you."

"You smell really good," Ramie said out of the blue. "Like vanilla and spring lavender."

"I'm glad you think so," Emma said with a smile as she watched the nurse work. "Where are your parents?"

"Long drive," Ramie answered as her eyes began drooping. "Daddy's a slow driver."

"It won't be long before she's asleep," the nurse said.

An hour passed and Emma stayed by Ramie's side as her bed was rolled out of the room and down the corridor. A service elevator carried them to the third floor and toward the operating rooms. Ramie, although remaining a little out of it, kept her eyes on Emma. Finally, they stopped and Emma had to let her go.

"Good luck," Emma said as Ramie was pushed through the doors to the operating suites.

"There's a waiting room down the hallway," a nurse pointed out.

"How long will she be in there?"

The nurse looked at a clipboard in her hand. "The surgeon has set aside six hours for this procedure."

"Six hours!" Emma said.

"It's micro-surgery and he has to be extremely careful."

"Will she be all right?"

"This might not be the last surgery she'll need to repair everything, but she should be fine. The doctor will speak to you after the surgery."

SEVEN HOURS LATER, Emma was dozing in the waiting room when a hand on her shoulder awakened her. She sat up and looked around.

"Are you Laramie Sunderlund's aunt?" a tall man dressed in blue scrubs asked.

"What? Of course not," Emma responded with a frown. Then she rubbed her eyes and cleared her throat before standing to correct her statement. "Sorry. Yes, yes I am," Emma muttered. "Is she all right? It took longer than anticipated."

"Putting all her bones back together took some time, but everything turned out fine."

"Will she need more surgery in the future?"

"We'll wait and see how well the bones knit back together.

Hopefully we won't need to do anything else."

"That's good, isn't it? Will she be able to sculpt again?"

"Very good. Too soon to know about her dexterity until the swelling goes down. She's in recovery right now and should be back in her room after they're sure she's stabilized. Probably a few hours. If you want, the nurses will let you sit with her."

"I don't want to interfere with what they're doing," Emma said. "I think I'll try to find a cup of tea."

"If you decide to sit with her later, just knock on the recovery room door and tell them Dr. Phillips said it's all right for you to be there."

Emma took the time to eat before returning to the recovery room upstairs and knocking gently on the door. A nurse opened the door and stared at Emma. "Yes," the nurse said.

"Dr. Phillips said I could sit in here with my...um...niece, Ramie Sunderlund," Emma said softly. "She had surgery today."

The nurse led Emma into a changing room and handed her a hospital gown and a head cover. Emma carefully covered her head and pulled the gown over her own clothing. When she opened the door and stepped out, the nurse led her behind a curtain barrier and into the recovery bay. Ramie looked pale and drawn, Emma thought, her skin unbearably white against her healing bruises. She wanted to reach out and touch Ramie's cheek, but hesitated.

"She came through the surgery fine," the nurse offered as she checked the IV lines running into Ramie's arms.

"She looks...terrible," Emma said.

The nurse looked at Emma for a moment. "When she does wake up, she might experience some pain. It was very delicate surgery, but Dr. Phillips is the best."

"Will she be able to use her hands?" Emma asked. "She's a sculptress."

"We hope so," the nurse answered. "It will be very important to keep her spirits up and make sure she does her therapy after you get her home and after the casts come off."

Emma looked up. "Miss Sunderlund doesn't live with me. She's a student at Overland University and lives in a dormitory."

"Oh, I see," the nurse frowned. "Hopefully, she will do everything she's supposed to do then. I heard her parents are coming to take her home to Vermont."

"Perhaps that will be for the best," Emma muttered.

"Call me if you need anything," the nurse said.

Emma pulled a chair next to Ramie's bed and sighed as she sat. If what the nurse said was true, she wouldn't be seeing Ramie Sunderlund much longer. In all likelihood, Ramie would not graduate in the spring. Her portfolio had been destroyed during the attack and the marble slab intended for her final project had been smashed. Emma rubbed her eyes and gently placed her hand on Ramie's arm. It felt cold, so unlike the young woman herself. Fatigue overcame Emma and she dozed periodically, unable to maintain her concentration on what she was reading. God! Was English literature really as boring as this individual made it seem. To Emma it had always been alive. She smiled. Perhaps she had only buried herself in literature so she wouldn't have to face life as it was, settling for temporary liaisons to distract her, avoiding any relationship that threatened to disrupt the tidy, uncomplicated life she had fashioned for herself since she lost Fran.

An anguished moan snapped Emma out of her solitary musings. Her grip on Ramie's arm tightened as Ramie's discomfort grew. Emma stood and looked around for a nurse. Everyone appeared to be busy caring for other patients. Emma leaned closer and conjured up the calmest voice she could.

"Listen to me, Ramie," she said. "I know it hurts and it will for a while. But you're a strong woman. You can face it and conquer it. No one can stop you. Take a deep breath, then another and another until you conquer the pain. It cannot beat you."

Gradually, Ramie stopped the whimpering cries that broke Emma's heart. It wasn't fair for someone so young to suffer so much. Ramie scrunched her forehead into a frown and opened her eyes.

A nurse asked Emma to step aside while she checked the medications dripping into Ramie's veins. "Can you hear me, Ramie?" the nurse asked. "You're fine and waking up from your surgery now. Is there anything you need?"

Emma stood behind the nurse as she worked, forced to break her tenuous connection with Ramie. The nurse injected something into the IV line and within minutes Ramie lapsed back into a peaceful sleep.

"I think she'll be ready to be taken to her room in a couple of hours," the nurse said as she shoved the needle into a red box next to Ramie's bed. "But she'll probably sleep the rest of the night."

"Will she be returning to the same room?" Emma asked.

"Yes, unless something happens that we aren't expecting. Now she just needs time for her hands to heal."

Nearly an hour passed before there was a tap at the recovery room door. A nurse pushed it open and Emma saw an older man and woman, both of whom looked exhausted, standing at the door. The nurse admitted them and handed them gowns and head covers. Emma instinctively knew they were Ramie's parents. She waited until the couple left to put on gowns. Emma looked down at the sleeping blonde, knowing she would never see her again. On an impulse she leaned down and kissed her softly on the forehead. Then she quickly left the sterile room, discarding her gown in a laundry container in the hallway. Emma left the hospital and turned her thoughts away from her recovering student.

Emma didn't see Ramie Sunderlund again. She turned in her final grades, including one for Laramie Sunderlund based on her work up to Thanksgiving, and began preparing her lectures for the coming semester. She didn't see Ramie at the spring graduation ceremony and felt certain the young woman had been withdrawn and returned to Vermont. Emma couldn't be sure whether or not Ramie would return to complete her studies and graduate. Perhaps the price of her dream had been too high.

Chapter Eight

May, 1990, Burlington, Vermont

"ARE YOU SURE that damn thing won't cut my arm off?" Ramie asked as the doctor approached her with what looked like a miniature circular saw.

Dr. Jaeger, who had been overseeing her care since her return to Vermont, frowned. He was a tall, white-haired man with bushy eyebrows and a deceptively gruff exterior. He had been her physician since her birth, but he never seemed to change. "The manufacturer guarantees it will not cut skin," he said. "But there's always a first time for everything, I suppose." He shrugged and flipped the switch on the cast saw, grinning maniacally at his patient as he approached.

"Your bedside manner sucks," Ramie muttered.

"That class cost extra," he said as he lowered the spinning blade to the cast on her right arm. "You're not going to pass out on me are you?"

"I wouldn't give you the satisfaction," she quipped.

"Damn," he breathed. "I thought I had a sucker on the line for sure."

Ramie gritted her teeth as the blade dug into the cast. A small cloud of debris covered her arm. The saw smoothly cut through the cast that extended from her hand to nearly her elbow and Ramie held her breath. She looked over her shoulder at her mother. "Big day, Mom. It won't be long before I can actually dress myself and wipe my own ass again."

"I wiped your fanny for years, ya know," Amie Sunderlund said with a wink. "There's just more of it now."

"I appreciate the jab, Mom."

"My pleasure." Amie smirked.

"Turn your arm over, please." He quickly ran the saw up opposite the first cut and set the tool aside. He used a different hand tool to separate the two halves of the cast that had encased her hand and lower arm for nearly six months. "Does your hand hurt, Ramie?" Dr. Jaeger asked.

"No," Ramie said. "It stinks though and looks disgusting."

"A lot of dead skin has accumulated while your hand healed. We'll wash it thoroughly after we check everything. Try not to be too shocked. You haven't used or exercised these muscles for quite a long time."

Ramie watched as Dr. Jaeger cut through the padding and stocking that was used to protect her hand and arm. As the protective layers fell away, tears dripped down her cheeks as she stared at what looked like an alien arm attached to her body. "Ohmygod," she said, her voice trembling.

"Can you wiggle your fingers?" Jaeger asked softly.

Ramie shook her head. She stared at the atrophied muscles above her wrist and the healed, pink incisions across the back of her hand. She slowly turned her wrist and took in the ugly, red starburst scar that puckered the skin in the center of her palm. Feeling a sudden wave of nausea roll through her stomach, she closed her eyes and struggled to take deep breaths to calm down. The feel of her mother's hand rubbing circles over her back oddly made her feel better.

"Remove the second cast, Dr. Jaeger," Ramie managed.

"You're sure?" he asked.

"It won't look any better in another hour or another day," she choked out. "Just do it. Please."

Without further discussion, Jaeger picked up the cast saw again and began the two cuts to free Ramie's left hand.

Thirty minutes later, Ramie followed her mother to their car and waited for Amie to open the door. Amie had a list of instructions for beginning the rehab of Ramie's hands in her purse, as well as prescriptions for pain medication and a referral for at-home rehabilitation.

"I thought we might stop by the pharmacy and perhaps convince your father to join us for lunch. We'll have to wait for your prescriptions anyway," Amie said.

"Can't we just go home, Mom?" Ramie whined. "I'm tired."

"You're depressed and feeling just a tad sorry for yourself. What happened to you was horrible, but it happened. Now the real battle begins. No one can fight it but you."

"If that's your version of a pep talk, it sucks," Ramie snapped.

"Best I can do," Amie huffed.

"What if I can't sculpt again...ever?" Ramie blinked and a tear dropped onto her cheek.

"If you want to sculpt again, you will."

"Emma said I would," Ramie muttered.

"Who?"

"One of my professors. She visited me at the hospital...I think. I wasn't thinking too clearly," Ramie said, staring down at her hands.

"Is that the woman who passed herself off as your aunt?"

Ramie shrugged. "I guess so." Ramie closed her eyes, straining to remember the tall, attractive woman who had captured her interest so many months earlier. Vaguely she recalled a soothing voice telling her she believed Ramie would sculpt again. *You were born to sculpt.* She had successfully purged the memory of that night from her mind, but continued to cling to the sound of Emma Rothenberg's voice, sweet and gentle, chasing away her fears. She also remembered the softness of Emma's lips against her forehead. Or, had she only dreamed that brief, intimate moment?

FIVE LONG MONTHS later, sweat beaded across Ramie's forehead, despite the cold, snowy weather blowing outside the Burlington Rehab Center. A droplet occasionally dripped onto her cheek. Her face was the picture of concentration as she forced each finger of her right hand into a fist around a rubberized elastic strip about six inches wide and two feet long. She raised her arm and pulled the elastic as she swung it to her left.

"Don't let it slip out of your hand, Ramie," her physical therapist, Lynn Piersall, said. "That's good. Adjust your grip if you need to."

"How many more?" Ramie asked, exhaling and inhaling deeply.

"Five more, then you can rest for a minute."

In her time at physical therapy, Ramie worked to improve her fine motor skills by feeling various sized beans inside a small container of a substance similar to Silly Putty. She removed them one at a time, using her thumb with different fingers. Gradually, she progressed to other tasks that required the use of her fingers, working together or separately. Despite periodic fits of rage and frustration, Ramie learned to perform simple tasks such as making a sandwich, cutting vegetables for a salad, cracking an egg and beating it for an omelet. The most exciting day for Ramie was the day she could actually use toilet paper to wipe her own ass. For more than a year, she'd been forced to rely on others to perform that simple task for her. She found it embarrassing at the least and humiliating at its worst.

"God, you're a fuckin' Nazi!" Ramie hissed. She bent forward and cradled her hands against her chest after releasing the elastic band. Sweat ran down her face and dripped from the tip of her nose as she rocked back and forth, willing the pain away.

"Grab the band one more time," Lynn said, lightly massaging Ramie's shoulder. "You're almost done."

"It hurts, dammit!"

Lynn knelt down in front of Ramie and took her hands into her own. "I know it hurts, Ramie. I wish it could be easier, but it can't be," she said softly.

"I'm never going to be the same, am I, Lynn?" Ramie asked.

"Not the same, but maybe better. We have to find a way for you to adapt." She shrugged. "Aside from sculpting again, what do you want?"

Ramie laughed. "I want to touch a woman again...or really for the first time. I want her to know how I feel by the softness of my touch on her skin."

"Got a particular lady in mind?"

"Not anymore," Ramie muttered.

Lynn stood and pulled Ramie up with her. "Let's get out of here and get some fresh Vermont winter air."

Twenty minutes later they were in Lynn's car, driving around. Ramie was quiet, absorbed by her own thoughts, not paying much attention until she realized they were entering the campus of the University of Vermont. Lynn creeped past the buildings before she pulled into a spot and parked the car. Ramie looked around, her eyes narrowing as they landed on the Fine Arts Building.

"What the hell are we doing here, Lynn?" Ramie demanded.

Lynn shrugged. "I have a former patient here and need to check on him. Today seemed like as good a day as any since you decided to poop out on me."

Lynn opened the back door and removed a small black bag. She smacked Ramie on the shoulder over the seat.

"Open your door and get out. I know you can do that for yourself." Lynn slammed the back door closed and moved to the passenger side of the car, waiting patiently as Ramie glared at her.

"You can do this, Ramie," Lynn encouraged.

Ramie nervously rubbed her left thumb against the scar on her right palm. She slowly worked her fingers around the door handle. She curled them into a partial fist and pulled until the door mechanism popped apart. Lynn grabbed the door and pulled it open, a brilliant smile flashing across her face. She held her hand out to assist Ramie from the car.

"I've got it, Lynn," Ramie said as she swiveled in the seat and used her hands to push her body up. She teetered slightly in an attempt to gain her balance before Lynn wrapped her hand around Ramie's bicep to steady her.

"Good job, kiddo," Lynn beamed as she closed and locked the door.

Ramie followed Lynn across the lawn and into the Fine Arts

Building. Once inside the building's lobby, Ramie was distracted by the art that covered the walls. Lynn stopped at a desk along the far wall and spoke to the student seated behind it. A few minutes later, she returned to Ramie's side.

"Ready?" Lynn asked.

"For what?" Ramie answered.

"Follow me and you'll see."

Ramie followed Lynn down a brightly lit corridor, continuing to look at the artwork hanging along the walls. When Lynn stopped to unlock a door, Ramie bumped into her. "Sorry," she muttered as Lynn guided her into the room. It was obviously a studio and a small slab of stone rested on the turntable of a waist high work bench.

Ramie spun around and glared at Lynn. "This isn't funny, Lynn."

"It's not intended to be funny," Lynn said. She set her black bag on the workbench and opened it, withdrawing a hammer and small chisel. She held them out to Ramie, wiggling them in her hands. "Take them, Ramie."

Ramie shook her head, tears filling her eyes. "I...I can't. This is cruel."

"No. It's the first step. I can be cruel later."

Ramie was terrified when Lynn handed her the hammer and chisel, convinced she'd ruin a perfectly good piece of stone.

"You are out of your mind."

"It's what you want, isn't it? To sculpt again?"

"Of course, but I'm not ready yet," Ramie protested.

"Just hit the damn thing. You have to start somewhere, Ramie."

Ramie reached out and let her right hand glide over the small piece of stone. "It's cool. I can feel it," she said.

"That's good, right?"

Ramie smiled. "I used to love the feel of the stone as it warmed under my touch." A tear ran down her cheek and she shook her head. "I can't do this, Lynn."

"Why not?" Lynn asked softly.

"Be...because the last time I saw a chisel it was nailing my hand to the floor." She shook her head again. "The pain was indescribable."

"Were you mad?"

Ramie whipped her head around to glare at Lynn. "I was fucking furious that something that should coax beauty from a piece of rock had been used for something so...so...perverse!"

"Then make it return to producing something beautiful. You control it," Lynn urged.

Ramie wiped her eyes with the back of her hand as her other hand drifted over the stone. She picked up a pair of goggles and adjusted them over her eyes. "Here," she said as her hand found a place in the stone. Her knuckles were white as she tightly grasped the chisel and placed it at an angle against the slab. The first time she struck the chisel nothing happened. "Too light," she mumbled to herself.

"Come on, Goldilocks. Make it just right," Lynn encouraged her.

Ramie took a deep breath to calm her trembling hand, loosening her grip on the chisel slightly before striking it. She smiled as a small piece cracked away from the slab. She rubbed a finger over the marble. "It's here. I can feel it wanting to be released from the rock."

Over an hour later, Lynn touched Ramie's arm and said, "Better stop now. I don't want you to overuse the muscles in your hand on the first day. I promise we'll be back. What will it be?"

"A gift, maybe," Ramie said.

"For someone special?" Lynn asked.

"For someone who believed I would sculpt again."

"It may take longer than you'd like, but you have to believe it too."

Ramie walked toward the exit of the building on the beautiful campus, stopping periodically to study a drawing or photograph hanging along the walls. "I miss this so much, Lynn," she said.

Lynn wrapped an arm around Ramie's shoulders and squeezed lightly. "I know you do, sweetie."

As they reached the main hallway, a tall, thin man stepped out of an office and stopped as he saw the women approaching him.

"Good afternoon, Dr. Fredericks," Lynn said cheerfully.

He nodded at Ramie. "Is this the patient you told me about, Lynn?"

"Yes. Dr. Fredericks, this is Laramie Sunderlund. Ramie, this is Dr. Barry Fredericks, the chairman of the art department."

Ramie reluctantly withdrew a hand from her pocket to take his hand when he extended it. "You have a nice facility here, Dr. Fredericks," she said.

"Well, it's not Harvard, but I think we have quite a bit to offer. Lynn told me you were almost finished with your degree in Art History before your injury. Is that right?"

"Yes, sir."

"A sculptress, if I'm not mistaken."

"I was, but it will be a long time before I sculpt again." Ramie felt tears beginning to form and rubbed her eyes.

"Have you considered completing your degree with us? Perhaps working toward your Master's in Fine Arts? As it happens we have an instructor's position in art history opening in the fall. It would leave you time to recuperate while advancing your education."

"I'd have to think about it. Right now I'm concentrating on recovering from my injuries."

"Of course. I understand. If you'd like to consider it, just contact my office. Good to see you again, Lynn. Have a good afternoon," Fredericks said before turning away.

"Did you set that up?" Ramie asked.

"Not exactly, but it sounds like a way for you to get involved in art again," Lynn answered with a shrug. "Dr. Fredericks was one of my patients a couple of years ago. Stroke."

"I don't think I could handle being around all these people actively pursuing art and not being able to join them," Ramie said, a frown creasing across her forehead.

"I understand."

"I don't think you do, Lynn. When was the last time you had to have others do practically everything for you?" Ramie snapped.

"I haven't and can't imagine what you're going through, but I know I can make life easier for you." She stopped and tapped a finger against the side of Ramie's head. "As soon as you can get your mind in the right place, you'll be amazed at what you can accomplish. There's always a way, honey."

RAMIE SAT AT the kitchen table watching her mother preparing their dinner. She worked her index finger into the handle of a coffee mug and wrapped her other hand around the cup to steady it. She had just managed to lift it to her mouth when the phone rang.

"Can you get that Ramie? I'm up to my elbows in flour here," Amie said as she pushed hair away from her face with her wrist.

"Sure. As long as whoever they are is willing to wait until I get there. You expecting a call?"

"Nope. Just tell whoever it is we already gave, have found Jesus, or already have three of whatever they're sellin'. One of those usually works," Amie said, returning to her work.

Ramie made her way to the living room and picked the receiver up carefully. Pressing it against her cheek for balance she said, "Sunderlund residence."

"Good morning," a man's voice said. "May I speak to Laramie Sunderlund, please?"

"This is Ramie Sunderlund," Ramie answered.

"My name is Detective Marsden with the Middleton, Ohio police department. I'd like to speak to you about your assault, if you have a moment."

"That was months ago, Detective," she replied softly.

"You're lucky to be alive, Miss Sunderlund," the detective stated rather matter-of-factly. "Would you mind if I ask you a few questions?"

"I couldn't identify my attackers then and I still can't."

"I understand, but I have been assigned to re-visit your case based on new information we've recently uncovered," the detective explained.

"Honestly," she said. "I've tried to forget about the whole thing."

"Forget about what?" Amie asked as she entered the front room wiping her hands on a kitchen towel.

"My attack," Ramie said softly. "The police in Ohio want to ask me a few questions."

"Well, it's about time," Amie huffed. "Sit down, dear. I'll bring you a fresh cup of coffee."

As if sensing Ramie's reluctance, Marsden said quickly, "I only have a few questions, Miss Sunderlund, The first officers on the scene didn't have many notes."

"I couldn't tell them much," Ramie said as she sat on the couch. "Too much pain. All I could remember was the pain. It was horrible. Even now, it's pretty much all I can remember."

"We can go through it slowly and maybe a memory you've been repressing will find its way to the surface again," Marsden said. "What were you doing before the attack?"

"I was going over the projects for my portfolio."

"Did you see anyone following you as you walked to the Fine Arts Building?"

"No. Everyone was gone already for the Thanksgiving break. I would have noticed something unusual. I stopped to make a snow angel," she said with a smile. "I saw one of my professors. She was...uh...walking her dog. I think she lives close to the campus."

"Did you speak to her?"

"No."

"Which professor was it?"

"Dr. Rothenberg, my English professor."

"I'll speak to her. She might have noticed someone. What did you do next?"

"I went to the Fine Arts Building, let myself in, and then went to the studio I'd reserved over the holiday," Ramie said.

"Was anyone else there?"

Ramie shook her head, "I didn't see anyone. I ate an apple and went through my portfolio for about an hour. Then I started working on my sculpture project. Before I could even strike it with the chisel, the lights went off. After that everything is a blur. I don't remember anything until I woke up after they found me."

"You're doing really good," Marsden said after he heard Ramie take what sounded like a deep breath.

Ramie laughed. "I haven't told you shit that will help find the guys."

"Ramie! Language," Amie reprimanded as she set a cup of coffee on the end table next to the couch.

"He's a policeman, mother," Ramie snorted. "I'm sure he's heard worse than that."

"A time or two," Marsden said. "I can call back tomorrow if you need a break," he offered.

"No. I just needed to catch my breath, but thanks. Next question."

"Was there more than one person involved? I know it was dark, but..."

"There were two. I managed to stab one with my chisel, I think. I must have because he released me for a moment. I tried to get away, but they'd locked the studio door," Ramie said.

"Did either man speak?"

"I don't remember. I was afraid. One of them hit me...or maybe they both did. I don't know. It was dark."

"Did they blindfold you?"

"No, but they had a flashlight or something. It was in my eyes until the beam moved to my hand and I saw what they planned to do. I tried to scream, but no one would have heard me. He said something right before he...uh, hit the chisel."

"What did he say?"

"I don't remember exactly. Something about going along. I should have gone along." Ramie said. "Something like that, whatever it meant." Ramie swallowed hard before she continued. "Then he...he nailed my hands to the floor and I passed out." Tears ran freely down her cheeks as she recounted the worst day in her life to Marsden. "Not much help."

"Did you have a disagreement with anyone before you were attacked?"

"Not really. I had a run-in a couple of weeks earlier with a graduate student, but it wasn't bad enough to cause him to attack me."

"What happened?"

"He was Dr. Rothenberg's assistant. I was having some

problems in her class and he knew it." Ramie said, taking another deep breath. "He offered to improve my grade if I slept with him. I refused, but he may have thought I told Dr. Rothenberg about it, although I didn't."

"Well, since you didn't actually see him or anyone else, I'll look into it. I'll give you my number. Feel free to contact me any time if you have a question or remember something else I should know."

After writing the number down, Ramie sat on the couch and sipped her coffee. Did she really want to relive that terrible Thanksgiving weekend over and over? All she could remember were the hours of pain and months of rehabilitation so far to regain the use of her hands again. She rubbed her thumbs over the scars in the center of her palms and looked at her still slightly crooked fingers. Despite the damage, she would eventually be able to work, but she could have died from blood loss after being nailed to the floor by her own chisels. She closed her eyes again and scrunched her forehead as the memory of the excruciating pain returned. She had been unable to move without increasing the pain. Thank God her dorm director reported her missing or she could have lain there in her own blood another three days. She tried to remember anything else her assailant had said. She saw very little, the blinding pain consuming her thoughts, blocking out voices. She hadn't really heard anything except the sound of the fragile bones in her hands shattering. She hurt him, which led to her being hurt in return. She made him mad, never dreaming of the horrible consequences. She shook her head to drive the memory away. Her mother's hand on her shoulder snapped her back to the present.

WHEN EMMA TURNED down the corridor toward her office, she saw a ruggedly handsome young man leaning against the wall next to her door. He was absorbed in reading something in a pocket-sized black notebook.

"May I help you?" she asked as she stopped to unlock the door.

"Are you Dr. Rothenberg?"

"I am," she answered as she opened the door and stepped inside. She dropped the papers in her arm onto her desk and turned to face him.

He extended his hand and showed her his wallet. She examined it for a moment before moving behind her desk to be seated. She removed her suit jacket and hung it neatly on the back of the chair. "What can I do for you, Detective Marsden?" she asked as she removed her glasses and leaned back.

"Do you remember a student named Laramie Sunderlund? It's been about a year since she was here."

"Of course I remember her. She was a student in one of my classes. She left Overland under rather...unfortunate circumstances."

"And do you remember a young man named Travis Whitman?" Marsden examined his notebook.

"He was my assistant until I had him terminated," Emma said, her voice calm.

"May I ask why you terminated his employment?"

Emma shrugged. "I suppose it would be a matter of public record anyway. I discovered, quite accidentally, that he had violated the code of ethics established for our graduate assistants. I informed human resources of that and told them I no longer required his services."

"Did this violation involve Miss Sunderlund?"

"Somewhat indirectly, I suppose. I saw Mr. Whitman speaking to her privately outside of class. When I spoke to him about it and informed him it was unethical, he told me she approached him and offered to have an intimate relationship with him in exchange for raising her grade."

"But you didn't believe him?"

"I seriously doubted it," Emma said, the corners of her mouth lifting slightly.

"Why?"

"I believed Miss Sunderlund preferred the company of other young women, although I had no proof of that. Merely intuition, I suppose. You'd have to ask her to be sure."

"Was there any animosity between them that you were aware of?"

"I can prove that he altered grades for my classes and I heard Mr. Whitman threaten Miss Sunderlund once, although it could have been a meaningless threat hoping to frighten her."

"How long after his threat was she assaulted?"

"About two weeks, I believe."

"She remembers seeing you the evening she was attacked."

"I don't recall seeing her."

"She said she was on her way to the Fine Arts Building and you were walking your dog, but she didn't speak to you."

"It's possible. I take Louie for a stroll almost every night."

"Even if you didn't see her, did you notice anyone else? Anyone who might have been following her?"

Emma looked up and eventually shook her head. "Honestly, detective, too much time has passed and I can't tell you much."

"Do you know what happened to Mr. Whitman?"

"He completed his degree at the end of that semester. I heard he may be pursuing his doctorate now at another university. I wasn't asked to provide a reference," Emma said. "I didn't file formal charges against him. After he left, I no longer saw the purpose."

"I will pass this information to the prosecutor's office. They may want to subpoena your records or ask further questions. Do you object to that?"

"Not in the least. I assume you've spoken to Miss Sunderlund. Has she recovered from her injuries?" Emma asked.

"I believe she's still undergoing rehab. Otherwise she sounded well enough," Marsden said.

Emma believed Detective Marsden had understated Ramie Sunderlund's attractiveness. Emma was certain that her beauty had not diminished with the passage of time.

IN MID-MAY Ramie made her way up the steps of the county courthouse in Ohio. She was nervous about coming face-to-face with the man accused of attacking her over a year earlier although there hadn't been a night when the incident didn't invade her dreams. She had relived it even more often recently as she answered questions from the police and prosecutor's office as they put their case together. They had told her the case against Travis Whitman relied primarily on the testimony of a man who confessed to acting as Whitman's accomplice. However, he had agreed only to roughing Ramie up a little and scaring her, nothing more serious. Because he had accepted a plea deal in exchange for his testimony there was the possibility the jury might not believe his story and fail to convict Whitman. No one considered the case a slam-dunk. Due to Ramie's continuing limitations with her hands, Amie accompanied her to Ohio to assist if needed, but she would be alone in the courtroom.

Ramie sucked in a deep breath in an attempt to settle the butterflies in her stomach as the elevator came to a stop on the third floor of the courthouse. She glanced around as she and her mother stepped into the wood-paneled hallway. Three women and a couple of older men, none of whom she knew, were seated on benches lining the walls. They all looked in her direction briefly before returning to their quiet conversations. A clean-shaven, ruggedly handsome young man came out of a room to her left and smiled when he saw her. He came toward her and extended his hand.

"Miss Sunderlund? I'm Detective Marsden and have spoken

to you on the phone once or twice. You made it right on time," he said as he grasped her hand lightly. "How are you feeling?"

"Nervous," she admitted. "It's nice to finally meet you."

"Do you have any questions for the prosecutor before we begin?"

"No."

"I've seen the witness list and you will be the final witness, but the others, except the presumed accomplice, shouldn't testify very long, so you might as well have a seat and try to relax. I'll let the prosecutor know you're here," Marsden said as he patted her on the shoulder. "You look great by the way."

"Thanks," she said.

Marsden left and returned to the room he had exited only moments earlier. Amie glanced around and guided Ramie to a vacant bench farther down the hallway. Once they were settled, Amie opened the bag she was carrying and took out a book, handing it to Ramie. Ramie stretched out her legs and crossed her ankles. She looked up from her book several minutes later when the ding of the elevator announced its arrival. Her eyes widened as the door slowly opened and she saw a tall woman step out, running her fingers through her wind-blown cinnamon hair. Dr. Emma Rothenberg acknowledged a few of the people seated in the hallway with a brief nod. Then her eyes met Ramie's and she smiled before taking a seat. Her eyes hadn't changed a bit, Ramie thought. They were still the deep greenish-brown she remembered. The last time she'd seen them they were gazing down at her warmly before Ramie was taken into surgery. Ramie clinched her hands into fists and opened them to rub the scarred tissue on her palms until she felt pain stab through them. Sweat began to form on her brow and nausea began roiling in her stomach.

"Stop, Ramie," Amie said softly as she placed a hand over Ramie's. "Take a deep breath and calm down, sweetie."

Ramie nodded and took a breath. "I think I'm going to be sick," she said.

Amie looked down the hallway and located the restroom. Ramie stood and followed her quickly down the hallway. A few minutes later she rinsed out her mouth and splashed cold water on her face before leaving the restroom minus her breakfast. She sat down and closed her eyes, leaving them closed until she heard her name called. When she opened her eyes, she and her mother were the only ones still seated in the hallway and it was darker outside. She ran a hand over her face and saw a man motioning to her.

"Did you enjoy your nap?" Amie asked as Ramie stood.

"I feel better," Ramie said. "Wish me luck."

"You'll do great, honey," her mother assured her with a hug.

EMMA LEFT THE courtroom through a side door and saw Ramie and the woman with her exchange a brief embrace. Ramie didn't look up and her view was blocked as she joined the bailiff and entered the courtroom. Emma wished she could have spoken to Ramie for a moment, but she had been cautioned not to speak to other witnesses. Ramie still looked amazing even though she had been obviously nervous. Her eyes were still the beautiful, vibrant Delft blue Emma remembered. She had been casually dressed in a cowl-necked sweater and contrasting slacks that were relaxed over her slender hips. Emma didn't know the woman with Ramie, but she resembled the woman she had glimpsed entering the recovery room after Ramie's surgery nearly a year before. She hoped Ramie was happy as she pushed the elevator button to return to her life again.

RAMIE STARED STRAIGHT ahead as she walked toward the witness stand. She raised her right hand to be sworn in and sat facing the attorney for the prosecution. She avoided looking in Travis Whitman's direction as she waited for the questions to begin. She concentrated on keeping her answers concise, but was unable to stop tears from dropping down her cheeks as she described the pain she'd suffered from her injuries and the long rehab that followed. She only stared at Travis for a moment near the end of her testimony when she was asked to show the jury her scarred hands. She brought them up for the jury to see before swiveling her body toward the defense table.

"This is what you did to me," she spat. "You stole my future. For what?"

"Objection!" Travis' attorney said.

"Sustained," the judge droned. "The jury will ignore the witness' outburst."

When Ramie left the witness stand, she was escorted from the courtroom by Detective Marsden. She was stopped momentarily by a handsome young man she didn't recognize. "I'm sorry," he whispered. "I didn't know it would go so far or get so out of hand. I'm so sorry."

Once they were out of the courtroom, Ramie turned to Marsden. "Who was that?"

"The accomplice, Ted Sumner."

Stunned, Ramie didn't know what to say. "Why would he

help Travis Whitman? I only hung out with him once!"

"Claimed he was upset because you made inappropriate advances toward his sister and she was traumatized."

"That's a lie," Ramie said. She frowned, remembering kissing and groping Gloria Sumner while wishing she was someone else. "Did he tell that to the jury?"

"He did," Marsden answered.

"Then they'll probably give Whitman a fucking medal," she muttered. "Can I leave now? I'm very tired."

Chapter Nine

April, 2000, Burlington, Vermont

RAMIE STEPPED BACK from her work bench and pulled off the bandana holding her hair back. She wiped her face as she examined the marble figure taking shape in front of her. Thus far she was pleased with the result, but her hands ached. It had been over ten years since her hands had been injured and the daily aches she suffered would not let the memory die. She clenched her hands into fists, waiting for the pain to distract her. Travis Whitman was more than halfway through his fifteen-year sentence for assault while she had received a life sentence due to his actions. It didn't seem fair, she thought, but life wasn't always fair. At least she could still work, doing what she loved.

She released her fists and went to a small machine perched on the desk of her studio in the university art department. She had a class in less than an hour. Still enough time for a hand treatment and a quick lunch. She flipped the lid of the machine open and slowly lowered her hands into a vat of warm wax. She sighed as the heat penetrated the scars on her hands, driving the ache away, at least momentarily. She closed her eyes and rubbed the heat over her palms with her thumbs. She smiled as she tried to think of a word to describe the relief the heat brought to her hands. Orgasmic, she thought. Yes, that was the word.

"Do you have a moment, Ramie?" Barry Fredrickson asked.

"Of course, Dr. Fredrickson." Ramie lifted her hands from the soothing wax and began peeling it from her skin, allowing it to fall into the warming vat to melt again. "What can I do for you?"

"I brought a friend who insists on meeting you."

"Just give me one minute," Ramie said as she dropped the last of the wax back into the vat. Then she picked up a bottle of lotion and covered the skin of her hands. She was still rubbing the lotion in as she turned to see a tall, attractive older woman examining the marble piece taking shape on her workbench.

"No hurry," Dr. Fredrickson said. "What's the subject for your new piece?"

"Hopefully a wood nymph for the botanical garden downtown."

"It's lovely," the woman said. "Very expressive facial features."

"Thank you," Ramie said, looking at Dr. Fredrickson.

"Ramie, this is Dr. Sylvia Joyner, a colleague and old friend of mine. Sylvia, this is Laramie Sunderlund, an associate with us," Dr. Fredrickson said.

"Except for the old part, it's a pleasure, Miss Sunderlund," Sylvia said with a smile as she extended her hand.

Ramie wiped the excess lotion with a rag and took the offered hand.

Barry laughed. "Actually, Sylvia's rather taken with your work and is hoping to steal you away," he said. "Temporarily, of course."

"I don't have any plans to leave, Dr. Fredrickson," Ramie said.

"Overland University now has an artist-in-residence program and we have a vacancy next fall. While we can't offer you a fortune, the university can offer you a place to live and a small stipend for your time," Sylvia explained. "You would be our first sculptor. It would be a wonderful chance to influence young artists."

"Overland?"

"Unless I'm mistaken, you're an alumnus of Overland, aren't you?" Sylvia asked.

"Almost," Ramie said, rubbing the scars on the palms of her hands. She glanced at the clock on the wall. "I have a class," she said as she turned away.

"Think about it, Miss Sunderlund. Perhaps you'd allow me to buy you dinner this evening," Sylvia said.

"No thanks," Ramie said. "I already have plans."

"No problem. I'll leave my contact information with Barry, but will need your decision by the end of this semester so we can arrange to ship a few pieces of your work to Overland."

"I'll think about it, but you shouldn't hold your breath. Thank you for the offer though," Ramie managed as she fled the room.

THAT NIGHT OVER dinner, Ramie told her parents about the offer from Overland.

"How long is the residency?" her father asked.

"What's the difference?" Amie snapped. "She's just now getting her life back to normal."

Larry rested his hand over his wife's. "It might bring her a sense of closure, Amie." He looked at Ramie and smiled. "It's your decision, honey, but it might be a good thing."

"What about your work here?" Amie asked. "Will your job

here still be available when you return?"

"Dr. Fredrickson said it would," Ramie answered. "He thinks I should accept the offer. He says it would expand my horizons, whatever that means, and make my work better known outside of this region."

"You're making enough money now, aren't you?" Amie asked.

"Yes and I'm staying busy enough for two sculptors. Maybe too busy. I need to think about it before making a decision."

After dinner, Ramie drove to her favorite place on the shore of Lake Champlain. Despite the fact that it was early spring, a cool breeze blew off the water and not many people were venturing near the lake. Ramie pulled her sweatshirt closer to her body and made her way toward the beach. She sat and wrapped her arms around her legs, pulling them close to her chest and resting her chin on her knees. She drew in a deep breath as she looked out over the lake toward the hazy coastline of New York in the distance.

She hadn't seriously considered returning to Overland since her trip to testify at Whitman's trial. She had hoped since then that she'd forget about him and what he'd done to her. She hadn't turned him in for grade fixing and never understood the reason for his attack. Even though she tried to forget that night, something seemed to happen to dredge it all up again more often than she liked. All that banished her bad memories were happier ones of Emma Rothenberg.

Ramie remembered how scared she'd been before her first surgery. The sight of Emma's cinnamon hair and the feel of her breath flowing over her ear as Emma whispered encouragement to her were all the balm Ramie's soul needed to get past her fear and pain. Was Emma still at Overland? Still frightening students? Ramie smiled, wondering if Emma had changed much over the years. Would she remember Ramie, the girl who didn't really belong in her class? Why would Ramie consider returning to Overland? Was the chance to see Emma again enough?

September 2000, Overland University, Middleton, Ohio

THE BEGINNING OF the new fall semester at Overland University wasn't any different from the previous years. Emma had been assigned a new graduate assistant named Louise. She was a somewhat timid girl with mousy brown hair, who seemed to hide behind large round glasses. However, she was a reliable worker and Emma trusted her to lecture in her absence as well as grade her students' work without bias. Occasionally, Emma took time off to travel for research purposes. She was busily working under the 'publish or perish' mandate the university had adopted when they moved from college to university status. That change had allowed more monies to be sought for growth and development. However, little of that money had trickled down to the English Department and Emma still worked out of the same third story office in Donlevy Hall.

Against her better judgment, Emma had resumed occasional liaisons with Millicent Carver. Overland University hosted an annual conference, which was attended by the spouses of university chancellors and presidents. Another conference at various sites hosted a similar meeting of the chancellors and presidents themselves. When Millie contacted Emma about possibly having dinner together during the first conference they had easily fallen back into their earlier relationship. For the last four or five years they met semi-annually for a long weekend of re-acquaintance. At the end of each liaison they parted amicably, Millie returning to the security of her loveless marriage and Emma to the security she found in the sameness of her work.

Apparently donations to the Art Department had been lucrative and in mid-October Emma received an invitation to an exhibition of pieces by former students. She accepted the invitation even though she had much work of her own to finish before their November deadline. She convinced an old friend in the English Department, Dr. Howard Trammell, to escort her. She knew how much he hated such events, but he owed her a favor.

Emma checked her appearance in the full-length mirror in her bedroom and used her fingers to put a few stray hairs into place. She frowned as she noticed an occasional gray hair that screamed out the years of her life that had passed almost unnoticed. She refused to color her hair, deciding instead to take her descent into aging as gracefully as possible.

The invitation called for formal attire. She chose a forest green cocktail dress that fell to just above her knees. She was slipping on a silver, collarless jacket when the front doorbell rang. The weather was still relatively warm, but fall was definitely in the air. She opened her front door and smiled at her colleague.

"You look very handsome in your tuxedo, Howard."

"It's as uncomfortable as hell though," Howard said as he entered. He jammed his index finger into his collar. "I wouldn't do this for anyone but you, you know. You realize, of course, that the last time I was forced into this particular piece of clothing I was a few pounds lighter," Howard groused.

"Perhaps you should consider purchasing a new suit or give up the daily slice of pie you seem so fond of. Despite that, you look quite dashing."

"Thanks, Em," he said as he took in her dress. "You look ravishing as usual."

"It's comfortable, but probably not ravishing." She laughed lightly as she threw a shawl around her shoulders.

"I thought you'd prefer to walk," Howard said.

"It's a pleasant enough evening," she nodded.

During what turned out to be a leisurely stroll, the two academics discussed their new classes and what they were personally involved in, subject-wise. Emma was fascinated by the topic Howard was researching even though he lamented having to take time away from teaching.

"I should have stayed at the public school level," he said. "Fewer problems, but the paperwork and unwanted social interactions were enough to drive one to drink."

"I don't think I would care for that," Emma agreed. "It's bad enough here, especially in the lower level classes."

As they turned onto the sidewalk leading to the recently renovated Fine Arts Building, Emma slid her hand into the crook of Howard's arm. He leaned closer to her and whispered, "My first stop will undoubtedly be the wine and cheese bar. May I bring you a glass, as well?"

"Thank you, Howard. I'd appreciate it."

"Planning to buy anything?"

"I wouldn't call it a plan, but if something strikes my fancy it might return home with me. Just my small contribution to the arts," she said with a grin.

As they entered the finely decorated building, Emma accepted a program from a young man inside the main doors and studied each photograph in a collage hanging in the lobby. She was amazed at the changes that were made to the old building to modernize the interior. The front hall was expanded and divided into sections for the exhibit to give each discipline its own space. Howard presented Emma with a flute of champagne before wandering off to mingle with other faculty patrons. Emma promised to catch up to him somewhere along the way.

She carefully examined the art projects beginning with pencil drawings and progressing through watercolors and oil painting. She saw two or three that captured her attention and she examined them from various vantage points. She didn't always win when she placed a bid on the pieces offered during the limited auction, but she would probably make an offer on one or two.

She eventually located Howard, ensconced at the hors d'oeuvre table. She gingerly placed three or four items on a plate. They wandered through the pottery and metal section. The last section showed off the sculptures presented by students since the last exhibition. Emma froze when she saw a particularly beautiful piece. In the center of the area, spotlighted by muted beams from overhead recessed lighting, was a gleaming pink-hued marble statue of a nude female captured in the throes of ecstasy. Her hand obscured the face as she appeared to brush short hair back. Sensuous lips were parted to release her cries of pleasure. Her small-breasted torso appeared relaxed, alive, and incredibly touchable. The lighting created deep shadows on pre-determined portions of the woman's body. Emma could almost feel the heat of arousal wafting from the figure

"Wow," Howard said. "That's what I call one hot mama."

Emma glanced at the title of the work. *Untouchable*. Artist: *Anonymous*.

A light hand skimming semi-intimately down Emma's back distracted her. "Magnificent, isn't it?" said Dr. Sylvia Joyner, the new chairman of the university's Fine Arts Department.

"It's unbelievably beautiful," Emma said. "Quite exquisite." Sylvia Joyner was only slightly shorter than Emma and in her mid-forties. She had intimated on more than one occasion since joining the faculty that she was open to spending time with Emma. However, despite Sylvia's beautifully angled face, smooth raven hair, and languid blue eyes, Emma remained aloof, unwilling to explore a possible relationship other than friendship.

"It's completely hand polished. No machinery whatsoever involved. Most sculptors today use small electrical tools to smooth the stone and fashion the features. This artist chose not to use them for some reason," Sylvia said, leaning closer. "Touch it. It's remarkably smooth and feels oddly alive under your fingers."

Emma balanced her plate of snacks and her drink in one hand and let the tips of her fingers glide down the surface of the sculpture. "It has an unusual warmth to it, unlike other marble pieces I've admired," she said. "Is there a reserve on it?"

"Although we could probably get a significant number for it, it's not available," Sylvia answered, shaking her head. "The artist told me it wasn't for sale, but refused to reveal more than it was special to her."

"Do you know the meaning behind its title?"

Sylvia laughed. "Personally, I don't know if the title means the piece itself or the artist. She's quite private, but I'll keep working on her."

"You know the artist?"

"Indeed. I was able to spirit her away from her position at another university. She's agreed to join our faculty this year as a guest lecturer and artist-in-residence."

Howard finally wandered off with Sylvia and Emma was left to entertain herself. She chatted with a few other patrons, but kept returning to the stunning statue.

"Do you like it?" a voice behind her asked quietly.

"Very much," Emma answered without looking back.

"It was supposed to be my senior project several years ago, but the original was destroyed, so this is actually a reproduction."

Emma turned to look at the woman and knew she hadn't been able to hide the surprise on her face. She felt her muscles tighten as she resisted her body's impulse to embrace the young woman. Clearing her throat, she asked, "Can you tell me the story behind the work's title?"

"My model was afraid to let anyone close to her. Let anyone know the sensuous and passionate woman she could be." Ramie smiled as she gazed at the statue again. "I simply released her."

Emma raised her eyebrows slightly and glanced down briefly toward Ramie's hands, which were buried in the pockets of the gray linen slacks that hung loosely from her hips. The soft curves of the feminine body Emma remembered were still revealed.

Continuing to look at the statue, Ramie moved to stand next to Emma. She shifted her eyes to take in Emma's dignified profile and smiled. Emma had changed little in the last decade.

"*Untouchable* was my rehabilitation project after I left Overland," Ramie said, withdrawing a hand to touch the gleaming stone, then quickly made a fist and returned it to her pocket. "I was so angry and defeated before she worked her way into my mind. I owed it to her to force my hands to work again." Ramie glanced at Emma. "It probably sounds ridiculous, but she believed in me even when I didn't believe in myself."

Emma couldn't stop her eyes from drifting down to Ramie's hands again. "It was your hands that brought her to life." She smiled. "That is something someone very young might imagine, but it was obviously rendered with great...affection."

Ramie held her previously mangled hands up for Emma to see. There were thin white scars across the backs of her hands and a round puckered scar marred the center of each palm. "My scars may eventually fade more, but I can still sculpt, at least for now."

"I had no doubt you would. Sylvia tells me you're returning to Overland as a guest lecturer," Emma said.

Ramie nodded. "I've been fortunate with my sculpting career

so far." She took a deep breath. "And I felt as if I had unfinished business here."

"Will you be sculpting while you're here?"

Ramie nodded. "It soothes my soul. I've been gratified by the response to my work the last few years. It's harder than it once was, but I think the effort has been worthwhile."

"I'm very proud of you for overcoming adversity and accomplishing your goal, Miss Sunderlund." Emma leaned a little closer. "Your comments in my class certainly made that semester much less boring."

"I'm surprised you still remember that time, but thank you, even though I wasn't sure I could back up what I was saying most of the time," Ramie said with a laugh.

"Oddly, I recall that time quite vividly," Emma said. "It was a semester well worth remembering." It was all Emma could manage to stop from staring at Ramie Sunderlund. She was an attractive young woman, now a stunning woman. Loose curls of blonde hair framed her face delicately and fell almost to her shoulders, highlighting the blue eyes Emma remembered well.

"How's it going, ladies?" Sylvia asked as she joined the two women and slid an arm around Ramie's waist. "Are you all right, my dear?"

"A little tired," Ramie answered with a smile. "Dr. Rothenberg was one of my professors when I was an undergraduate here."

"Obviously before my tenure as department chair," Sylvia stated with a light laugh. "I would never have allowed such a gifted artist to escape. It took me several weeks to persuade her to return to Overland."

"I can understand that," Emma said politely. "Her time at Overland ended prematurely."

"Your hands?" Sylvia asked. Then she looked at Emma and said, "She refuses to tell me what happened."

"It's not something I care to remember," Ramie said with a sad smile.

Emma saw her clench her hands. "I understand completely." Emma looked over Ramie's shoulder and waved at someone. "I think my escort has seen all the art he can endure for one evening," she said. "I'm glad you're back at Overland and hope the future will be everything you deserve."

"Thank you for your patience with me, Dr. Rothenberg. It was an honor to study under you."

Emma laughed. "I doubt you would have said that ten years ago," she said as she squeezed Ramie's shoulder lightly before joining Howard once again for the walk home. Emma was surprised, but glad to see Ramie Sunderlund. She would look forward to seeing her again. But what would be the purpose? The very idea of being attracted to a woman nearly half her age bordered on the ridiculous.

"A SUCCESSFUL EVENING," Sylvia said as she guided her car through the streets of Middleton. "Emma seemed quite surprised to see you again. How long has it been?" she asked with a smile.

"About ten years," Ramie muttered. "She hasn't changed much."

"Well, she definitely remembers you. Did you notice how she looked at you? Although I can't blame her. You do look stunning tonight."

Ramie turned toward Sylvia, changing the subject. "When can I get my schedule?"

"Still working on it. It should be ready by the end of the week," Sylvia answered with a smile as her eyes scanned over Ramie briefly.

Sylvia signaled and pulled into the drive of the small house Overland provided for their artist-in-residence. She turned the vehicle off and walked around it to open the passenger door to help Ramie out. Sylvia escorted Ramie to her door and waited as she unlocked it. When Ramie pushed the door open, she turned and said, "Thank you for the ride, Sylvia. I spent most of the day unpacking and am a little tired."

"Could I interest you in dinner this weekend?" Sylvia offered.

"Perhaps another time. I hope to finish unpacking and check out the studio facilities to reacquaint myself. I'm sure it's changed since I was here last."

"Drop by my office and I'll give you a set of keys," Sylvia said. Before she stepped away, she added, "I saw the way you looked at Emma as well."

"I don't know what you mean," Ramie blushed.

Sylvia laughed lightly. "She's unavailable, you know. God knows I've tried. She's quite deeply closeted. Other than her questionable relationship with Millicent Carver, she remains aloof and untouchable."

"What was questionable about their friendship?"

"At one time there was a rumor they were more than friends. That they were lovers," Sylvia semi-whispered. With a brilliant predatory smile she added, "God! I would have paid good money to exchange places with Millie for a night or two."

Ramie stepped into what would be her home for the next year and closed the door, leaning against it, her eyes closed. She should have invited Sylvia in and Sylvia probably expected it, but the only thing Ramie wanted at that moment was to remember everything about that night. Of course she was happy to see Emma again, but was shaken by how much it affected her. Emma Rothenberg was still as attractive and desirable as the first day Ramie saw her despite the passage of a decade. When Emma's eyes met hers, Ramie saw a glimpse of something deeper than surprise, something...inviting. Or had Ramie only seen what she wanted to see. Emma would never know about the fantasies that kept Ramie going through everything, clinging to an attraction that refused to die. That lingering attraction was what drew Ramie back to Overland and while Sylvia was an attractive woman, Ramie couldn't pull her mind away from her ever-present thoughts of Emma Rothenberg.

Ramie hadn't touched a woman in the last ten years without remembering the cool feel of Emma's hand as she comforted her. If she breathed deeply enough, Ramie could smell the scent that belonged to only Emma. She ached to feel Emma's touch and fill her lungs with Emma's scent again.

EMMA WALKED DOWN the hallway of offices Monday afternoon and stopped in front of Howard's open door. His forehead rested on his fingers while he chewed his pipe stem as he read the paper in front of him.

"You look extremely studious, Howard," Emma commented as she leaned against the door jamb.

"I don't hear you offering to read this juvenile drivel for me, my dear," he huffed.

"My days teaching Introduction to Anything are hopefully a thing of the past, but alas, I remember them well." She pushed away from the door. "I thought I might be able to persuade you to join me for a very large cup of coffee at the Union," she said.

"What? And tear myself away from this stack of utterly forgettable writing?" Then a smile split his face. "I thought you'd never ask. You are truly a life saver."

"They'll still be there when you return, you know."

"I do, but I hopefully will have acquired a caffeine-infused attitudinal realignment by then."

Emma stepped into the hallway and waited as Howard closed his office door.

"Aren't you going to lock it?" Emma asked as Howard held her coat for her.

"Why?" Howard shrugged, buttoning his suit jacket. "A gerbil with two semi-functioning neurons that occasionally run into one another could get into any of these offices," he chuckled. "The locks only make you feel safe up here," he said, tapping a finger against the side of his head. He held his arm out and Emma took it. "Perhaps we can add a decadent slice of pie to our coffee," he beamed. "My treat."

Emma and Howard walked at a leisurely pace down tree-lined sidewalks. Emma loved the way the trees were gradually changing into their vibrant fall wardrobe. She smiled and took a deep, cleansing breath, filling her lungs with cool, but refreshing air.

"This background truly suits you, my dear," Howard noted casually. "You look like a university professor."

"I remember my own professors and hope I don't look anything like them. Most were white-haired, wrinkled, and just old. I can't do anything about getting older, but so far have managed to avoid the white hair and wrinkles."

"I, on the other hand, don't mind looking like a stereotypical university professor, portly tummy, mustachioed, three-piece suit, etcetera."

"Except for the portly tummy and mustache, I am also stereotypical. But who knows, in a few years I might gain weight and have a mustache too," Emma chuckled.

"You will always be devastatingly attractive, Emma," Howard said affectionately.

They entered the two-story Student Union Building, placed their order, and quickly located a vacant corner table. Emma sat back and crossed her legs, watching Howard wolf down a calorie-laden chunk of apple pie.

"How can you live on coffee alone?" Howard asked after wiping pie crumbs from his mustache with a napkin.

"I drink tea at home," she said with a shrug.

"You know, Emma, if you loosened up just a tad, there would probably be someone waiting with a cup of tea when you arrive home."

"I know how to boil water, Howard," she sniffed.

"That's not the point and you know it. I'm worried about you. It's not healthy to be alone so much."

"I have plenty to keep me busy," Emma said after another sip. "But I do miss Louie terribly."

"You know that wasn't what I meant," Howard said with a frown. "I miss the old boy too, but was referring to someone who would keep you warm in the evenings."

"Louie did that without demanding much of my time," Emma answered with a wistful smile at the memory of her beloved pet.

"Speaking of demanding your time, have you heard from Millie recently?" Howard asked, leaning back and sipping his coffee. "Shouldn't be too much longer before Stanton is away from home again, eh?"

"I'm doing fine alone and I have no intention of discussing Millie Carver with you."

"She's using you, dearie. I'm sure she'd be able to find someone closer to home willing to occupy her time while Stanton is gone if you stepped away. Sylvia Joyner is available and has made her interest obviously obvious, if you'll pardon my wording. You have more to offer than a woman like Millicent Carver can ever appreciate."

Emma glared at him. "That's enough, Howard," she snapped. "I enjoy your friendship, but could survive without our daily discussions."

Howard held his hands up in surrender. "*Mea culpa.*"

"You're forgiven. Are you planning to attend my little gathering the first of the month?" she asked as she gave him a friendly attempt at a smile.

"I have it marked on my calendar," Howard announced cheerfully, apparently his moral lesson concerning Millicent Carver forgotten. "The first home game of the season is this weekend. Are you planning to attend? If so, perhaps we could meet there. I'll even bring my own pom-poms."

"If you bring pom-poms, you can sit by yourself," Emma chuckled.

Howard glanced across the dining area and a wide smile broke across his face. "Now there is a choice morsel for any woman of the Sapphic persuasion."

Emma let her eyes scan the main room of the Student Union. They passed, stopped, and backed up a little when she saw a head of curly blonde ringlets, its owner holding a tray containing a club sandwich, chips, and a small drink. Ramie scanned the room for a vacant seat in the crowded dining area. Emma felt a small but intense surge of desire shoot through her system. She hadn't seen Ramie Sunderlund since the art department's exhibition. Ramie located a table occupied by a young man preparing to leave and quickly set her items down. She casually scanned the room before Emma was able to react and avert her eyes. The rich blue of Ramie Sunderlund's eyes seemed to laser into Emma's, producing the warmth of an embarrassed blush on her cheeks. Ramie began making her way toward Emma and Howard's table, staring intently at Emma as if she were afraid she might disappear if she looked away.

Howard stood when Ramie came to a stop in front of them. She stuck her hand out. "Wonderful to see you again, Dr. Trammell," she said as Howard accepted her hand.

"Miss Sunderlund," Howard acknowledged.

"How are your classes this year, Dr. Rothenberg?"

"Satisfactory thus far."

"None of your students could possibly be as terrified as I was," Ramie said with a laugh.

"We were just discussing this week's football game and making plans to attend. Do you enjoy football, Miss Sunderlund?" Howard blurted out.

"Very much, Dr. Trammel. I never missed a game when I was a student here," Ramie answered.

"Then perhaps you could join us Saturday afternoon. There is a rather good section reserved for faculty members and I'm sure you would qualify to sit there. Don't you, Em?"

Emma continued sipping her coffee, but managed to nod. What the hell is Howard doing, she thought. She knew Ramie and Howard were staring at her and expected a response when all she wanted to do was magically disappear. She swallowed and forced herself to respond. "Um, there are always vacant seats in the faculty section if you care to join us."

"Thank you. I'll certainly think about it, but right now I'd better get back to my lunch before my next lecture. It was nice to see you both again."

Emma's eyes followed Ramie as she moved gracefully between tables toward her own. The memory of a younger woman leaving the auditorium after Emma's lecture ended caused a brief lift of her lips.

"A delightful young woman," Howard said when Ramie was halfway back to her table.

"Indeed," Emma said. "I assume you will bring additional pom-poms."

Howard grinned and waggled his eyebrows. "I didn't see anything wrong with the pom-poms she already has. In case you hadn't noticed she's quite a magnificent specimen of womanhood. Ripe for the plucking."

Emma looked back at him and squinted. "You're an old man with a dirty mind," she huffed.

"Perhaps you should consider inviting Miss Sunderlund to your soiree next month. You know, to welcome her back to Overland." Howard grinned. "Or for some other reason."

"You're impossible, Howard. It's time to get back to work."

"YOU CANNOT BE serious!" Emma exploded when Franklin Douglas, the head of the English Department, announced at an impromptu department meeting that the next year he was planning to assign lower level classes to all members of the faculty, including those with seniority. His announcement was met with much grumbling around the table and threats to quit.

"The demand that we be published already leaves us with precious little time, Franklin. The additional preparation time for classes none of us have taught for years would simply be too much," Emma argued.

"It's English, Emma, not rocket science," Douglas sighed.

"Regardless of what you think," Emma spat. "Keeping up with the most current research does take considerable time. And incorporating that material into any lecture does as well. We cannot be expected to simply toss out a new idea and hope our students catch it as it flies by."

"Now there's an interesting new concept," Howard chuckled. "Drive-by teaching."

"The new thinking is that less can actually be more," Franklin said, glaring at Howard.

Emma shook her head, but responded, her voice strong. "I've read that as well, but less is always less. My students cannot be expected to learn when given fly-by information. It makes the subject seem potentially unimportant. Besides, that study was intended for secondary public education. Our students already come to us essentially ignorant and now you are suggesting we make it more so."

"By having our best teach our newest students, you will have the chance to bolster their knowledge level sooner," Franklin argued.

"Possibly," she admitted. "But we run the risk of dumbing down the curriculum, in my opinion."

"It is only a consideration at this point," Franklin chuckled. "Perhaps you should put together something to convince the dean of its flaws."

"Where was the new dean before he came to Overland?" Howard asked

"The University of Washington-Seattle. Actually, I believe he was an English professor."

"Why would he leave Washington to come here?" Emma asked. "Washington has an excellent program, and while Overland is growing, its status is less well-known."

"He wanted to be closer to his wife's family, who live in Indiana," Franklin stated.

"Anything else of importance on our agenda?" Emma asked

crisply as she rose and grabbed her purse and coat. "I need to begin preparing my grades for the current quarter."

RAMIE LOOKED DOWN at the notes in front of her. She still had work to do before meeting with a class of graduate students who hoped to pick her brains about what they could expect in order to become successful commercial and freelance sculptors in their own right. She had spent most of the day and early evening setting up her office and the studio assigned to her in the Fine Arts Building. Several members of the art faculty dropped by to welcome her or to discuss various aspects of sculpture. While it was nice to become acquainted with her new colleagues, she was resigned to spending most of the weekend finishing tasks that should already be completed. Plus, she had already agreed to meet Howard Trammel and Emma Rothenberg for the football game the following afternoon. Maybe accepting this position was going to become more work than she had imagined. Her mind was restless. She missed her private studio and its adjacent comfortable loft on the second floor of the old, unused barn behind her parents' home in Vermont. And, she realized, she was starving. It wasn't uncommon for her to lose track of the time and miss meals. She would have to keep better track of the time.

She pressed her thumb into the palm of her hand and held it there as long as she could tolerate. The pain would gather her wandering thoughts and allow her to concentrate again. She gasped when a flash of discomfort began in her palm and shot through her fingers. She quickly removed her thumb and stared at the ugly, puckered scar on her palm. It throbbed for a moment, matching her heartbeat, as she took in deep breathes. She leaned her head back and waited for the momentary pain to pass. She clenched her fingers, imaging the feel of cool stone gradually warming as her fingers touched it and brought it to life. She smiled remembering working to bring *Untouchable* to life with gentle strokes and tender caresses. She stood and shook her hands vigorously until the final flair of pain subsided. She had given life to *Untouchable*, but it had never touched her back, other than in her fantasies.

Perhaps it was a mistake to return to Overland after so many years. What had she hoped to accomplish? She had been in the same place ten years earlier. Was this what her students could expect? Creating fantasies with no hope of truly fulfilling their dreams or desires? Life expected more and she needed more. She grabbed her keys and her jacket. She was positive her energy level would improve after a decent meal and a good night's rest.

A few minutes later, she pushed through the glass doors of the building, pausing to lock them.

The night air was colder than usual for late September. Ramie breathed in a lungful of cold air and tilted her head back to exhale a stream of white past her lips as she stared up at the refurbished Fine Arts Building while she pulled on her denim jacket. A decade earlier, her world had been shattered in a senseless act of violence in this very place. Her mind dredged up the pain of that night, but she willed her feet forward and made her way toward the parking lot. She was stronger now. More certain of what she wanted. Of what she had always wanted. Seeing Emma again had only confirmed what she'd known even before that terrible night.

The sound of a door slamming shut at a building nearby drew Ramie's attention. She turned toward the sound in time to see Emma Rothenberg gaze up at the cloudless sky as she brought the collar of her coat farther up her neck.

Without thinking, Ramie raised her hand to wave and took a step forward. Her foot caught on a sprinkler head and she tripped. Her forehead bounced on the walkway and she curled her hands around it, momentarily stunned. She blinked rapidly to clear her vision before she attempted to get up.

"Are you all right?" Emma asked as she placed a hand on Ramie's back and brushed her hair back with the other.

Ramie nodded as she tried to catch her breath. "Thank you. I'm fine now. I just need a minute." She lifted her head and looked at Emma.

"Miss Sunderlund," Emma breathed. "What are you doing here this late? Can you stand?"

"I...I was arranging my office," Ramie gasped as she began shivering.

"Are you sure you're all right?" Emma asked.

Ramie struggled to her feet. "I'm positive." She smiled. "I feel slightly stupid though for not watching where I was walking."

"Let's get you someplace warmer for now," Emma said quietly as she wrapped an arm around Ramie's shoulders.

"I have my car. I can drive home," Ramie said, although she enjoyed the feel of Emma's arm around her.

"I don't think you're in any shape to drive right now, my dear. You can retrieve your vehicle tomorrow."

"Actually, I'm hungry and was planning to find a nice place for a quiet meal. Would you care to join me? My treat," Ramie asked.

"Well, I...uh...was just—" Emma started.

"You said I shouldn't drive right now and the apple I had for lunch is long gone." Ramie shrugged. "If it would make you feel better, you could just watch me eat."

"There's a pleasant little family restaurant not too far away, if you enjoy simple food. It should still be open. Truthfully, I wasn't looking forward to having to cook tonight."

"Great," Ramie said. "If you wouldn't mind, you could drop me here after we eat so I can get my car."

"Certainly," Emma said.

THE RESTAURANT WAS small and sat off a side road not far from the campus. Candles flickered on each table and cast dim intimate lighting over the interior. Ramie was impressed with the décor, which lent a homey atmosphere to everything. It reminded her of home, especially the fireplace. She and Emma found a cozy table to one side of the fireplace. The low rippling flames sent shafts of red, orange, and yellow across the white linen tablecloth and reflected off Emma's glasses.

"What do you recommend?" Ramie asked as she studied her menu.

"The roast beef dinner is excellent. Very tender. I've never had a bad meal here," Emma replied.

A pleasant, middle-aged waitress appeared with two glasses of water. "It's nice to see you again Dr. Rothenberg," she said with a warm smile.

"A meal here is always a pleasure, Janet," Emma acknowledged.

"The usual?" Janet asked Emma.

"Please. And a cup of hot tea."

"Miss?" Janet asked, turning to Ramie.

"The same only with a cup of coffee, please," Ramie said as she closed her menu.

Once Janet left to turn in their order, Emma said, "You don't even know what you're getting."

"I trust you. You said everything here was good." Ramie shrugged. "Plus I'm so hungry right now, I'd eat just about anything that didn't attempt to eat me first," she laughed.

Ramie glanced around the restaurant and rubbed the palm of her hand. "I don't remember this place."

"It's only been here about five or six years, I think. It's not very busy this evening, but there's usually quite a wait on the weekend," Emma explained.

"It doesn't look like a student hang-out."

Emma smiled. "More of a faculty hang-out, I believe. A few

students come by if they want an evening to be a special one."

Emma's usual turned out to be an open-face hot roast beef sandwich with a large serving of mashed potatoes surrounded by bread and roast beef, all generously slathered with rich brown gravy.

Emma choked slightly when Ramie groaned, "God. This is orgasmically delicious." She looked at Emma and grinned. "Is that even a word?"

Emma cleared her throat. "I don't think so."

"Well, it should be. Some things are just that good."

Eventually Ramie's rate of devouring her food slowed. "I should have asked before, but how is Louie?"

Emma wiped her mouth with her napkin before answering. After a drink of her tea she said, "Regrettably, Louie passed away a few years ago. I still miss his company terribly, especially in the evenings."

"Have you considered getting another dog?"

"No. I'm getting too old to train another and it still wouldn't be Louie. I wouldn't be as lucky with another animal."

"I'm sorry, Dr. Rothenberg. He was a beautiful animal." Ramie reached across the table and placed her hand over Emma's, squeezing it lightly.

"Thank you," Emma said as she withdrew her hand and placed it in her lap. "Are you ready to go?"

"Yes," Ramie said as she picked up the check. "My treat, remember?" she added.

After Ramie paid the bill, Emma escorted her to the car. They chatted a few minutes while the vehicle warmed up. Ramie leaned her head against her seat as Emma backed out of the parking slot.

A hand on her shoulder awakened Ramie with a jerk and she was startled to see Emma leaning over her. When their eyes met, Emma cleared her throat and extended her hand to help Ramie from the vehicle.

Ramie took the offered hand. A spark of electricity arced between them and Emma flinched slightly, feeling warmth flow through her body. "Must be static electricity because of the cold air," Emma finally said. "Sorry."

"I didn't mean to fall asleep," Ramie said. "Must have been that filling meal."

"No harm done. Are you sure you can drive? I could take you home if you'd feel safer," Emma offered

Ramie shook her head. "I'm fine, Dr. Rothenberg. I don't live far from here."

Ramie fished her keys from her jeans pocket and opened the

driver's door of her car and scooted inside. She leaned back and ran her hands through her hair and rubbed her face. She winced when her fingers felt a knot on her forehead. Perhaps a hot shower would ease the throbbing. What a wonderful way to impress a woman like Emma Rothenberg, Ramie thought. "Next time," she whispered to herself as she waved goodbye to Emma before she backed from her parking spot.

RAMIE AWOKE THE next morning with a thundering headache. She made her way into the bathroom and was shocked by the large bruised area on her forehead and the beginning of a black eye. Lovely, she thought. She didn't own enough make-up to make the huge purple splotch on her face less obvious. She popped a couple of aspirin into her mouth and prayed the headache would disappear soon. She had been too tired to shower when she arrived home the night before, so after eating a bowl of cereal, she stripped and stepped into the shower. The water running over the discolored lump on her forehead felt good and her headache began to lessen. She was almost cheerful and looking forward to the game by the time she zipped her jeans and pulled a brand new Overland sweatshirt over her head. The fleece touching her skin was soft and warm.

When she stepped outside, preparing to leave, an unexpectedly brisk, cold wind struck her and she hurried back into the house to grab a jacket. She remembered from her days as a student that the first game each year was well attended. Her house wasn't far from the campus and she decided to walk the few blocks to the stadium rather than search for a possible parking spot. She crammed her hands into her jacket pockets and set out for the stadium an hour before the two o'clock kick-off time, hoping she'd be able to find Howard and Emma. She was surprised to find her colleagues waiting for her at a gate marked "Faculty Entrance".

"I hope you haven't been waiting long," Ramie said as she stepped up to them.

"A few minutes," Howard replied. "My God! What happened to your head?"

Ramie laughed. "I tripped and fell last night. It was my own fault and looks worse than it is. Too bad we're not the Overland Pirates. I could have hidden the whole thing."

"How far away did you have to park?"

"I walked. My residence isn't far away."

"You should have told Emma. She always walks. You could have come together," Howard said with a smile.

"Perhaps next time," Ramie said, glancing at Emma with a grin.

Howard led the way up the concrete steps into the faculty seating area, stopping every few steps to look for three seats together. Eventually he pointed to a group of empty seats along the aisle about halfway up the metal bleachers. "Those are perfect. Easy in, easy out," he said with a smile. He climbed the steps and waited for Emma and Ramie to slide in. Emma pulled a blanket from the shoulder bag she was carrying and spread it over their seats so they didn't have to sit directly on the cold metal. It only took a few minutes for them to adjust their bodies into a reasonably comfortable position.

Howard rubbed his hands together and reached into his coat pocket. He withdrew his well-used pipe and stuck it into his mouth. "Do you mind?" he asked, turning toward Ramie.

"Actually I used to love the scent of pipe smoke as it wafted past me," she answered. "Feel free, Dr. Trammel."

"Howard, my dear, please," he said as he stuffed tobacco into the pipe bowl. He leaned forward slightly and pointed at Emma. "And that is Emma. Now that we are workmates, so to speak, it seems appropriate. Right, Emma?"

Emma seemed engrossed in reading the program she'd picked up on the way in, but managed to nod in response. "Certainly, Howard."

"Would either of you ladies care for popcorn or a drink before the game begins?" Howard asked between puffs while he lit his pipe. "I'd be happy to make a run to the concession stand. It's right below us."

Ramie laughed. "I can smell it and it smells wonderful." She wiggled around to remove her wallet from the back pocket of her jeans.

"No, no," Howard said jovially. "My treat. Emma?"

"Hot chocolate, please," Emma answered.

"That sounds good for me, too," Ramie said. She looked at Emma. "Hot chocolate and would you like to split a popcorn with me?"

"That would be fine," Emma said.

"Do you come to all the games?" Ramie asked.

"As many as I can," Emma replied. "I enjoy the competition."

Ramie smiled. "The competitive type, huh?"

"There's nothing wrong with a little healthy competition," Emma snorted.

Ramie grasped Emma's arm. "Oh, I agree. It's the spirit of competitiveness that drives us forward. Do you still play tennis? As I recall you were quite good at it."

Emma stared at the hand on her arm for a moment before answering. "From time to time," she said softly.

Emma couldn't remember the last time she'd been so uncomfortable. Until Howard left, Ramie's arm pressed against Emma's. She was certain she could feel the heat from Ramie's body against her own. It was most distracting, even though Ramie didn't seem to notice. Emma felt better when Howard stood and Ramie moved away slightly. Then she felt suddenly colder and missed the warmth of Ramie's touch. Emma brought her eyes up, pausing briefly at Ramie's mouth. Her lips were full and lush. Kissable. She blinked and her eyes met Ramie's for a few seconds.

Then Ramie removed her hand, breaking the spell. "Do you...uh...participate in any sports?" Emma choked out.

Ramie's cheeks flushed as she answered. "I used to ski before...before..." she struggled.

"Before your assault?"

"Yeah." Ramie looked down at her hands, compulsively fisting them. She took a deep breath. "They hurt in the cold now."

"I'm sorry. I didn't mean to raise a painful memory."

"You didn't. It's something I thought I had under control, but occasionally it finds its way to the surface again."

Ramie rubbed her hands together and slipped them into her jacket pockets.

"I have hand warmers if you need them," Emma offered.

"I'm fine," Ramie said. "Why did you tell the hospital you were my aunt?"

"Wha—" Emma started. Then she smiled. "They wouldn't let me see you the day of your surgery unless I was a family member. I knew you were scared and didn't think you should face it alone," she said with a shrug.

"My mother was pretty upset about that," Ramie chuckled.

"Give her my apologies. It seemed like the right thing at the time."

"It was. I went into surgery knowing someone was there who cared. Thank you, Emma."

The sound of Ramie's voice saying her name warmed Emma's heart. She wanted to say that she more than cared, but was stopped by Howard's reappearance and was somehow grateful for the interruption.

THE FOLLOWING MONDAY afternoon, Emma removed her glasses, tossing them onto the stack of essays on her desk, and leaned back in her chair to stretch. She smiled remembering

Ramie's face as the low candlelight gently flickered across her features during their impromptu dinner three nights earlier. She looked adorable dozing in the front seat of Emma's car. Her face was angelic, innocent, yet oddly desirable. She shook her head in an attempt to shake her thoughts away. They were totally inappropriate. The passage of ten years didn't change the fact that Ramie Sunderlund was significantly younger than Emma, as well as a former student. Saturday had been a difficult day as Emma fought against her own feelings of attraction to Ramie. She had always had difficulty fighting her feelings. Her inability to control them had gotten her into trouble before and she couldn't allow that to happen again.

Now Emma had been working for hours, trying to complete her grading and wishing she had allowed her assistant to shoulder part of the burden. Since the incident with Travis Whitman years before, she found it difficult to give anyone else control over her grading, even though she often felt stretched to her limit.

A light tap on her door pulled her attention away and she smiled when Howard's beaming face appeared.

"Time for our weekly snack," he said.

"I have all this grading to get through. Howard," Emma said with a frown.

"As a wise woman, who shall remain nameless, once sagely told me, it will still be there when you get back," Howard said, rubbing his chin in thought. "Now who could that have been?"

Emma chuckled as she opened her desk drawer and pulled out her shoulder bag. "Yes. I wonder indeed. One hour and no more."

"Of course, my dear," he said as he motioned her out the door.

Ten minutes later, Emma took a cup of coffee from the student server and waited patiently as Howard ordered his usual slice of pie to accompany his coffee. They found a table against a brick planter and settled into their chairs.

"Considering your rather staunch disapproval, Franklin has decided the less is more idea needs more research," Howard said as he carefully peeled the Saran Wrap from his pie. "He's considering selecting a panel to more thoroughly investigate the idea. Don't be shocked if he selects you to be on it."

"I'm afraid I'd have to turn down such a generous offer," Emma said coolly. "Change the subject, please."

"No need. A change of subject is approaching even as we speak."

"What— " Emma started.

"Dr. Rothenberg," Ramie said as she stepped up to their table. "How are you?"

"I should be asking you that question," Emma said as she stood. "I trust you have recovered, Miss Sunderlund."

"I have. I wanted to thank you again for assisting me Friday evening," Ramie said. "And to tell you both how much I enjoyed the game on Saturday."

"I see the bruise on your forehead is beginning to fade," Howard noted. "And a victory on the gridiron lifts everyone's spirits, even if it was colder than expected. We hope you'll join us again."

Ramie shifted from foot to foot and looked uncomfortable when Emma refused to meet her eyes. She smiled and then grimaced slightly at a twinge from the bump on her forehead. She cleared her throat and said, "Well, I should find a table before my break ends. Have a good day, Dr. Rothenberg, Dr. Trammel."

As Ramie turned away, Howard glanced at Emma and said, "Miss Sunderlund?"

"Yes, Dr. Trammel," Ramie responded as she faced the two professors again.

"Umm…Emma is hosting a small gathering of faculty members at the beginning of November, and now that you are one of us, even temporarily, I was wondering if you might consider attending. It's quite a good way to meet your colleagues in a more social setting. Although students don't believe it, we are people too, albeit smarter than the average student. Casual. Food and drinks provided."

"Are you asking me on a date, Dr. Trammel?" Ramie asked with a mischievous smile.

"No, of course not," Howard blustered, causing Emma to choke on her drink. "I thought you might enjoy the opportunity to mingle and relax with other faculty members."

Ramie laughed. "I'd love to join you, Dr. Trammel, as well as others I may not have had the pleasure of meeting yet. Thank you."

"I'll send you the specifics after I return to my office," Howard said.

Emma's eyes followed Ramie as she made her way to a recently vacated table. "That was very suave and debonair of you, Howard," she said.

"You could have invited her yourself, you know?" Howard said, leaning slightly over the table.

"Our hour is nearly up," Emma answered with a shrug before finishing her coffee.

"Admit it, she is quite attractive," Howard noted. "And

available," he added, wiggling his eyebrows.

Emma shook her head. "I grant that she is extremely attractive, but she is also half my age, Howard."

"Are you afraid, Emma?"

"Not afraid. Simply realistic." Emma glanced at Howard and changed the subject. "Ready? I still have grading to complete."

Chapter Ten

WHEN RAMIE ARRIVED at the address Howard had sent for what he described as an informal gathering, she was surprised by the number of vehicles packed into the cul-de-sac encircling Emma Rothenberg's modest country-style cottage. The first weekend in November was cold and she saw light gray smoke drifting into the dark sky overhead. She hoped the interior was warm. Although she had been instructed to dress casually, she elected to wear maroon slacks and a matching multi-colored sweater she hoped would be acceptable. Truly casual would have been faded jeans, her old, oversized flannel shirt, and scruffy work boots. Basically her work clothes. Tonight called for something better.

She stayed later at work than she wanted before racing home and jumping into a hot shower. Because she arrived at Emma's late, she was forced to park on the street that ran in front of the cul-de-sac and walk the block to the house. She heard talking and laughter as she stepped onto the porch and took a deep breath before ringing the doorbell. She smiled when the door burst open and she saw Howard's smiling face. He pushed the screen open and waved her inside.

"We thought you had decided not to join us this evening," he said.

"Sorry I'm late, but I was delayed by a student who needed help," Ramie explained as she shrugged off her coat.

Howard took the coat and hung it in the closet just inside the front door. "There is a fairly wide assortment of adult beverages in the dining room, as well as snacks if you're hungry."

Ramie spotted the fireplace and said, "I think I might warm up before I do anything else." She shivered and ran her hands up and down her folded arms. "It's a little brisk outside."

"Do whatever you wish, my dear."

Ramie made her way to the fireplace, sticking her hands out to warm them. They ached from the cold. Because she was running late, she hadn't taken the time to dip them in the warm wax bath as she usually did. The heat of the flames in the fireplace felt heavenly as she closed her eyes and rubbed her hands together. Satisfied her hands were warmed, she brought them up and pressed them to her still cool cheeks, sighing at the feel.

"Perhaps a cup of coffee will help warm you up," a woman's voice said.

Ramie opened her eyes as Emma set a steaming cup on the mantle.

"Thank you, Dr. Rothenberg."

"Tonight we are merely colleagues, Miss Sunderlund. Please feel free to use my first name," Emma instructed.

"Thank you, Emma," Ramie said softly with a smile.

"Please feel free to mingle, Ramie. There are probably a few people you'll remember."

Ramie watched Emma walk away, pausing occasionally to engage a guest in friendly conversation. She had never seen Emma so relaxed. Eventually, Ramie began to feel comfortable enough to mingle and introduce herself. Periodically, while chatting with others she would look up and see Emma gazing in her direction. Emma looked amazing in a two-toned velvet lounging suit that complemented her hair and brought out the color of her eyes. Ramie felt flushed with warmth when Emma looked at her.

"Ramie?" A warm hand on her elbow made Ramie turn to find Sylvia Joyner standing beside her.

"Hi, Sylvia. I'm sorry. I didn't see you when I arrived," Ramie said before leaning in for a brief hug.

"No problem. If you have a minute, I'd like to introduce you to a couple of people," Sylvia said as she guided Ramie across the room toward a knot of individuals who were engaged in a lively conversation.

As Sylvia and Ramie joined the group, a distinguished-looking man in a three-piece suit smiled.

"Perhaps you can give us your opinion, Sylvia," the man said.

"Well, Dean Campbell, I always have an opinion about most things and would love to share one as long as it doesn't involve the principles of physics or molecular science. I'd have to plead total ignorance about those disciplines," Sylvia said with a laugh and was joined by others around her who apparently agreed.

"I believe you're safe there, Sylvia," the Dean said.

"Before you ask for my opinion on any subject, however; I'd like to introduce you to this year's artist-in-residence, Miss Laramie Sunderlund. Miss Sunderlund did her undergraduate work here at Overland and has become a successful sculptress in her own right. Ramie, this is Dean Campbell, the dean of the College of Arts and Sciences."

Ramie extended a hand and said, "It's a pleasure to meet you, Dean Campbell."

Campbell covered Ramie's hand with both of his. "I'm familiar with your work, Miss Sunderlund. I hope your stay with us is a pleasant one and beneficial for our students."

"Thank you, Dean Campbell," Ramie said, her smile brilliant. "I'm sure it will be a challenge, but I'm enjoying myself so far. Everyone has been very welcoming."

As soon as the discussion turned to more serious topics, Ramie managed to drift away.

Nearly an hour or so later, Ramie made her way to the dining room where a wide variety of food was arranged on a large table. It all looked delicious and she chose several pieces to try.

"Is it what you expected, mingling with faculty members?" Emma asked as she joined Ramie and popped a canapé into her mouth.

"It's interesting, but I will confess that some of their discussions have been thoroughly over my head at times. I'm sorry to say my appreciation for literature probably hasn't improved over the years, although I do find reading relaxing."

"What do you like to read?"

Ramie laughed. "Nothing very academic I'm afraid."

"As long as you found them entertaining, they've served their intended purpose," Emma responded with a smile.

"What do you read…for fun?"

"Don't tell anyone," Emma said in a low voice as she leaned slightly closer, "but when I have time I enjoy a good mystery."

"Your secret is safe with me," Ramie said with a smile. The scent of Emma's perfume was light and alluring. Ramie caught herself before she leaned even closer. "You have a lovely home. I meant to tell you earlier."

"Thank you. It's a sound structure, but had been a little neglected until I purchased it. I had to do quite a bit of renovation work before it was where I wanted it to be. Now I'm quite comfortable here." Emma picked up another canapé and chewed it slowly before speaking again. "If you're interested, I'd be glad to give you a quick tour."

"I'd like that."

Emma glanced around. "I don't have anything important demanding my time at the moment if you're interested now."

"Now would be great, but I don't want to take you away from your other guests," Ramie said.

"Unless the food or liquor runs out, I doubt I will be missed. Give me a moment to let Howard know on the off chance I'm needed."

Emma crossed the room to speak to Howard. Ramie saw him smile and nod as he looked past Emma in Ramie's direction. He patted her lightly on the shoulder when she turned to leave. Ramie swallowed hard as she watched Emma approach. She was so beautiful and dignified and walked with a grace Ramie hadn't noticed until then. Ramie stuffed a cracker topped with cheese into her mouth and washed it down with a cup of punch.

"You can take your snack and drink with you, if you wish," Emma said with a devastating smile as she returned to Ramie's side.

"I'm good and don't want to risk making a mess. I can be a klutz."

Emma smiled at her benignly. "Then follow me."

They strolled leisurely through the downstairs rooms, which included the kitchen, a guest room with an attached full bath, and Emma's library and office. Ramie had already seen the living and dining areas. According to Emma, the house was built in the early twentieth century and had originally served as the home of an early mayor. She had many of the original rooms removed and the current rooms enlarged for her needs. The mayor and his wife had several children and those rooms upstairs and down were repurposed, along with a former parlor. Quarters for a housekeeper and one child's room became the guest room and accompanying bath. The parlor was joined with the living area and another bedroom allowed room for an expansion of the kitchen and pantry areas.

"It must have cost you a fortune," Ramie noted. "But it was so worth it."

"I love the architecture of older homes such as this one. Once it was opened up, there was more than enough space. The biggest change was upstairs. There I removed virtually everything and incorporated the space into a master suite with a sitting area, walk-in closet, and the bathroom of my dreams. Until the construction was completed, I slept in the downstairs guest room for what seemed like forever," Emma said with a laugh.

"Then I'll definitely have to see that," Ramie enthused.

Ramie followed Emma up the front stairs, giving her an appreciative view of Emma's ass. A small landing at the top of the stairs opened into what Emma called the master suite. Emma opened a set of light oak French doors for Ramie to enter the room. Ramie's eyes widened as she turned in a circle, attempting to take it all in. A king-size bed sat at an angle against two walls. Large floor-to-ceiling windows created virtually an entire wall with a second set of French doors in the center that led to a balcony overlooking a garden below. The furnishings were what Ramie could only call minimalist, yet contemporary.

"It's magnificent," Ramie breathed. "Everything is so

understated, yet very elegant."

Emma paused to light a candle on the nightstand next to the bed.

"In the spring and summer, the scent of flowers from the garden drifts up and fills the room at night," Emma said, the timbre of her voice soft and intimate. "It's...intoxicating."

Ramie turned to face Emma and their eyes met.

"You are so incredibly beautiful," Emma whispered and raised her hand to let the backs of her fingers stroke Ramie's cheek.

Ramie took Emma's hand and pressed it to her lips. "I came back to Overland because of you, Emma. You were my unfinished business." She released Emma's hand and gazed into her smoldering eyes. "Put your hands on me, Emma," she murmured as she moved closer.

Another long moment passed before Ramie felt Emma's hands move up her back and into her hair. Emma's eyes were filled with unmistakable desire. Their lips were centimeters apart. Emma seemed to be engaged momentarily in some kind of internal argument, struggling with her own desires. Ramie saw a change flicker across Emma's eyes as a hand cautiously touched her cheek. And then it happened. Emma kissed her. Her lips were soft and full and warm. Ramie felt her heart soar as she drank in the incredible feeling of happiness she had dreamed of for so long. She parted her lips to invite Emma inside as she deepened the kiss slightly. Emma accepted her silent invitation. The silky feel of Emma's tongue gliding over hers made her weak in the knees. Ramie never wanted to lose this connection, but Emma abruptly broke the kiss and stepped back slightly, her eyes filled with doubt as they searched Ramie's face.

"I...I'm so sorry," Emma choked out.

"I'm sorry that you're sorry," Ramie said. She cleared her throat, unsure of what to say. "I...uh... should leave. It's been a long day and I'm a little tired. You have a lovely home."

"Of course. I understand," Emma said.

"I doubt it," Ramie mumbled under her breath before following Emma out of the room and downstairs again. Emma was quickly drawn into a discussion by Howard and could only watch as Ramie located her coat. Then she was gone.

RAMIE SPENT THE remainder of the weekend attempting to put together her next lesson and moping around the small house that was serving as her temporary home. Emma was never out of her thoughts, nor the too-brief kiss they'd shared. She would do anything to be with Emma again, feel the desire, the tenderness as Emma's lips pressed against hers. She needed to see Emma and make her understand how much she meant to her. Surely she could make her understand.

She mentally imagined herself entering Emma's office, locking the door behind her, marching behind her desk, and smothering her with a hungry kiss before leaning her back onto the desk and revealing her deepest feelings. Well, maybe not that far, Ramie thought with a smile, but as close as she could get to expressing her feelings.

At the end of her final class, Ramie strode resolutely to Donlevy Hall and climbed the stairs to the third floor. She stopped in front of Emma's office and stood for a moment to catch her breath, then knocked. Receiving no answer, she tried the doorknob to make sure before turning to make her way back the direction she'd come. Perhaps Emma was gone for her regular coffee break with Howard at the Student Union. She glanced into several open offices on her way toward the staircase. Looking into the next to last office, she spotted Howard searching through a file cabinet behind his desk and stopped.

She leaned against the door frame and smiled. "Where's your partner in crime today, Dr. Trammel?"

Howard glanced over his shoulder and smiled when he saw Ramie. "It would seem I've been abandoned, my dear girl."

"Too much partying?" she asked as she pushed away from the door and stepped inside the office.

"Please have a seat, if you can find one. I'm devoting today to the filing I've obviously neglected for far too long," he said as he sat behind his cluttered desk. "I've only been at it for an hour or so, but am grateful for the interruption. How can I help you?"

"I thought while I had a little free time I'd drop by to thank Dr. Rothenberg for inviting me to the party Saturday. Obviously I've missed her."

"She developed a frightful headache late Saturday and called me Sunday to say she was going out of town for a few days. Needed to get away even though we'll have a break before too long."

"Then I'll try to catch her after she returns. It's nothing urgent."

"She'll be sorry she missed you."

Chapter Eleven

EMMA STROLLED ALONG the rock-strewn shoreline of the lake a few hundred yards from her cabin. She brushed a small branch through the grassy knobs that had sprung up over the summer and stopped periodically to skip a flat rock over the still surface of the lake. She missed it more than she realized. She missed having time to herself as well. She'd lived a self-enforced life of loneliness since her mid-twenties except for an occasional weekend with Millie Carver. Those weekends reminded her she was still alive. She never allowed herself to become involved in a long-term relationship with anyone. Her work was enough to fulfill her life. This was the life she chose for herself after she lost Frances. It was almost everything she'd always wanted...almost.

The simple little cabin had been her father's. He called it his retreat. Nestled on a heavily forested parcel of land, it was near the lake where he would go to fish and think. Emma accompanied him once she was old enough to bait her own hook and entertain herself. After his death, Emma fought to get the only things that mattered to her, her father's office furnishings and the little cabin. Her sister, Olivia, had no interest in them and Emma relinquished any claim to the stately home outside Columbus where they grew up. Emma knew she would never return to her childhood home. It was where the dreams of an idealistic young woman died. Now this cabin was her retreat.

As the sky began to darken, she pushed the hood of her jacket from her head and smiled at the idea of a warm, comforting fire, accompanied by a cup of hot tea and a good book. The light breeze off the lake was chilly and as darkness fell the temperature would as well. She rubbed her hands briskly up and down her arms to generate a little heat. She needed this time to center herself again, to clear her mind, and to forget the feel of Ramie Sunderlund's lips as they met hers. She licked her lips without thinking and imagined she could still taste the smooth, vanilla flavor of the lip gloss Ramie wore. Why couldn't she forget that?

As she turned toward the cabin, the sound of gravel crunching beneath tires startled her. No one knew she was at the cabin and she had no neighbors for miles this time of year. Only someone impossibly lost could have located her cabin. She carefully approached through the trees that separated the cabin from the lake. She didn't recognize the vehicle in her drive. All she saw were ringlets of curly blonde hair sticking out from beneath a knitted cap. Ramie stood silently on the covered porch, her hands buried in the pockets of her faded jeans. An over-sized Overland sweatshirt covered the upper half of her body.

"May I help you?" Emma called out as she approached after Ramie knocked on the door and waited for someone to answer.

Ramie jumped slightly at the voice behind her. She turned and smiled when she saw Emma striding toward her. "It's getting chilly out here now that the sun is setting," she said.

"What are you doing here?" Emma asked.

"I was hoping we could talk," Ramie answered with a shrug while Emma paused at the bottom of the porch steps.

"I have an office. Make an appointment," Emma said in a voice that sounded brusque, even to her.

Ramie frowned. "I've been there, but you weren't. Howard said you wanted some time alone."

"That was my intention," Emma muttered as she made her way up the steps. "How did you know about this place? It's not registered in my name."

"I've been here once before, sort of accidentally. I...uh...saw you here, with Mrs. Carver." The look in Ramie's eyes changed at the memory. She brought her hands out of her jean pockets and allowed them to rest loosely along her sides.

"I see," Emma said. She entered the cabin, removed her jacket, and hung it before kneeling in front of the fireplace. She placed a log on top of the embers she banked before leaving the cabin earlier. She plucked an andiron from its holder and shifted the log around to settle it into the glowing embers. "What did you wish to talk about?"

Ramie bit her bottom lip. When Emma stood, Ramie stepped forward and took Emma's face between her cool hands, guiding her closer until their lips met. Taking advantage of Emma's attempt to object, Ramie slid her tongue into the warm cavity and searched its depths thoroughly while Emma stood there stiffly. Her arms moved to embrace Emma's body, but before she could enclose her Emma's hands fisted in Ramie's sweatshirt and spun the young blonde around, forcing her back against the wall, her thigh pressing between Ramie's legs. A groan worked its way up Ramie's throat as Emma deepened the kiss hungrily. Feeling the heat of Ramie's crotch as it moved against her thigh, Emma found the bottom of Ramie's sweatshirt and slid her hands beneath, kneading the warm, pliable flesh. She ran her fingers up Ramie's sides and over the fabric of her bra, feeling the nipples react to her touch. Ramie tore her mouth away and leaned her head back.

"Is this what you came for?" Emma rasped as she pushed

Ramie's bra up and let her lips encircle an already tight nipple.

"Oh God…yes," Ramie whimpered.

"Tell me what else you want," Emma whispered.

"You. All of you," Ramie moaned as she arched harder against Emma's mouth and buried her fingers in Emma's soft hair "I want…you. So much."

Desire flashed through Emma's body like stabs of lightning. The heat consuming her was quickly overwhelming her. She kissed down the side of Ramie's face to her neck, eliciting another needy groan. "You're impossibly irresistible. Why did you have to come back to tempt me like this?" Emma rasped as she fondled Ramie's softness.

"Please, Emma. I want to feel you against me. I need to touch you," Ramie said, her voice quivering.

Emma flipped the switch on the wall, then took Ramie's hand and led her toward the sofa. She openly admired Ramie's face as it seemed to glow in the reddish-orange light from the now flaming log. Emma kissed her tenderly before drawing Ramie down onto the sofa. Ramie's lips found Emma's lips for a demanding kiss.

"I want you," Ramie panted. "God, I've wanted you for so long."

Emma held her, absorbing her warmth as her hands lightly traced over Ramie's body. Her mouth savored the taste of the young woman in her arms. Emma's tongue teased Ramie's lips lightly. When Ramie opened her mouth in response, Emma ran her tongue across the back of Ramie's teeth and licked at her palate slowly.

"I'm old enough to be your mother," Emma said as her fingers ran through Ramie's hair.

"You're nothing like my mother," Ramie groaned as she cupped Emma's breast through her shirt. Emma's small breast reacted to her touch and she arched harder against Ramie's hand.

"This is so wrong," Emma managed, "but you are so tempting and I am so very weak when I'm near you. I could kiss you all night."

Soon what had begun as gentle and tender exploded into a frantic need to kiss and touch one another. A need repressed for too long. Emma pushed her roughly onto her back and covered her body with her own before crushing her lips in a desperate, hungry kiss.

"Yes, baby," Ramie panted as she began to squirm. "I've waited so long."

Emma smiled as she cradled Ramie. She stroked Ramie's hair as she rested against her shoulder. She felt warm breath on her neck and closed her eyes, savoring the feel of the body beneath hers. She drifted into a peaceful sleep holding Ramie in her arms.

Chapter Twelve

EMMA WAS ROUSED before dawn the next morning when the body resting against hers moved and a hand slid under her shirt and over her stomach. Her hand slipped into soft curls and hugged the warm body closer against her own. Hands floated softly over her and she relished her body's response. The thrill of hands on her skin again made her shiver with want.

"Em?" an unexpected voice murmured.

"What?" Emma answered as her eyes snapped open and she saw deep blue eyes looking at her. But they couldn't be there.

Ramie smiled and kissed Emma lightly before saying, "I'm sorry, darling, but I'm starving. I haven't eaten since lunch yesterday."

Emma cleared her throat. "Why don't you take a shower and I'll fix something so you can get your strength back."

"Join me?" Ramie asked as she nuzzled against Emma's neck.

"I thought you were starving," Emma said.

"I am," Ramie answered as she stood and lightly tugged at Emma's hand. "I'm starving to feel your hands and mouth on me again," she added.

"I'll be there in a moment," Emma said.

Ramie nodded and leaned down to kiss Emma's lips fully. "I'll be waiting, love," she whispered softly.

Emma watched as Ramie made her way toward the bathroom. Emma sat up, and exhaled loudly as she ran a hand over her face. My god, what have you done? How could you have lost control like that? Ramie is a desirable woman. Incredibly desirable, but you know better than to act on your feelings. Damn it! You can't allow it to go any further. She took that chance once before, but couldn't allow it to happen again. Ever.

EMMA WAS SITTING on the front steps with a steaming cup of coffee when Ramie, wrapped snuggly in Emma's robe, stepped onto the porch. She sat next to Emma, holding a cup of her own and leaned over to bump her shoulder against Emma's.

"Change your mind?" Ramie asked before taking a tentative sip of her coffee.

"Yes," Emma mumbled. She cleared her throat and stared

into the forest that encircled the cabin. "You should leave after breakfast."

Ramie took a long drink from her cup before speaking. "If that's what you want," Ramie said as she began pushing her body up.

"I can't give you what you want," Emma said.

"You don't know what I want," Ramie said as she stood, looking down at Emma. She brushed her fingers through Emma's hair. "Can we discuss this after breakfast?"

Ramie refilled their coffee cups and sat silently at the small kitchen table, sipping her coffee and watching Emma as she prepared a simple breakfast for two. Periodically Emma would glance to where Ramie sat. She was beginning to feel uncomfortable, knowing that Ramie was observing her. The silence was deafening and she tried to fill the void by thinking about the things she needed to do once she returned home. She was still thinking when she set a plate filled with scrambled eggs, ham, and toast in front of Ramie.

"More coffee?" she offered.

"I'll get it," Ramie answered as she stood.

When Ramie returned with the carafe of coffee, she rested her hand on Emma's shoulder and squeezed it lightly. Emma tried to ignore the feeling the touch generated inside and the coldness she felt when the hand left her shoulder.

"What's wrong, Emma?" Ramie asked when she sat again. "This looks delicious, by the way. Thank you."

"It's not exactly a gourmet meal," Emma said with a shrug.

"Is it me?" Ramie asked. "I know I'm not very experienced, but wi—"

"It's not you," Emma said more forcefully than she intended. "You are beautiful, desirable, and...and..."

"And what?"

"Everything any woman could dream of."

Ramie reached across the table and took Emma's hand. "Yet you want me to leave."

"Yes."

"And if I refuse?"

"Why would you?"

"You really don't know?" Ramie frowned. "I've dreamed of you touching me and wanting me to touch you for so long. I'm not a child anymore and those dreams have never changed. Now that I've had a taste of the passion you hide so carefully from everyone, I don't want to lose it. Please don't send me away."

"I can't promise you...anything," Emma rasped. "I believed in forever once, but not anymore. This is wrong and you know it."

"And Dr. Emma Rothenberg never does anything wrong," Ramie said in frustration.

"Not when it can be avoided."

"What about Millicent Carver?"

Emma glared at Ramie. "That was a mistake," she answered quietly. "And none of your business."

"Did you want her?"

"I allowed my libido to overcome my good sense." Emma's eyes grabbed Ramie's. "I'd appreciate it if you left now."

"Is that what you really want?" Ramie asked.

"Yes," Emma said.

"I don't believe you. I think you're afraid, Emma."

"You don't know a damn thing about me," Emma snapped. "You need to find someone your own age to satisfy your...needs."

"I don't want anyone else." Ramie took a deep breath and slowly exhaled. "And I won't give up, Emma."

Why am I fighting the attraction I've had for this girl since the first day she walked into my class, Emma thought. Because she is no more than a girl! Emma straightened and said, "I am flattered, Miss Sunderlund, but I cannot do this." Emma paused and steeled her eyes before looking into Ramie's. "More importantly, I *will not* do it."

Emma saw the flash of hurt on Ramie's face as she stood to gather their dishes. "Finish your coffee. I've got these. Then I'll get dressed and leave you to your precious solitude."

Ramie filled the sink with hot water and crossed one foot in front of the other as she washed dishes and placed them in the small drainer. Emma finished her coffee and carried the cup to the sink. She caught the fresh scent of Ramie's hair and body. As if drawn by a force she couldn't resist, she slid her hand into the front of Ramie's robe. The heat of Ramie's skin flowed through her fingers, warming her deep inside in a place that had remained cold and untouched for so long.

"I'm sorry," Emma whispered as she fisted her hand and stepped away.

Ramie spun around, but before she could say anything, Emma covered her mouth in a passionate kiss that took Ramie's breath away. She brought her hands up between them and pushed Emma back.

Emma blinked and turned away.

"Please leave," Emma choked out. "I can't let this happen again." Emma didn't speak again as Ramie dressed or as she watched her walk out the front door of the cabin. Once she was certain Ramie was gone, she collapsed on the sofa and dropped her head into her hands to cry until the sadness and loneliness she carried deep inside finally drifted silently away.

RAMIE MOVED FROM student to student in the studio in the Fine Arts Building and carefully examined the piece each was working on, trying to forget the events of the last few days. She drove home from Emma's cabin with a strange mixture of emotions. Exhilaration from the desire she was certain she felt in Emma's kisses. Incredible sadness she saw the next morning when Emma demanded she leave. A touch of anger at being rejected. She had clearly expressed her feelings. She didn't understand the sudden change from passion to sadness, but vowed to find the reason. Emma's kisses only made Ramie want more from the stand-offish woman. The feel of Emma's hands on her skin refused to go away.

The remainder of the day, Ramie tried to take her mind off Emma and concentrate on her sculpting, but nothing seemed to work longer than a few minutes. She wasn't accustomed to being so distracted. There had been women in her life occasionally after she recovered from her assault, of course, but none who interfered with her ability to sculpt. Until now. And with a woman who was apparently uninterested in exploring a relationship with her.

Frustrated beyond belief, Ramie left her studio, pulled her coat on, and slammed the door on her way out. It was already dark and she didn't see Emma's car in the faculty parking area. It was time to confront the situation head on, she fumed as she entered her vehicle. She backed up and drove off campus, filled with resolve.

She pulled to the curb and sat for a few minutes observing the quiet home, thinking about what she would say. Perhaps this wasn't such a great idea after all. What if Emma slammed the door in her face? What if she refused to speak to her? Ramie ran a hand over her face and let her fingertips linger on her lips. Emma must care. Anyone who kissed the way she did had to care. Didn't they? Pushing away her doubts with a deep breath, Ramie opened her car door and stepped out. Her knees felt funny for a moment, refusing to take the first step that could lead her to the future she dreamed of. She jammed her hands into her coat pockets and lowered her head, forcing her legs forward.

When the front door opened Ramie reached out and pulled Emma into her arms. Before Emma could speak, Ramie kissed her slowly, her lips telling Emma everything she felt. When their lips parted, Ramie held Emma close and caressed the softness of her hair. "I need you so much, Em," she whispered. "Please give me a chance. Give *us* a chance."

Emma brought her hands up between them and managed to step back, her face unreadable as she said, "Come in. We should talk." Ramie opened her mouth to speak, but Emma held her hand up to stop her. "And you have to listen. If you won't then you'll have to leave and never return."

Ramie's protest died before the words formed when she saw the seriousness in Emma's eyes. She could only nod and mutter, "Okay."

"Give me your coat and have a seat," Emma said, motioning toward the living room couch. She hung Ramie's coat in a small closet behind the front door before sitting comfortably in a patterned wingback chair facing the couch. She entwined her fingers and leaned her elbows on her knees before clearing her throat quietly.

"First of all, and most importantly, I apologize for what happened at the cabin." She smiled. "I've never done anything like that before and can't explain it now." Emma appeared to be thinking and frowned before she continued. "When I was in my twenties, I was deeply in love with another woman. I would have done anything to be with her." She glanced up quickly at Ramie. "You...you look amazingly like her. The same blue eyes and curly blonde hair. The same youthful eagerness to experience life. To taste it, savor it as perhaps only the young can." Emma sighed and shook her head slightly. "Her enthusiasm for life never ceased to fascinate me. Then she chose a path that didn't include me. I accepted her decision, it was what she wanted, but I should have fought to keep her. I never fully recovered from my loss. Over the weekend I succumbed to my desire to touch her and kiss her again. Regrettably, I hurt you in the process and am sorrier than you know. It wasn't my intent." Emma stopped speaking and leaned back in her chair. "As for this unrealistic infatuation you seem to have at the moment, I advise you to cease your efforts. While I may be flattered, I would never risk such a liaison. I don't mean to sound cruel or heartless, but you are still a child. I simply don't have anything to offer you. My lifestyle is not compatible or acceptable to mainstream society. If it became general knowledge, I risk losing my position and possibly my career. Nothing you could offer me would trump those things. It's a shame, but that's life at the moment. I have learned to live with it."

When Emma didn't speak again, Ramie asked, "Are you finished?"

"Yes," Emma said.

"You're right. Not being able to live and love as we choose is a shame. A terrible burden that forces us to live in the shadows, but the difference between us is that while you can live with things the way they are, I don't want to. But if that's what I have to do to be with you, I will. I don't give a damn what anyone else thinks and I don't let others make decisions for me. I don't care about your age. It's just a number to me. It's not who we are." Ramie tapped the spot over her heart. "Who we are is in here. I'm sorry you lost your first love, Em. I can't be her for you. I'm not perfect. I know that. But what I feel inside is clawing to be set free. Only you can do that."

"For the moment," Emma said. "Eventually, you will find someone closer to your age to satisfy you."

Ramie laughed. "That would take one helluva remarkable woman."

"She's out there somewhere, waiting for you. I guarantee it."

"I'm here now, Em. Desperate to show you how very much I love you," Ramie said softly.

"You're blushing," Emma noted with a slight smile.

"I've never said that to anyone before, but I've never felt this way before either," Ramie acknowledged. "Is this how you felt about the woman you loved? Like you couldn't breathe if you didn't have her."

Emma swallowed hard and drew in a deep breath. "Yes," she exhaled. "Every day."

"Is it why you become involved with women you know you can't have, like Mrs. Carver? So your heart will be safe and you risk nothing?"

"That is none of your business," Emma persisted.

"You're right. I'm sorry. I should go." Ramie stood to leave and started toward the closet to retrieve her coat.

"Don't leave," Emma said, her voice strained.

"Why should I stay? So you can have your wicked way with me," Ramie said with a slow smile.

"Isn't that why you came?"

"I'm planning to come later tonight," Ramie said, moving closer to Emma and tracing her lips with a finger. "Hopefully more than once."

Emma drew Ramie closer. "Umm...but not for only one night," Ramie hummed when her lips found Emma's pulse point and sucked it gently. "I won't be a one-night stand," Ramie said. "Not even for you."

Emma took Ramie's head in her hands. "I surrender" she said, breathing heavily.

AFTER LOCKING THE doors and windows, Emma took Ramie's hand and led her silently upstairs. Emma paused to light candles on the nightstands and Ramie started to undress. Before she was able to remove any clothing, Emma's hands on her shoulders stopped her. "Let me," Emma whispered as she kissed the side of Ramie's neck softly. Ramie turned to face Emma and watched as she released the buttons on Ramie's shirt.

"You seem a little nervous," Emma said, meeting Ramie's eyes. "Tell me if you want me to stop. It's not too late to change your mind."

"Don't stop," Ramie said. "But there's something you should know."

"What's that?" Emma asked as she pushed Ramie's blouse over her shoulders and let it drop to the floor.

"I...I'm not very experienced at this sort of thing," Ramie admitted.

Emma smiled slightly then reached around Ramie to unhook her bra. "Don't worry," she said softly as she released the clasp to let the lacy red bra fall away. "I am."

Ramie sucked in a deep breath and closed her eyes when Emma's hands caressed her breasts. Warm lips covered her nipple and she gasped, her hand coming up to grasp the back of Emma's head and press it more firmly against her skin. All too soon, Emma released the connection to unsnap and unzip Ramie's jeans. Her thumbs traced along Ramie's waist and hooked the waistband to push the pants down, leaving her panties in place.

Emma knelt to push the jeans to Ramie's ankles She skimmed her hands lightly up the backs of Ramie's thighs and over her buttocks. Ramie stroked Emma's hair and enjoyed the controlled attention her body was receiving. Unlike younger lovers Ramie had been with, Emma was taking the time to appreciate the body before her. Emma kissed the material and cupped Ramie's sex as she stood. "You're unbelievably wet," she breathed.

Ramie kicked off her shoes and stepped out of her jeans as Emma guided her back onto the bed. "Now lie down and let me appreciate you," Emma whispered as she kissed along the side of Ramie's face.

Ramie stretched out as Emma began removing her own clothes. She was soon fascinated by the smooth curves of Emma's body and she couldn't tear her eyes away from her small breasts. She loved women with small breasts. Her mouth watered at the thought of them in her mouth...eventually.

Emma traced her finger slowly down Ramie's neck and body until she came to her heated center. Emma pressed her finger against Ramie's covered sex, then brought it to her nose and inhaled its scent. "Delicious," she whispered as she knelt on a padded bench at the foot of the bed. She kissed Ramie's ankles and the tops of her feet before sucking her toes into her mouth one at a time, eliciting a groaning giggle.

Encouraging Ramie onto her stomach, Emma ran her hands up Ramie's legs and inhaled deeply as she kissed the length of each leg, pausing to suck and lick the sensitive area behind the knees. Her fingers crawled up the flesh along the inside of Ramie's thigh while her tongue licked up its back. She slipped a finger under the edge of Ramie's panties and into the wetness beneath, stroking the sensitive clit with her fingertip.

Ramie twitched. "Please, baby," she begged.

"Patience," Emma murmured. "There's so much of you that needs my attention."

Emma took the waist of Ramie's red hi-cut bikini panties between her teeth and tugged them down to gently knead Ramie's buttocks. Suddenly, she lifted her body and ran the pads of her fingers over the area between Ramie's hip and buttocks. "What have we here?" she asked as her lips teased the slightly raised area she'd discovered.

"That would probably be my tattoo." Ramie laughed.

"The Little Devil?" Emma asked, then licked the tattoo. "There has to be a story."

"More like there were a couple of drinks too many."

"Did it hurt?"

"A little the next morning when I woke up. But honestly, I think the hangover was worse."

Emma kissed the tattoo again. "It's sort of cute. Now where was I?" she said as she slid the panties down Ramie's legs and dropped them to the floor.

"You were driving me crazy with your talented hands and lips," Ramie said, rolling onto her back again.

"Ah, yes. I remember," Emma said, as she dipped her head and swiped her tongue the length of Ramie's sex before sucking Ramie's clit into her mouth and teasing it with her tongue. Her hands slid up Ramie's body as it arched to meet her mouth, enclosing her full breasts and teasing the nipples into hardened points. Ramie grasped Emma's forearms tightly as she panted heavily and groaned through gritted teeth. "Oh my God. Please, Emma. I've waited so long."

"Do you want me to stop?" Emma asked as she lowered her head before dragging the tip of her tongue slowly over Ramie's sex again.

"P...please, n...no," Ramie stammered. "Oh, baby, you make me f...feel so damn g...good."

Emma managed to remove her arm from Ramie's grip. Her fingers joined her mouth and slipped smoothly inside. "Please, baby, I need more," Ramie begged as her hips moved faster. Emma obliged with a second finger as she stroked. "More!" Ramie demanded as she took in what Emma offered. On the next stroke a third finger joined the others and Ramie felt the muscle walls contract tightly in an attempt to hold Emma's fingers deeply inside. Emma drove into Ramie's body until it began to open and spasm. Then she withdrew her fingers, curled her tongue, and plunged it into Ramie's body. Before Ramie's body stopped twitching sporadically, Emma lowered her head, teasing Ramie's clit with her tongue and drawing it between her lips once again. Ramie jerked, but the feeling overwhelmed her. Her hands found Emma's shoulders and pushed against them.

"Oh God, Emma," she groaned. "I...I can't take any...more. But you make me feel so good!"

Emma increased the pressure gradually, reducing Ramie to a whimpering mass of want, her hips gyrating uncontrollably against Emma's mouth. Ramie's fingernails dug into Emma's shoulders. Her mouth opened soundlessly and the breath rushed from her lungs as the pleasure of what she was feeling took control and consumed her in a second thundering orgasm.

Emma prowled up over Ramie and pulled her into a deep, consuming kiss. Ramie smiled and licked her lips, her eyes still closed.

"That's how you taste," Emma whispered. "So sweet."

Ramie opened her eyes, still hazy with the aftermath of pleasure, and gazed into Emma's. "Give...give me a minute, baby. That was more than I ever thought possible," she said.

A second kiss ended suddenly as Emma's fingers entered Ramie's slick center again. Ramie's hips moved to greet Emma's fingers as they entered and withdrew slowly, the speed and depth gradually increasing. Ramie begged Emma to release her again as her hips swallowed Emma's fingers. Ramie whimpered as Emma slowly withdrew her fingers. "Nooo. Not yet," she whined.

Emma kissed her way down Ramie's neck and shoulder to lie behind her and wrapped her arm around her waist to hold her. "I promise they'll return soon," Emma whispered. Her fingertips stroked the soft skin beneath Ramie's breasts, then cupped them to feel their weight fill her hand. Ramie cuddled against her, took a deep breath, as her body shook with laughter.

"What?" Emma asked.

"Old enough to be my mother, my ass," Ramie said between bursts of laughter. "I can barely move!"

Emma pushed up and supported herself on her elbow. Ramie covered Emma's hand and shifted to look over her shoulder to see Emma.

Emma leaned down and took Ramie's mouth gently. "You're so responsive when I touch you," she said, running a hand down Ramie's body, causing muscles to twitch. "Everywhere," Emma added with a kiss to her neck, which led to a moan. Ramie pressed Emma's hand against her breast as she shifted onto her side.

"Sleep, sweet girl," Emma whispered as she spooned against Ramie's back.

"But—"

"Later, sweetie."

EMMA WOKE UP the next morning and glanced down at the disheveled mass of blonde curls nestled against her shoulder. She was awakened in the middle of the night by slightly callused yet strong hands running over her body. She smiled at the memory of the passionate night they spent pleasuring one another. She hadn't felt such deep satisfaction since the last time she'd made love to Frances. The week before Frances left her.

She kissed Ramie's forehead and stroked her fingers along her side. Ramie mumbled as she felt for the fingers teasing her awake.

"I have a departmental meeting today," Ramie groaned as she rolled onto her back and fluttered her eyes open.

"That should be fun," Emma chuckled. "I should make your coffee extra strong this morning then."

Ramie pushed her upper body up, the sheet falling to her waist and exposing her full breasts. "You'd do that for me?" she asked.

"It's the least I can do to repay you for making me feel so alive again," Emma said with a smile, her eyes obviously appreciating the sight before her.

When Ramie rolled onto her stomach, Emma swatted her on the ass. "Don't tease me, baby. Work beckons. Off to the shower now," Ramie said as she swung her legs off the bed,

"There are extra towels in the cabinet behind the door," Emma said.

By the time Ramie joined her in the kitchen, Emma was pouring a cup of black adrenaline for her. Ramie took the mug with both hands and sighed with relief. "What time will you be home tonight?" she asked between sips.

"Why? I can barely walk now," Emma said, adding sugar to

her cup of tea.

"Wasn't it the most intense feeling you've ever had?" Ramie's eyes sparkled as she looked at her new lover.

Emma leaned over to kiss her. "I wouldn't have missed it for the world. Thank you, my dear."

"My pleasure," Ramie said proudly with a smile. "Literally." She turned to look out the window over the sink. "What's that?" she asked as she slurped her coffee.

"What?" Emma asked, looking over her shoulder into the large back yard.

"That building."

"Oh, it's the shed where I keep my garden tools. It's really too big, but I don't know what else to do with it. It was here when I purchased the property." Emma brushed blonde hair from Ramie's neck and kissed the newly exposed skin as she slid a hand around Ramie's waist and under her oversized t-shirt seeking to feel the smoothness of Ramie's breast in her hand once again.

Ramie's hand covered Emma's and pressed it against her tender breast. "As much as I want you, darling, don't start something we're both too tender to finish," she hissed.

"You're no fun," Emma chuckled.

"Can I see your shed?" Ramie asked as she turned in Emma's arms and pushed onto her toes to kiss her. Ramie's eyes twinkled and she looked like a kid on Christmas morning.

"If you want," Emma shrugged. "Let me find the key."

Emma tugged her robe closer to her body as she opened the back door and led the way over round stone steps set into the grass to create a walkway. Ramie jumped in front of her when they reached the building, forcing Emma to reach around her to fit an old key into the lock. Ramie held her hands up to the glass in the door and looked through. When the door finally creaked open Ramie stepped inside and looked at the assortment of tools hanging everywhere. A large worktable took up the center of the building and shelves lined the walls.

"It's perfect," Ramie breathed.

"For what?" Emma asked, wrapping her arms around Ramie and hugging her close to keep her from shivering.

"A studio. There's plenty of room to sketch and paint." She left Emma's arms and went to the worktable. "And this is a perfect height for sculpting. If there were running water and a sink, it would be ideal for working with clay, too." She looked at the ceiling and sucked in a surprised breath. She grasped a cord hanging down and pulled it. A sunroof popped open and allowed fresh air into the enclosed space, along with a few frozen chunks of snow. "This is wonderful, Emma," she beamed. "It's an artist's dream."

Emma shrugged. "If you think you can use it, come over any time. I can have a smaller attachment added for my tools. Maybe install a sink and water line."

"Really?" Ramie asked. Then she frowned and looked at Emma seriously. "How much?"

"Call it my contribution to the arts," Emma said with a smile

"Are you asking me to move in with you?" Ramie asked, her eyes wide.

"Of course not," Emma said with a nonchalant shrug. "But because you clearly told me you wouldn't be a one-night stand, it might afford me the opportunity to see you from time to time," she added.

Ramie seemed to think for a moment. She stepped closer to Emma. "It sounds like a practical plan. Could I spend the night if I worked too late?"

Emma rubbed a hand over her face before she drew Ramie into a passionate kiss. "I would like that," she whispered. "Even though you do snore a bit."

"I do not!" Ramie protested, looking insulted.

"Like a buzz saw." Emma laughed. "But I could get used to it."

"Only when I'm exhausted and *that* is your fault," Ramie snorted. She shivered. "It's freezing out here. Let's go back inside. I need to go home and change."

As they held hands and walked back to the house, Emma said, "If you don't have plans already, I can prepare dinner for us this evening. What would you like?"

Ramie smiled. Her voice was low and husky when she answered. "Just you, baby."

Emma's face turned more serious as she searched for a reply. They stepped into the warm kitchen. "I appreciate the sentiment, Ramie, and while I do care about you very much, one or two nights together doesn't mean whatever is between us at the moment is anything more than lust. One day you'll meet someone else or grow bored and move on." She smiled. "I have to accept that and will miss you terribly, but confess I do enjoy how you make me feel."

"I'm not going to leave you, Emma."

"You believe that now, but our lives change when we least expect it."

Nearly an hour later, Emma stood in her driveway and watched Ramie leave. She never believed anyone as young and beautiful as Ramie Sunderlund would find her desirable. She was certain that the day would come when Ramie would be attracted to another woman closer to her own age. For now, there was nothing Emma could do to stop how she felt. She would deal with a broken heart when it happened. And she knew it would.

Chapter Thirteen

"YOU SEEM UNCOMFORTABLE tonight, Em. Is something wrong?" Ramie asked later in the week as she plucked a chunk of potato from the bowl of stew in front of her.

"Of course not," Emma replied.

Ramie shrugged and put a spoonful of vegetables into her mouth. "We should discuss whatever is obviously bothering you." She set her spoon down and rubbed at the scars on her hands.

"Do your hands hurt?" Emma asked, reaching out to take one of Ramie's hands. She stroked it gently.

Ramie shook her head. "Just a nervous habit. What's wrong, Em?"

"Nothing's wrong," Emma insisted.

"Don't lie to me," Ramie snapped. "If it's me then spit it out."

Emma frowned and shook her head. "It's not you. It's something I have to work out up here," Emma said tapping the side of her head.

"Do I make you feel trapped because I'm here virtually every night?"

"The beauty of my previous liaisons was that I wasn't responsible for anyone else's well-being. There was only me and the relationships I had were temporary, fleeting, and insubstantial." She looked at Ramie. "Being with you makes me happy, but I'm afraid when this euphoria fades away you will be hurt. I don't want to hurt you, but you should be prepared when it happens."

Ramie stood and moved to stand next to Emma. She cradled Emma's head against her body. "It won't happen and I promise to never hurt you."

"You can't promise that, Ramie. No one can."

Ramie forced Emma to look at her. "This is new to both of us, but thinking about you got me through my rehab." She smiled down at her. "That doesn't mean we won't argue or disagree. What we really feel is inside. As long as we can talk about what bothers us or what we feel or want, we'll be fine."

"You make me care about you more than I should," Emma said.

Ramie leaned down and kissed Emma softly. "Did you bring work home, darling?"

"Of course," Emma sighed.

"Then why don't you get busy while I clean up the kitchen before I leave?"

Emma stood and hugged Ramie before she turned toward her office as Ramie started gathering the dishes. Ramie ran water into the sink and stacked the plates and utensils on the counter. By the time she placed the leftovers in the refrigerator, the water was ready. The hot water felt wonderful on her hands and she let the heat soak into the scars on her palms. She closed her eyes and luxuriated in the feeling. Hands slid around her waist and she leaned back against the solid body behind her.

"Finished already?" Ramie chuckled. "God, you're fast."

"Couldn't concentrate," Emma answered. "Come upstairs with me."

"Why?"

"Because I want to feel you against me once more before you leave."

Ramie lowered her head, exposing the back of her neck. "Convince me," she breathed.

Hot lips pressed against her neck. "Can you feel my body trembling?" Emma asked.

Ramie leaned her head back onto Emma's shoulder. "Yes."

"Because I want you. I need you to calm the trembling."

"Am I the only one who can stop it?"

"Yes," Emma said as she pulled Ramie tighter against her.

"I love to feel you tremble knowing it's because of me." Ramie moved her hips to rub against Emma, eliciting a gasp. "Touch me, darling," she said.

Unexpectedly, Ramie spun around in Emma's arms. She pushed Emma back until she was pressed against the refrigerator. She claimed Emma's mouth roughly and kissed her thoroughly. When Emma finally brought the kiss to an end, she panted breathlessly. "God, I want you."

Ramie took her hand and pulled Emma up the stairs, stopping every few steps to deliver another hungry kiss. "Promise me it will always...be this way between us," Ramie said, breathing heavily.

"I can't," Emma said as her lips found Ramie's again.

"No," Ramie said, pushing Emma away. "Promise me it will *always* be like this."

"I...I can't. Please, Ramie." Emma reached toward her.

"Promise me!" Ramie said loudly, keeping Emma away.

Emma brushed Ramie's arms away and grabbed for her. She lifted her off the floor and carried her into the bedroom, where she shoved her onto the bed. She looked down at the younger woman and climbed onto the bed, grasping her wrists, and pressing them into the mattress. Her eyes were dark as she stared down at Ramie. "Don't ever tease me like that again. Don't ever make me ache for you so badly."

"Release me," Ramie said calmly.

Emma released Ramie's arms and met her eyes. "That's how I want you to want me," Ramie said. "Desperately. Like you'll die if you can't touch me." Ramie reached up and pulled Emma into a soul-shattering kiss, followed by frenzied love-making that left both women drained.

EMMA GROANED WHEN she tried to roll over the following morning. She finally forced her body onto her stomach and allowed her arm to flop onto the woman beside her.

"I wish you hadn't done that," Ramie moaned. "I really need to pee, but am almost too sore to move."

"Me, too," Emma said with a soft chuckle. "But damn, it was good." She forced her body up slightly and leaned over for a deep morning kiss. "It was so damned good."

Ramie ran her hands through Emma's hair. "You're good, baby." She bit her lower lip as she looked at Emma.

"What?" Emma asked.

"It's nothing," Ramie said as she cuddled closer to Emma's body. "Last night you...well...you surprised me...a little. You were so...passionate. Commanding, Possessive."

"You mean not the staid, boring woman you saw in class," Emma said as she stroked Ramie's face with her fingertips.

"I would never have called you boring. Maybe disciplined, but definitely not boring," Ramie chuckled. "If anyone knew how...uninhibited you could be—"

Emma stopped her with a kiss that quickly deepened. After they separated, Emma said, "Don't tell anyone or you'll ruin my reputation."

"I wouldn't share this with anyone, darling."

They helped one another out of bed and into the bathroom. Emma glanced at the clock next to the bed while they clung to one another. "I have a class in ninety minutes," she groaned.

"I want to be there to see that," Ramie laughed as she gasped. "But unfortunately, I have a lecture as well. Jesus! I desperately need coffee before I go home to change."

RAMIE WAITED AS Emma pulled her car into its usual parking slot before approaching. She opened the driver's door and laughed at the surprised look on Emma's face.

"I thought you had a class," Emma said.

"In a few minutes, but I have enough time to greet you properly," Ramie answered before leaning down to kiss Emma, holding the kiss longer than necessary.

When Ramie broke their connection, Emma growled, "That was foolish. Anyone could have seen us. What were you thinking?"

"It was harmless," Ramie replied with a shrug. "No one saw anything or would have cared if they did."

"Perhaps we need to discuss a few boundaries," Emma hissed as she stepped from her vehicle.

"Any time, any place," Ramie retorted.

"Tonight. I'll come to your place."

"Fine." Ramie spun around and strode purposefully toward the Fine Arts Building.

Emma climbed stiffly up the three flights of Donlevy Hall. Her sore muscles reminded her of the night before, but made her smile. Her past liaisons had been tame compared to time spent with Ramie. She had never lost control with anyone before. Nor had she ever allowed herself to surrender so completely to another. She stopped on the second floor landing. She hadn't planned to sleep with Ramie Sunderlund. She had overreacted when Ramie greeted her with a kiss, but she needed to know there would have to be rules if their tenuous relationship were to continue. She was certain others speculated about her personal life, but she would continue to guard it fiercely.

RAMIE PUSHED THE tall glass door into the Fine Arts Building open and waved at the student worker behind the front desk. She quickened her pace as she pulled off her jacket. She unlocked her office door and tossed the jacket inside. She ruffled her fingers through her hair in frustration and sucked in a deep breath to calm herself before walking into the studio at the end of the hall. Fifteen students were gathered in clumps, discussing an unknown topic. Ramie jumped onto the raised platform at the front of the classroom and clapped her hands together to get their attention. "Anyone with a particular problem this morning?" she asked. A couple of hands went up at their workstations. Ramie stuffed a few grease pencils into the pocket of her work apron after she finished tying it together. "I'll circulate and examine your work after I assist these students," she announced as she walked toward the first student with a question.

Most of the morning passed with few complications. Ramie

was pleased with the progress her students were making. One or two showed definite promise as sculptors. Overall, it was a good day and allowed her enough time to work on her own project. She was considering what her next move would be. Because of the damage done to her hands, sculpting was still difficult for her, especially as the weather cooled. She wasn't sure Middleton was where she truly belonged. But she couldn't leave after she was finally establishing a relationship with Emma. She could continue to produce the sculpture she loved at her own pace, but had to admit the tedious work was hard on her hands. There were days when she couldn't grip her chisels correctly. Every choice in life had a consequence. By choosing to be with Emma, she would limit her opportunities. She shook her head. No, she wanted to be with Emma. That was more important than becoming a well-known, sought-after artist. She had consciously made that decision and would accept any consequence their fledgling relationship demanded.

IT WAS ALREADY after dark when Ramie heard a knock at her front door. When she opened it, she was surprised to find Sylvia Joyner standing on the stoop.

"Sylvia! This is a surprise!"

"I hope I didn't interrupt your dinner," Sylvia said.

"No. I was just trying to think of something to fix. Please come in."

Sylvia stepped inside and glanced around before turning to face Ramie. "Do you have company?" she asked.

"Should I tell my secret lover it's safe to crawl from under the bed?" Ramie answered with a laugh.

"I wasn't prying into your business, Ramie," Sylvia said as she removed her gloves.

"If I had company she would be visible, Sylvia. I make it a rule not to hide any part of my life."

"Love what you've done with this place. A little Spartan for my taste though." Sylvia said, changing the subject abruptly. "How are your classes?"

Ramie pushed her hands into the back pockets of her jeans. "Since I'm only here temporarily I didn't think it was wise to put more holes in the walls. As for my classes, they are fine, so far. A couple seem to have a definite talent for the work." She looked down at the floor and cleared her throat. "You could have asked that in my office anytime. What do you really want, Sylvia?"

"Smart girl," Sylvia said with a half-smile. "What's your relationship with Emma Rothenberg? And before you say anything, you should know I saw you kiss her this morning."

"I don't believe my relationship with anyone is your business," Ramie said. "Dr. Rothenberg and I are friends."

"I have many friends, my dear, but greet very few with a rather lengthy kiss to the mouth," Sylvia chuckled. "Listen, you know I don't care. I've made my intentions quite clear, but this is a conservative university in a very conservative town. Many of the biggest contributors to our programs are also very conservative in their beliefs. All I'm saying is that your apparent affection for Emma could be misconstrued if noticed by the wrong person."

"That's strange coming from you. Maybe coming back to Overland was a mistake on my part."

"I don't think so. Our students can learn so much from you. I can't tell you what to do, but I do care about Emma as well. If she is involved with you and the wrong people found out, it could damage her career irreparably. Just be careful, please."

"I love her, Sylvia, but I won't do anything to jeopardize her career."

"And how does she feel about that?"

Ramie shrugged. "Too soon to tell. She's afraid."

"Eventually things will change, I hope. It's getting too crowded in that damn closet we're forced to call home for the moment."

"I'm not sure I can go there," Ramie said with a frown.

"To have what you want you may have to. That's up to you. Maybe the price is too high right now. Well, I'll let you get back to whatever you were doing before I interrupted. Feel free to drop by my office anytime if you need to talk."

"Thanks, Sylvia. I will," Ramie said as she escorted Sylvia to the door.

As soon as she was sure Sylvia was gone, Ramie grabbed her jacket and drove to Emma's home. It was a little late, but Emma should still be awake. She pressed the doorbell and waited. She winced when the porch light suddenly blinked on, temporarily blinding her. She heard the lock on the door flip as she tried to clear her vision. As soon as she saw Emma staring at her through the screen, she said hurriedly, "You wanted to talk to me. I assume you didn't stop by because I had unexpected company."

"Please come in," Emma said as she pushed the screen open to allow Ramie to enter. When Ramie turned, Emma said, "Let me take your coat."

"Could you kiss me first? It's been a long and trying day," Ramie sighed as she shrugged off her jacket and tossed it onto a chair. When she turned her head again, Emma was standing in front of her. She brought one hand up and ran it into the hair along Ramie's face. Her other hand pressed against Ramie's waist and pulled her closer. Ramie raised her head to meet the softness of Emma's lips. Emma's hand slipped to the back of Ramie's head as the kiss deepened and tongues slid over and around one another in a dance of desire. When the dizzying kiss finally came to an end, Ramie managed to ask, "Um...wow. What...what did you want to talk about?"

"That's how I wanted to kiss you this morning, but I can't and neither can you. Not publicly."

"Is that what you want?"

"Of course not! But that's how it has to be. I've spent my life building a career and I can't afford to jeopardize it for a few moments of lust."

"Is that what this is to you, lust? It's a helluva lot more to me and you make it sound like a tawdry affair I should be ashamed of, but I'm not." Ramie laughed, but there was no humor in it. "Don't worry, Emma, I won't do anything to jeopardize your precious career again." She turned and snatched her jacket from the chair.

"What would you like me to do?" Emma asked.

"I'd like you to treat me like a thinking adult with some common sense. I'd like you to acknowledge my feelings. I'd like to know you care about this 'moment of lust' between us." Tears filled Ramie's eyes and fell to her cheeks when she blinked. "I love you, Em. Tell me I'm wasting my time and don't give me that crap about your age. I know your age and I couldn't care less. I just don't."

Emma moved closer and wrapped her arms around Ramie, drawing her nearer. "Sh-h-h-h," she shushed softly. "Don't cry."

"But you were right. Sylvia saw me kiss you this morning," Ramie mumbled against Emma's chest.

Emma laughed. "Well. I wouldn't worry too much about Sylvia."

"I know. She's been trying to get into my pants since I met her." She looked up at Emma and sniffed.

"Should I be jealous?"

"Never. Can we go to bed now so I can show you how I really feel?"

Before Emma could speak again, Ramie pushed onto her tiptoes to kiss her deeply. Then, giggling, she took Emma's hands and began backing toward the stairs.

Chapter Fourteen

A BLACK-AND-WHITE city cab pulled to the curb in front of the cottage on Parsons Circle, five blocks from University Drive. A thick white cloud from the heated exhaust pipe lazily lingered over the rear of the vehicle as it idled. Millicent Carver leaned over the front seat to hand the driver a crisp twenty-dollar bill. She hadn't seen Emma since mid-May and the idea of reuniting with her brought a smile to her lips.

"Keep the change," she said as she reached for the door handle. She stepped out and her foot sank into the newly fallen, and as yet undisturbed, snow. Emma's cottage was picturesque with its snow-covered roof and cut-out gingerbread ornamentation that ran along the peaked covering over the front porch and outlined the eaves around the house. Millicent hoped Emma hadn't already left for her classes. There was no evidence of footsteps away from the home. Millie drew her coat closer to her body before making her way onto the porch. There was just enough early sunlight to begin a gentle melting that dripped onto the steps, creating dots in the fresh snow.

Maybe I should have called before dropping by, Millie thought as she brought her gloved index finger up to press the door chime. She shook her head and grinned at the idea of surprising Emma so early in the morning. Some of the most memorable times she'd spent with Emma Rothenberg had been early in the morning. The thought of their times together warmed her while she waited. Her anticipation grew when she heard footsteps from inside the house, followed by the clicking of the front door lock. A brilliant smile cut across Millie's face as the door opened and she saw Emma.

The look on Emma's delicate features was one of surprise and shock. She set her teacup on a table next to the door and unlatched the screen, finally smiling when she recognized Millie. She pushed the screen open to allow Millie inside. Millie engulfed Emma in a warm hug before leaning back and laughing.

"Aren't you glad to see me, darling?" Millie asked.

"Of course I am, Millie," Emma responded. "This is quite a surprise. If you'd called I would have made plans for my assistant to take my classes to allow me to meet you for breakfast."

"No need. It's a last minute trip. I barely had time to pack. I'm supposed to attend a luncheon with that dreadfully tedious

Carolyn Brooks," Millie said as she removed her gloves and unbuttoned her coat. She turned for Emma to help her remove it.

"Would you like a cup of tea? I'm sure the water is still hot. Or I might have coffee," Emma offered, clearing her throat while placing Millie's coat over the back of a living room chair.

Millie came up behind Emma and wrapped her arms around her waist to press against her back. "Not when I have a warm body near me to drive away the cold."

Emma patted Millie's hand and attempted to move away. "Unfortunately I have to leave for class in a little bit."

"It's a little early isn't it, darling?" Millie purred as her hands tightened and drifted up toward Emma's breasts.

Emma finally turned to face Millie and grasped her by her upper arms to keep her at a distance. "I'm sure you noticed the new snow outside," she said. "I always leave earlier in case there are slick areas."

Millie rested her hand in the center of Emma's blouse and played with one of its buttons. "You don't seem very happy to see me, dear. Hopefully you haven't forgotten me so quickly," she pouted as she slipped a finger into Emma's blouse and brushed it against her bra. "I certainly haven't forgotten *you*, my sweet."

"Of course I haven't forgotten you, Millie," Emma replied. "However..." she started.

The conversation was interrupted by the thudding of footsteps charging down the staircase from the second floor master bedroom.

"Ohmygod! Why didn't you wake me, baby? I can't be late for this month's departmental meeting," Ramie babbled as she flew down the stairs. Emma rolled her eyes when she noticed Ramie was still wearing her usual sleeping attire—skimpy panties under a green faded, holey, cut-off t-shirt that advertised the University of Vermont and exposed most of her abdomen, barely covering her breasts. "Is there any coffee?" she asked as she dashed toward the kitchen.

"I made a fresh pot," Emma called out.

She saw Millie's eyes widen as she gaped at the half-dressed young woman disappear into the kitchen, returning a moment later sipping from a half-filled cup. Emma felt the familiar warmth of Ramie's body as she ran a hand smoothly up her back and pushed onto her tiptoes to place a light kiss on Emma's lips. Ramie then turned her attention to Millie and reached up to remove Millie's hand from Emma's chest. She smiled and held out her hand.

"We haven't been formerly introduced," she said sweetly. "I'm Laramie Sunderlund. And you are?"

"Millie. Millicent Carver," the stunned woman managed as she took Ramie's hand and stared at Emma.

Ramie squeezed Emma's arm and turned away. "I'd love to stay and chat," she started with a glance at Emma before finishing what she was saying, "*Mrs.* Carver, but I'm running late for a meeting. I'm sure you understand. Oh, and please give my regards to the Dean." She smiled and added, "Great coffee this morning, darling. You're getting better every day."

When Ramie was gone, Emma asked, "Would you like some tea…or coffee now, Millie?"

Millie nodded. "Tea please," she said, pressing her hand against her reddened cheek and lowering her body into the closest chair.

Emma picked up her teacup and carried it into the kitchen. She prepared two fresh cups before rejoining Millie in the living room. She sat, crossing one foot behind the other and waited. She wasn't expecting a pleasant conversation with her former lover.

Millie took a sip and cleared her throat. "I didn't realize you'd taken up babysitting, Emma," she finally said.

"That was uncalled for, Millie," Emma replied calmly.

"Well, what do you expect me to say? That girl can't possibly be over twenty," Millie huffed. "Couldn't you at least find an adult to share your bed?"

Emma smiled benignly and rested her teacup on her leg. "I can assure you Miss Sunderlund is an adult."

"I grant she's attractive enough, stunning actually, but you must know she'll leave you eventually."

"Just as I knew you would."

Millie looked hurt by Emma's statement. "My marriage provides me with a certain measure of…security."

"But not happiness."

Millie harrumphed. "Is that what you think you've found? Happiness?"

Emma closed her eyes and thought. "For the moment."

"I hoped I'd made you happy."

"You did, Millie, but I needed more," Emma said with a shrug. "I would never compare you and Ramie. You're both very special to me in your own way."

"Is the English chairman aware of this…liaison?"

"There's no reason for Franklin to be involved in my private life. It doesn't affect my teaching or my responsibility to the university and has not been a topic of discussion."

"And Ms. Sunderlund?"

"She's a guest lecturer in another department. It's a temporary position. We rarely see one another during the day."

"Does she live here? In your home?" Millie gasped.

"No. The university provides a residence for their visiting artists."

Ramie bounded down the stairs again, pulling on her jacket. Emma smiled and stood in time to exchange another brief kiss.

"Later, baby," Ramie said in a low voice.

"Be careful of ice on the road," Emma said, brushing the backs of her fingers over Ramie's cheek as she tugged a toboggan over her ears.

"Love you, Em," Ramie called out as she left through the back door and slid into her car.

"God, Emma. You're so...domesticated," Millie said.

"Be happy for me, Millie, for however long this lasts."

Millie stood and moved to stand in front of Emma. "You know I am, dear, despite my concerns."

Emma held Millie's coat and pulled it over her shoulders. "You know you enjoy the chase more than the relationship," she laughed.

"That's true," Millie said with a nod. She brushed her fingertips over Emma's lips and bit her lower lip. "If I'd been braver, we could've been extraordinary together."

Emma hugged Millie tightly. "We were. You'll always have a special place in my heart."

"But not in your bed."

Emma released her and shook her head.

Emma called a cab and waited on the front porch until Millie was gone. A potentially bad situation had been averted, she hoped. Millie had been reasonably decent with only a modicum of catty remarks. Emma had to smile at the memory of Ramie's reaction to seeing a woman she knew perfectly well had once been Emma's lover standing in the living room. Perhaps later that evening, Emma would need to reassure Ramie there would be no further surprises to greet her another morning. Emma glanced at her wristwatch. Although it was still ninety minutes before her first class, she would have to hurry.

MID-MORNING, EMMA dialed the number to Ramie's office in the art department.

"Sunderlund," Ramie answered brusquely.

"Is this a bad time?" Emma asked cautiously.

"Just a sec," Ramie replied.

From the muffled sound, Emma believed Ramie had simply placed her hand over the receiver to continue another conversation. Periodically she picked up a word or two, but couldn't deduce whether or not Ramie was angry. A few moments later, Ramie's voice was back. "Idiot," she muttered and then Emma heard her taking a deep breath.

"Did your early morning visitor leave without violence?" Ramie asked pointedly.

"Of course." Emma smiled. "Millicent Carver would never create a scene."

"Think she liked my panties and t-shirt?"

"She didn't say."

"Can I assume there won't be any other early morning visitors I should be aware of? Or do you have a long line of former lovers waiting in the wings?"

"There won't be anyone else."

"Promise? I do have a jealous streak—you know?"

"I promise."

"Hey! Wanna do lunch?"

"I have a meeting at one-thirty," Emma answered, flipping the pages of her desk calendar.

"How about I pick up a couple of sandwiches and bring them to your office. Then I'll have time to ravish you before your meeting and you can go with damp panties and a smile on your face."

"That does sound tempting, but I'm afraid there wouldn't be enough time."

"It would be just an appetizer until you get home. That's when you'll get the remaining courses," Ramie said with an evil laugh. "God, we've got to stop this! I'm getting extremely turned on and may attack the next unsuspecting student who wanders into my office." Emma heard a sound, followed by laughter. Then Ramie said between fits of laughter. "Scratch that, sweetie. The last person through my door was some pimply-faced freshman boy who was so totally not worth my effort."

"Does that mean I'll see you again this evening?" Emma asked.

"Well, I guess that depends on whether you want to or not," Ramie kidded.

"I'm serious, Ramie."

"Is something wrong, darling?" Ramie asked, her voice now serious.

"No. I just wanted to hear your voice before my next lecture," Emma replied. She leaned back in her chair and took a deep breath. Ramie was like Millie in many ways. She was lovely, passionate, and, like Millie, would probably be leaving at some point in the future. Millie's sudden departure had come as something of a surprise, but at the end of the coming spring,

Ramie's time as a visiting artist would end and Emma would be alone once again. She was forced to admit that her feelings for the young artist ran deeper than was wise. How many times could she endure being left?

RAMIE WAS POINTING out a problem area on a piece of sculpture that still needed work and offering suggestions for a remedy. She took a grease pencil from the back pocket of her jeans and deftly marked the stone as a student observed.

"We have a visitor, Miss Sunderlund," Ramie's student leaned forward and whispered.

Ramie glanced over her shoulder and saw the well-dressed woman waiting patiently near the workroom doors.

"Use a small chisel and strike it gently to remove the section I've marked," Ramie instructed. "I think that will solve your problem, Jeffrey." She patted him on the back. "Your work is much better now that you've become less heavy-handed."

The young man rubbed his hands on the front of his jeans. "Guess I'm in a hurry to see what it will look like," he said with a bashful grin.

Ramie walked away, but turned to walk backwards for a moment. "It has to look like the vision in your mind, and that's worth a little patience." Ramie turned toward Millie Carver and wiped her hands on a towel. She extended her hand and, to her surprise, Millie took it.

"I didn't mean to disturb your class," Millie said.

"You didn't, Mrs. Carver. This is simply a place for students having difficulty perfecting a new technique."

"And you teach them how to perfect it."

"I try," Ramie said with a smile. "Poor Jeffrey seems to suffer from an attention deficit problem." She shrugged. "Probably become a world renowned sculptor one day," she added. "What can I do for you, Mrs. Carver?"

"I'd like to speak to you privately, if you have a moment," Millie said.

"My office is down the hall. Follow me." Ramie stopped a student instructor and said, "I'll be back in a few minutes, Linda. Can you watch them for me?"

"No problem," the young woman said as she glanced at Millie.

Ramie led Millie to her office and waited until she entered before closing the door and making her way behind an old desk, plopping down, and taking a deep breath. She looked at Millie and waited for her to speak.

Millie pulled the gloves from her hands one finger at a time and crossed her legs. "First of all, I wanted to apologize for earlier this morning. I should have called before dropping by Emma's home uninvited."

Ramie shrugged.

"And second," Millie said, "I wanted to implore you not to hurt her."

"I would never do that, at least not intentionally."

"I'm assuming you are aware that Emma and I were involved before I moved."

Ramie brought a leg up into her chair as she nodded. "I saw you together once," Ramie admitted. "Before I knew who Emma was."

Millie tilted her head and stared at Ramie.

"At her cabin on the lake," Ramie clarified.

Millie closed her eyes and smiled to herself. "I remember the cabin very well," she said softly. "Emma is a rather remarkable woman, Miss Sunderlund. She has a way of making those closest to her feel...special."

"Yes, she does."

"Well, I only wanted to clarify what happened this morning," Millie said as she stood and picked up her belongings.

"You care for Emma very much, don't you?" Ramie asked.

"More than I should. We both knew what our relationship was and that it would eventually end. I, however, wasn't quite prepared for the end when it came. Since then we have managed to meet periodically. If I'd been aware that she'd taken a new...lover, the embarrassing meeting earlier could have been avoided," Millie said stiffly.

Ramie cleared her throat. "She deserves more than occasional happiness."

"And you're giving her that? I've been told that your position at Overland is temporary. So you see, my dear, you'll be leaving her just as I did. When you do and if she turns to me for solace, I might not be able to convince myself to walk away from her again."

"I'm not planning to leave, but I don't think she believes that yet. She's been left too many times already. You come back when it suits you and she expects you to leave. Just so you know. Emma won't be available in the near...or distant future."

Millie smiled. "A bold statement, but time will tell. I'm a patient woman."

"I'm sorry you're so unhappy with your life, Mrs. Carver," Ramie said.

Millie shrugged. "It is what it is. Thank you for your time,

Miss Sunderlund." When Millie reached the door, she looked back at Ramie. "She knows how to reach me."

Ramie nodded and watched Millicent Carver leave her office. Ramie lowered her chin to rest on her knee and sighed. She loved Emma. Of that, she was certain. Yet in less than six months her time at Overland would end and she would be free to resume her life as a working artist and an instructor at Vermont. Her parents thought she'd lost her mind when she accepted the temporary position at Overland, but had been unaware of her lingering attraction to Emma Rothenberg.

LATER THAT AFTERNOON, after going home for a shower and changing into clean clothes, Ramie used a spare key to let herself into the back door of Emma's house. She glanced at the clock on the kitchen wall and pulled chicken from the freezer. By the time she slid dinner into the oven and set the timer, she heard the front door open.

Emma walked up behind her and, as usual, pulled Ramie's blonde curls aside to kiss the nape of her neck. "I'm surprised to see you here," she whispered.

Ramie wiped her hands on a towel and turned to meet Emma's lips, drawing her into a deep kiss. Before Emma could say anything else, Ramie slid her hands into Emma's jacket and jerked down, trapping her arms. Her hands wandered along Emma's sides until they reached her breasts, feeling Emma's nipples react and harden. Emma grunted at her arousal as Ramie forced her back. "I want you, Em," Ramie breathed raggedly. She took a deep breath and exhaled. "I can smell your arousal and know you want me, too." She looked up at Emma. "It's...intoxicating."

Emma's legs ran into the kitchen table as she struggled to free her arms. "Ramie," she said.

"Hmm," Ramie managed as she unbuttoned Emma's blouse and pushed her bra up to reveal her small, tempting breasts. Emma cried out as Ramie's mouth teased the tempting, erect nipples while her hands squeezed Emma's ass, pulling her closer until Emma had no choice but to lay back onto the table top.

"You smell so good," Ramie murmured as she unfastened Emma's slacks and pushed them down along with her panties. She ran her hands up Emma's thighs and lifted her to meet her mouth.

"God, baby! Please," Emma begged as her body reacted. "Please, Ramie."

"You're mine, Emma Rothenberg. You don't belong to

anyone else. No one has or will ever love you more than I do. You drive me crazy. I want you all the time." Tears ran down Ramie's cheeks as she slowly entered Emma and watched the pleasure gather on her lover's face. "You're so very beautiful, baby," she said before meeting Emma's lips and savoring the desire she felt through them.

Emma finally managed to free one arm and dropped it to cover Ramie's hand. "I need you," she panted.

Finally, Ramie moved away slightly and pulled Emma up, hugging her fiercely. "You're everything to me, Em. I'll never give you a reason to turn to Millie Carver again."

"What?" Emma asked as she struggled to gain control of her breathing.

Ramie rested her forehead on Emma's shoulder and held her. When she finally looked up and smiled, she said, "She still wants you, but now she knows I'm willing to fight for you, if necessary, because you're so worth it. Now go upstairs and clean up. Dinner should be ready in about half an hour."

EMMA STOOD IN the shower, letting the soothing hot water run down her body, relaxing her muscles. She wasn't quite sure what to make of the greeting she received from Ramie. She would have to ask more questions concerning the apparent discussion with Millie. All she could really remember, besides the pleasure that had coursed through her body, was that Ramie was willing to fight for her. No one had done that before. Or had she not been willing to fight for what she wanted. Frances pushed her away and she had allowed it to happen. Millie selected security over happiness and Emma hadn't considered maintaining their relationship important enough to attempt persuading her to stay. There had been valid reasons for both losses, but shouldn't she have demanded more? Frances wanted what she called a "normal" life with the possibility of children of her own. Did that mean she considered loving Emma "abnormal"? Was she defective in some way because she couldn't give her the one thing she wanted, a family with children? Emma loved Frances so much that she gave her the opportunity to have what she wanted more than anything. More than she wanted Emma.

If she thought about it long and hard enough, Emma couldn't put a name to her feelings for Millie Carver beyond physical satisfaction. Millie presented no threat to Emma personally, although there was the idea that knowledge of their relationship could damage Emma's reputation. However, it was unlikely that Millie would make their relationship public knowledge. It would damage her own future irreparably and Millie was neither vindictive nor a fool.

Now there was a woman twenty years or more her junior who was offering her what would possibly be her final chance at finding what she had longed for all her life. She'd let it walk out of her life once. Could she turn it away again? And what would she have to give up to accept it? There were a million things that could go wrong. Emma could honestly say that where matters of the heart were concerned, she was hopelessly torn. How long could an intimate relationship last? And when it ended or faded, would what remained be enough for a still moderately young woman? As Emma stepped out of the shower and quickly dried, she had more questions than answers. She didn't like where her thoughts were leading her, but it was time she and Ramie had a serious discussion about what they each saw as their future.

"Are you staying tonight?" Emma asked over dinner.

"If you want me to," Ramie answered quietly as she speared her salad.

"Of course I do." Why was this so difficult? She and Ramie had been as intimate as two people could get so why couldn't she simply ask what she wanted to know. Was she afraid of what Ramie might say? "I was...um...wondering if you'd like to go out next weekend?" Emma asked.

"Are you asking me on a date, Dr. Rothenberg?" Ramie replied with a grin. "A real date? Where would we go?"

"I know a place in Columbus you might enjoy," Emma said with a shrug. "I have an old friend there. She called recently and invited me up for dinner. I'd love for you to meet her."

"Does she know you'll be bringing a date?"

"I told her I was seeing someone, if that's what you're asking. She was a little surprised."

"Why?"

"I don't discuss my private life with anyone. It's my business and no one else's."

"Is she another former lover?"

Emma jerked her head up and stared incredulously at Ramie. "God, no! Sarah and I have always been friends, but never anything more. Besides, her significant other, Pat, is a champion marksman," Emma sighed. "If she even thought I'd touched Sarah I'd have been a dead duck."

Ramie reached across the table and squeezed Emma's hand. "Then I'd be honored to meet your friends, darling. Thank you."

Chapter Fifteen

RAMIE WAS PRACTICALLY crawling out of her skin with nervousness during the ninety minute drive to Columbus the following Saturday evening. She spent all afternoon trying to decide what to wear, finally opting for semi-casual, but comfortable. Emma seemed relaxed as she drove her car along the highway. Ramie's hand rested comfortably on Emma's thigh. She chatted about her friends who were meeting them at an upscale restaurant in the heart of downtown Columbus. According to Emma, it was an Italian restaurant frequented by students from the university, but since this week's football game was away, it shouldn't be as overcrowded as usual.

As Emma left the main highway and turned onto a wide road that would take them into the downtown area, Ramie asked, "What do your friends do for a living?"

"Sarah's an attorney for the city and Pat is a chemist for a subsidiary of Dow. They couldn't have children of their own, of course, but adopted two girls who are now grown and live out-of-state. I'm the godmother for their eldest girl. We've been friends for as long as I can remember and they are anxious to meet you."

Great, Ramie thought. She knew virtually nothing about the law and absolutely nothing about chemistry. She hoped Emma could keep a conversation going. It wasn't exactly the evening Ramie was looking forward to.

Emma pulled into a multi-story parking garage and lowered her window to take a ticket before searching for an empty parking spot. "This area is what we called the main drag when I lived here," Emma said. "We'll have to walk a couple of blocks to the restaurant. Hope you don't mind."

"No. I'm good. There's a spot," Ramie pointed out.

After Emma pulled into the spot and set the brake, Ramie asked, "Do I look all right?"

"You look lovely, why?"

"I don't want to embarrass you in front of your friends. Guess I'm a little nervous about meeting them," Ramie admitted with a shrug.

"Don't worry. It will be fine. I promise. Just be yourself," Emma said with a smile as she stepped from the car. She walked to the passenger door and opened it, offering Ramie her hand.

They moved down the sidewalk at a leisurely pace. Emma

stopped to look at a display in the window of a lingerie shop. She leaned closer to Ramie and said, "I'd like to see you in that, but probably wouldn't leave it on you for long."

Ramie blushed, but nudged Emma's shoulder and said, "God. You've got quite a dirty mind, Emma Rothenberg." Then she pointed at a small sign in front of the mannequin. "It claims it comes with an edible crotch," she said.

"Huh," Emma laughed. "I've never tried that, but I can definitely see the possibilities."

Ramie grabbed Emma's hand and pulled her away from the window. "Let's go before that drool spot you're making on the sidewalk gets any larger."

Ramie took a long, deep breath as they entered the restaurant, preparing herself for a tiring evening with Emma's friends. The restaurant was busy with the wait staff rushing around taking orders to the kitchen or delivering steaming dishes to various tables. Small low-hanging lights cast a warm, dim glow over everything. Ramie was impressed with the décor and hoped the food was as impressive. Emma searched the dining area for her friends and then took Ramie's hand. "There they are," she said.

Emma placed her hands on Ramie's waist and guided her between tables, finally stopping at a table for four not too far from the kitchen. Ramie hoped the shocked look on her face wasn't too obvious as she stared at the two women already seated. Emma pulled a chair out for Ramie before taking one for herself. She turned to Ramie and said, "These are my friends." She gestured to a woman with smiling eyes and light brown hair that grazed her shoulders. "This is Sarah Potter, my roommate when we were innocent undergrads," she said with a laugh. And next to her, her partner, Patricia Bennett. Ladies, this is Ramie Sunderlund, my companion for the evening. Be gentle and try not to embarrass me too much."

Patricia extended her hand to Ramie. "Pat. No one except my mother calls me Patricia."

Ramie took Pat's hand and smiled at the woman with short dark hair that capped her head. Her inquisitive blue eyes seemed to study Ramie closely before returning her smile.

"Emma always did have excellent taste in women," Sarah said as she also took Ramie's hand. "I see that hasn't changed."

"Thank you, I think," Ramie said with a blush at the compliment.

"How are the girls?" Emma asked as a waiter poured them all a glass of wine before taking their orders.

Sarah sipped her wine. "They're doing well. Pamela is

clerking for a member of the Maryland Supreme Court at the moment, but she's met a young man. We think they're planning to get married even though she hasn't actually said so yet. Probably afraid Pat will drag out her gun," she chuckled.

"And Kris has left school and is off somewhere trying to find herself," Pat huffed. "Whatever the hell that means."

Sarah patted her hand. "She'll be fine, darling. We each have to find our own way."

"I remember when that meant finding something we liked and sticking to it," Pat protested.

"Emma tells me you're an artist, my dear," Sarah said to Ramie, gracefully changing the subject.

"Yes, I am. I sculpt primarily," Ramie responded.

"She's the current artist-in-residence at Overland," Emma added. "And incredibly talented."

"I would love to see your work sometime," Sarah said. Then she turned her attention back to Emma. "Have you heard from Livvie recently?" she asked.

Emma glanced at Ramie and for an instant Ramie saw barely controlled anger mixed with terrible sadness before Emma took a deep breath and spoke, her voice tight. "She hasn't bothered to acknowledge my existence in thirty years. Why would she now?"

"She's been quite ill. I thought you should know. After all, she is your sister."

"Olivia has obviously forgotten that," Emma hissed. "I came here tonight to enjoy myself, Sarah, not discuss ancient family issues."

Ramie placed her hand on Emma's forearm and squeezed lightly before moving it to cover Emma's clenched fist.

Although the food they ordered looked and smelled delicious, Emma only picked at it and barely managed to add anything to their dinner conversation. What had begun as a promising evening, other than Ramie's initial nerves, was going south rapidly.

"I need to work off some of this pasta," Ramie tried. "Is there someplace around here we can go dancing later?"

"There used to be a place near where we're parked," Emma said. "I guess it's still there."

"Can we go after dinner?"

"If you want," Emma said with a shrug.

"That sounds like fun. We haven't been dancing in ages," Sarah said. "Are we invited as well?"

Emma looked at her oldest friend for a moment and nodded. "Of course you're invited. It will be like old times again."

"Damn straight!" Pat, who had been quiet most of the

evening, announced. "I can still bust a move or two." Then she leaned closer to Sarah. "If I throw my back or hip out, you can take me home and help me work the kinks out, baby."

Sarah ran a hand down her face, blushing slightly. "No more drinks for you, sailor," she chuckled.

DANCERS WERE PACKED closely on the dance floor at The Ladies Room when Ramie and Emma, followed by Pat and Sarah, entered. It was late, almost eleven, by the time they arrived. As they looked for a place to sit, the driving beats of the anthem "I Will Survive" by Gloria Gaynor started and Ramie couldn't stop her body from moving to the beat of the music. The hands resting lightly on her hips made her smile.

Pat spotted an empty booth across the room. Emma waited for Ramie to slide in before joining her. She cast a warm smile at Ramie and leaned closer to whisper in her ear. Afterward they laughed before a waitress interrupted them. Emma looked more relaxed than she had been all evening.

Occasionally Emma engaged her friends in conversation and asked Sarah to dance. From the expressions on their faces they looked amiable again. Ramie felt a flare of curiosity begin in her stomach as she danced with Pat and watched the two old friends move around the dance floor easily, involved in a conversation.

"Emma's never discussed it with me, but what's the issue between Emma and her sister?" Ramie asked.

"It's really not my place to say," Pat answered with a shrug. "Actually no one but the two of them really knows what happened. I only know about it third hand at best. All I know is that Emma has never gotten over it."

Ramie scooted over when Emma returned and Pat stood to allow Sarah to slide back into the booth. Both women gulped down several swallows of their drinks.

"When did you two meet?" Sarah asked.

"About ten years ago," Emma said, looking at Ramie. "Ramie's a former student." With a smile she added, "Although she doesn't share my passion for literature, she did contribute to several interesting class discussions."

"Thank you," Ramie said quietly as she stared at Emma and ran a hand along Emma's thigh.

A slower tune began and Emma asked, "Would you care to dance, Ramie?"

"I'd love to," Ramie replied with a warm smile.

Emma slid out of the booth and held Ramie's hand as she moved across the seat and stood. When they reached the dance floor, a warm hand slipped around Ramie's waist as Emma stepped into the dance. Ramie closed her eyes and drifted along in Emma's arms, something she had only dreamed of. She brought her arm up to rest along Emma's shoulder, her hand stroking the nape of Emma's neck and gently massaging it as her head rested comfortably against Emma's shoulder, inhaling the scent she couldn't get enough of. She would be happy to remain in Emma's arms all night. She nuzzled closer against Emma, her fingers playing in the soft hair along Emma's neckline. She felt a change in Emma's breathing and an increase in the heat emanating from her body. "Thank you for tonight, baby. I love feeling your arms around me, your body close to mine," she said.

"I hope to be even closer very soon," Emma rasped as she stroked her hand down Ramie's back.

"Oh really," Ramie said. Then she added with a grin, "I'll look forward to that."

Emma pulled her closer and looked at Ramie's hand resting in hers as their fingers meshed together and she brought them against her chest.

"I THINK WE'LL be leaving soon," Emma announced once she was seated. "It's after midnight."

"Should you be driving?" Sarah asked.

"Don't worry mom," Emma laughed. "I made reservations at the Fairmont. We'll drive home in the morning after breakfast."

"Well, Sarah and I have had a long day, so I hope you don't mind if we split first," Pat said.

"We might stick around for one more dance. It might be a while before we make it back to Columbus. When you speak to the girls, tell them I said hello."

"We will. Now haul your ass up and give me a hug," Sarah said as she scooted out of the booth. "And it was a pleasure to meet you, Ramie. I hope we'll see you again soon."

Emma stood and engulfed Sarah in a full body embrace. "I'll call and we'll talk, okay," Emma said softly.

"Anytime, sugar. You'll never get rid of me," Sarah laughed. "Now let me go. I have a woman of my own I need to take care of."

Emma watched her friends melt into the still large crowd of patrons before sitting back down next to Ramie.

"You didn't tell me you had plans to spend the night," Ramie said as she sipped her drink. She rested a hand on Emma's, entwining their fingers. "I didn't bring a thing to wear," she said with a grin.

"You won't really need anything," Emma answered.

"Why, Dr. Rothenberg! Whatever are you suggesting?" Ramie asked, looking shocked.

"Not a thing. Finish your drink and let's get out of here."

"One more dance and I'm all yours, baby," Ramie purred.

As they finished their drinks, a handsome woman in her late thirties came out of the crowd to stand next to their table. She stared at Ramie and smiled. "Please don't tell me you're leaving," she said, her speech slurring slightly. "It's taken me a few drinks to get up the courage to ask you for a dance. That is, if your mom doesn't mind," she added with a brief glance at Emma. A lop-sided grin creased her face.

Emma cleared her throat and glared at the young woman standing over her. Slowly, she stood. "I can't speak for her mother, but *I* mind," she managed, looking at Ramie.

"No, thank you," Ramie said at the same time, staring at Emma.

Ramie stood and leaned closer to Emma, drawing her into a slow kiss. "Let's get out of here, darling," she murmured against Emma's lips as the embarrassed woman moved away.

Ramie wrapped an arm through Emma's as they made their way out of the club. Emma was uncharacteristically quiet as they walked to their car and during the drive to their hotel.

As soon as they entered their room, Ramie spun around and said, "Talk to me, Emma."

Emma tossed the room key onto a nearby table and leaned against the wall next to the door. "What do you want me to say, Ramie? I told you something like this would happen. And it won't be the last time. I guarantee that."

"That woman was drunk."

"But she wasn't blind. Drunk or sober, it's obvious I'm much older than you."

Ramie stepped closer and leaned against Emma's body. "You don't feel like my mother," she whispered, nuzzling under Emma's chin and kissing her throat. When Emma's hands rose to stroke Ramie's back and hair, Ramie murmured, "You don't touch me like my mother." She found Emma's mouth and nibbled along its edges before drawing her into a tender kiss. With her hands tangled in Emma's hair, Ramie ended the kiss and sighed, "I love my mother very much, but would never kiss her like that. You're the only one. Now take me to bed, darling, and let me prove it."

"Not yet. We need to talk first."

"I'll talk about anything you want as long as it's not your age or mine."

"There's more we have to discuss."

She took Ramie's hand, leading her to a chair near the room's curtained window. Emma sat and drew Ramie down to sit on her lap. As Ramie settled against her, she rested her head on Emma's shoulder. "What do you want to discuss?" she asked.

"Where do you see us in a year? Five years? Ten years?"

"Are you admitting there is an 'us'?"

"Yes," Emma acknowledged. "Isn't that what you want?"

"You know it is, but I want you to want it as much as I do," Ramie said. "I think you're waiting for me to leave you."

"Everyone leaves," Emma struggled. "It hurts and I have to know what to expect."

Ramie took Emma's face between her hands, forcing her to look at her. "I'll never leave you. Do you believe me?"

"You're leaving in six months," Emma said, her voice hard.

"I might, but that depends on you, honey."

Tears filled Emma's eyes and fell to her cheeks. "It's selfish and probably not the best for you, but I don't want you to leave. I...I can't imagine my life without you and I'll do everything I can to make you happy until my last breath."

Before she could say more, Ramie stopped her from talking by covering her lips with her own, her tongue searching Emma's mouth as if she never had before. When they parted, Emma embraced her tightly and kissed along her throat.

"Don't be afraid, my love," Ramie whispered.

"I'll try not to be, but you hold my future in your hands," Emma said.

"And you hold mine in yours. Trust me," Ramie said in return, kissing Emma's cheeks.

Chapter Sixteen

THE FALL SEMESTER was nearly over and Emma was wondering how she would occupy her time over the long, lonely three week break ahead of her. She had spent a long and boring week alone when Ramie flew to Vermont to visit her parents for Thanksgiving and she was sure Ramie would go home again soon. Even Howard, that traitor, had already made arrangements to fly to Atlanta to do research for an article he was preparing. As Emma rolled over in bed and rubbed her face with both hands, she was sure she could find a way to occupy her time. Donlevy Hall would be quiet and it would be a good time to read over notes to get prepared for the spring semester. There was new information that could be incorporated into her lectures and she had already put it off for too long.

Emma glanced at the empty place next to her on the spacious bed and ran a hand over it. She picked up the pillow next to hers and pressed it to her face, inhaling deeply and smiling at the familiar scent. The end of the semester was a busy time for everyone and Ramie had called Friday afternoon to let Emma know that something unavoidable, and unexpected, had come up in the art department, but she would be over Saturday. Emma sighed as she tossed the pillow onto the bed and swung her legs over the side to begin another day.

The sound of voices from downstairs caught her attention as she pulled a lightweight sweater over her head. Giggling, followed by shushing sounds, floated up the staircase and she considered calling the police, but decided to investigate first. She crept down the stairs to find Ramie and several of her students busily decorating her living room and scurrying in and out of her house. She gasped as she watched two young men in the process of moving the Christmas tree she and Ramie had already decorated across the room to a spot in front of the living room windows, its ornaments swaying precariously.

Before she could say anything, Ramie said, "If you break anything your grades will suffer. So be careful." Dressed in jeans and an over-sized sweatshirt with tinsel draped around her neck, Ramie was directing the students through various tasks. She glanced up and saw Emma frozen on the stairs and waved, a smile across her face. She stopped what she was doing and picked up a coffee mug, carrying it to Emma.

"Good morning, darling," Ramie enthused as Emma took the mug, which was still steaming.

"Elves, I assume," Emma said.

"Extra credit elves," Ramie said with a nod. "Do you like it so far?"

"Lovely," Emma muttered as she winced watching a young man dive to catch a falling glass ornament. He stood up triumphantly cradling it against his chest.

"Good catch, Jeffery!" Ramie called out. "Remember what I told you about rushing!" She looked back at Emma and winked. "We'll be through by noon."

Emma rested her hand on Ramie's shoulder and smiled. "Thank you. It will be beautiful."

Every time Emma looked at Ramie, she was amazed that the young woman had stayed with her almost an entire semester. When Ramie first began pursuing her, Emma had only listened to her libido as her desire drove her to do things she had never dared to think possible. But Ramie made the impossible possible.

After dinner that evening, Emma asked as they lounged on the couch in the living room, watching the lights on the tree twinkle, "Are you staying this evening? I missed you last night."

"I was planning to if you didn't have other plans," Ramie said, wrapping her arms around Emma and squeezing.

"I do have plans and they all involve you," Emma grunted.

"I thought maybe, if you were interested, we could start a new Christmas tradition."

"And dare I ask what that might be?"

Ramie broke away from Emma and rushed through the rooms turning off various lights, leaving only the lights of the Christmas tree on. As she returned to where Emma sat, she reached down and pulled her sweatshirt over her head and dropped it. Stopping in front of her lover and straddling her lap, Ramie began unbuttoning Emma's blouse. "I thought perhaps, only if you were interested, of course," she teased, "we might make love beneath the Christmas tree. I've always wanted to do that."

"No bows or ribbon?" Emma asked with a smile.

"Next year," Ramie breathed heavily, smiling as her hands stroked Emma's still covered breasts, feeling the nipples respond to her touch.

"I...love opening p-presents, but it's not really Christmas yet," Emma gasped.

"Details, details, darling. I've been thinking about you and me under that damn tree all day." Ramie unfastened Emma's bra and pulled it free. Her fingers spread over Emma's abdomen as her tongue teased the partially erect nipples into hard points.

"Oh, hell," Emma moaned as she lifted Ramie off her lap and into her arms. She moved toward the tree, setting Ramie down on the soft tree skirt. She watched as Ramie leaned back, the twinkling lights flickering over her skin. Ramie took Emma's hand and pulled her down, filling her mouth with a small breast and sucking greedily as her fingernails raked over her lover's back. Emma fought to bring her hand between Ramie's thighs, feeling the hot dampness.

Ramie arched beneath Emma and released her breast. "Take me, baby, the way only you can. I want you so much," Ramie begged. Emma quickly unzipped her slacks, followed by Ramie's. When they both lay naked, Emma lowered her hips and pressed her thigh into Ramie's center, sliding it slowly over the length of her clitoris. Her hands ran down the back of Ramie's thighs as she lifted them to encircle her waist. Ramie rode Emma's thigh and pulled her closer. "In me, now, Em," Ramie said. "I won't be able to wait much longer. You feel too good, baby. Oh God!"

Emma slowed the movement of her hips and slid down Ramie's body until she could smell her intoxicating scent. Ramie raised her hips searching for what she wanted, needed. The tip of Emma's tongue touched her quickly before withdrawing to touch another spot. Emma watched as Ramie's center, red and swollen with desire, pulsed with each teasing touch.

"Emma! Please. For God's sake! I need to come so much it's painful!" Ramie cried out.

Emma waited for the next pulse and smiled as her fingers were drawn in, the inner walls caressing them, holding them deep within Ramie's body. Emma withdrew her fingers halfway before leaning forward far enough to draw Ramie's breast into her mouth, teasing her nipple with her tongue as she drove her hand into her center again forcefully. She released the breast, whispering, "Now, sweet baby. Come for me now so I can taste you."

Two deep pumps later, Ramie's body stiffened and she bit her lower lip as her orgasm flowed over Emma's fingers, hot and slick. Emma removed her fingers and wrapped her arms around Ramie's sweaty, trembling body, holding her through a series of strong spasms followed by tremors that continued to roll through her body.

"I...I can barely breathe," Ramie croaked as she struggled to take a deep breath. "God, baby." She rolled her head to look at Emma, smiling as their lips met.

"Merry Christmas, darling," Emma whispered against Ramie's mouth. "I love you."

Ramie stared at Emma, her eyes serious as she brushed her hand through Emma's cinnamon hair. Emma frowned when she saw tears sparkling in Ramie's eyes.

"Did I hurt you?" Emma asked.

Ramie shook her head, blinking. "You've never said that to me before. Are you sure? It's not just because—"

"I'm positive," Emma whispered. "I should have said it a long time ago."

Ramie rolled onto her side and pressed her body against Emma's, forcing her onto her back. She slid her arm around Emma's waist and draped her leg across Emma's. "Don't ever stop loving me, Em. I couldn't stand it if you stopped loving me."

Emma kissed the top of Ramie's head and encircled her shoulders. "I won't," she promised.

Chapter Seventeen

"SUNDERLUND," RAMIE SAID as she picked up the phone in her office the next Monday afternoon.

"Hi, honey," Emma said.

"Hey, baby. This is a surprise," Ramie responded.

"Are you busy?"

"Just ran the last artist out. Why?"

"I have to attend the department's Christmas party this evening and wondered if you might accompany me."

"Short notice."

"I know. Sorry. I hadn't planned to attend, but we're apparently also welcoming a new associate joining the department and Franklin expects a full turn-out."

"It's not your fault, sweetie."

"I like that."

"What?"

"When you call me sweetie."

"I can think of a few other names as well."

"All good, I hope."

"Okay, Em, stop or I'll be in trouble."

"Anything I can do to keep you out of trouble?" Emma teased.

"Not if you plan to attend that English function. Is it formal? I know how you English types are. All stuffy and proper and grammatically correct."

"Occasionally," Emma laughed. "The invitation says professional attire, whatever the hell that is."

"You've seen my work clothes. I don't think I have anything suitable to wear."

"I actually appreciate you the most when you're wearing nothing, but that probably wouldn't be considered professional attire. Why don't I pick you up and we can go shopping for something more suitable?" Emma checked her wristwatch. "Say in half an hour."

EMMA FRESHENED UP and sipped on a cup of tea while she waited for Ramie to shower and dress. Emma had never taken anyone to a departmental function and was starting to feel her nerves kicking in. It had been several years since Ramie was a student in one of Emma's classes and she doubted anyone would remember that time. Still, escorting a woman twenty years her junior anywhere was bound to draw unnecessary attention. Over the last two months, she and Ramie had attended every home game, usually with Howard, as well as a couple of concerts given by the music department. Gradually, Emma became slightly more relaxed around others when with Ramie in public. She hadn't planned to place Ramie in an embarrassing spot, but thought the Christmas party would be a good way for Ramie to meet her colleagues.

"Well, what do you think?" Ramie asked, breaking into Emma's thoughts as she made her way down the stairs.

Emma set her cup down and walked over to see her. Ramie had agonized for nearly an hour over finding the right clothing. She and Emma argued over the price and eventually agreed to split it between them. When Emma saw her, she couldn't believe she was the same woman. Ramie looked gorgeous in the white suit, the jacket covering a metallic silver blouse with a dramatic plunging neckline that revealed a tempting cleavage. Her curly blonde hair lay along the tops of her shoulders.

"Oh my," Emma exhaled.

"Good enough to eat, huh?" Ramie laughed at the look on Emma's face.

"You have no idea," Emma said, gazing at Ramie's cleavage.

Ramie stopped on a step that let her height equal Emma's. "You look fabulous too, darling," she said as she rested a hand on Emma's shoulder. "We'll be the hit of the party."

"I predict we won't be there long," Emma said softly and leaned forward to kiss her.

Ramie's hand in the middle of her chest stopped her. "Oh, no. If you think I got all dolled up just so you could mess it up, then you are sadly mistaken, Dr. Rothenberg. I plan to get our money's worth out of this outfit. So cool your jets, wild woman."

"I plan to get you *out* of that outfit as soon as possible," Emma grinned.

"Later, baby, I promise," Ramie whispered as she leaned down to deposit a chaste kiss on Emma's cheek.

EMMA TOOK A deep, calming breath as she and Ramie entered the large banquet area on the second floor of the Student Union. Emma greeted the Dean of Arts and Sciences, Dr. Campbell, and his wife as well as her department chairman, Dr. Franklin Douglas, and his wife, introducing Ramie each time as a colleague and guest lecturer in the Art Department and nothing more. They had agreed on the way to the reception that was sufficient and all anyone needed to know. The last person in the receiving line was a dignified looking man who appeared to be in his mid-fifties. Although he looked vaguely familiar from a distance, Emma was certain they had never met, at least in a professional capacity. Next to him stood a well-dressed woman, also in her early fifties, with stylish salt-and-pepper hair. He extended a hand to greet Emma and smiled broadly. "You must be Emma Rothenberg," he said jovially.

Emma accepted his hand. "Yes, but I apologize that I don't recognize you," Emma said.

"Philip Westmoreland. I'll be joining the faculty here in January and will be teaching Historic Medieval Literature."

"Of course! I recently read your article in the *Midwestern Journal of English*," Emma said. "Very illuminating."

He turned to the woman next to him, who was looking intently at Ramie, and slipped his hand around her waist. "And this is my wife, Frances. Her assistance was invaluable during my research." Frances Westmoreland was a tall, slender woman. Curly medium length blonde hair curved around her cherubic face. When her blue eyes flickered to Emma, she managed a smile, but her face paled.

Emma was stunned and unable to draw a breath momentarily before she offered her hand to Mrs. Westmoreland. She didn't know what to say until she heard her voice introducing Ramie. "This is Laramie Sunderlund, the artist-in-residence with the art department at Overland this year." It sounded stiff and unnatural to her own ears. She felt lightheaded, as if she might faint when the periphery of her vision began to tunnel.

"Are you alright?" Ramie asked.

Emma looked at her and nodded. "I'm fine." Then she shifted her eyes to look at the hand resting in hers.

Frances' hand was warm, yet trembled slightly as she nodded at both women without speaking.

"I understand that your area of expertise is Twentieth Century American Authors," Westmoreland said. "My wife is quite an aficionado of the same period. Perhaps the two of you could get together to discuss it sometime. God knows it's not my favorite era," he chuckled.

"It would be my pleasure," Emma responded without looking at Frances. Of course it was her favorite area. She and Emma had read the same books and shared numerous lengthy discussions about the themes while Emma worked on her dissertation.

Emma, followed by Ramie, left the line quickly to mingle

with other professors, assistant professors, and instructors. Ramie became caught up in a lively conversation with a few of the younger staff members and drew the attention of the older male professors in particular. Emma was certain Ramie was flirting shamelessly with each of her colleagues and could only sigh in resignation.

Almost an hour later, as Emma refilled her cup with punch, a soft voice from behind her said, "I didn't know you were on the faculty at Overland." She turned to see Frances Westmoreland and wasn't sure what to say. All she could do for a moment was stare at the woman before her. She was older, of course, but still had the curly blonde hair she remembered sifting through her fingers. When her eyes fleetingly met the blue eyes that reminded her of a clear summer sky, she fought to drag her gaze away from the depths that still drew her in after thirty years apart.

"You're looking well, Fran," Emma managed. She flickered a glance in Phillip Westmoreland's direction. "I heard you had married, but never knew who the lucky...man was."

"You always talked about trying to get on at a school in California or Oregon. If I'd known..."

"This was as close as I could get to where...I was last with you. I needed that then."

Fran shifted her weight uncomfortably from one foot to the other and glanced toward her husband. "If I'd known you were here, Emma, I would have discouraged Phillip from applying for the position."

"No need. Overland is a fine university with a growing reputation."

Emma heard her name and looked over her shoulder to see Ramie motioning for Emma to join her. "Excuse me. It was nice to chat with you, Mrs. Westmoreland."

"Certainly," Fran said as Emma turned away. "Perhaps we can have lunch together one day."

"I don't think that would be wise," Emma said as she walked away.

She crossed the banquet area to where Ramie was standing. When their eyes met, Emma felt her heart thudding in her chest. Before she fully realized it she was standing next to Ramie, her hand resting comfortably against the small of her back, as if it had always belonged there. Ramie resumed her conversation while bringing her hand up to brush Emma's, assuring her she did, in fact, belong there. Ramie looked up at Emma and gave her a dazzling smile. The rightness of being with Ramie jolted Emma's mind. No one had made her feel this way since she had been in her twenties. Not since the last time she'd been with Frances. Her fingers meshed with Ramie's as she looked back across the room at Frances Westmoreland.

The woman tilted her glass back to drain it, then seemed to draw her body up and make her way toward where her husband was engrossed in a conversation with Howard Trammel. Emma felt her body stiffen when Frances glanced at her again. She couldn't help but wonder what she might eventually have to give up to remain with Ramie.

"Are you ready to go home?" Emma asked when the people Ramie was speaking with finally drifted away.

"You just can't wait to get me out of this outfit, can you?" Ramie teased.

Lowering her mouth closer to Ramie's ear, Emma said, "Nothing can deter me from my goal of removing that outfit. One delightful piece at a time."

"Jesus! Did it suddenly get warm in here or is it just me?" Ramie asked as she fanned her face with her hand.

Emma smiled. "I'll pay my respects to Franklin and his wife. Then we can leave."

RAMIE WAITED PATIENTLY for Emma to speak to Franklin Douglas and his wife. She leaned against the door into the banquet hall. She noticed Mrs. Westmoreland moving toward her.

"Leaving already?" Frances asked with a smile. Something about the smile made Ramie uncomfortable.

"I'm afraid so," Ramie said. "It's been a long day."

"I hope I'll see you again soon. Dr. Trammel said your work is quite exceptional."

"Howard might be a little prejudiced," Ramie said with a laugh. "He and I have become close friends this semester."

Ramie saw Emma glancing in her direction over Frances' shoulder and the look on her face was one of panic.

"Feel free to drop by the art department any time. I'm there almost every day," Ramie said as Emma approached.

"Ready?" Emma asked.

Ramie nodded as she clasped the hand Emma offered.

"We need to talk," Emma said quietly as she escorted Ramie to their car.

Chapter Eighteen

EMMA WAS QUIET during the drive to her house. As soon as they entered the back door she walked directly to her office and opened a cabinet behind her desk. She withdrew a cut crystal bottle filled with amber liquid. Removing the top, she filled a matching glass a quarter full and swallowed most of the drink in one large gulp.

Ramie had never seen Emma so upset. She came up behind her and ran her hand down her back. She felt Emma flinch as she touched her.

"What's wrong, Emma?"

"Nothing. Would you like a drink?" Emma asked as she threw the remainder of her drink into her mouth and poured another.

"No, but you're obviously upset about something. Is it something I did tonight?"

"No," Emma said. She placed the liquor container back in the cabinet and carried her drink into the living room, sitting heavily on the sofa. Ramie joined her and got comfortable before resting a hand on Emma's thigh.

Emma swallowed her drink and held the empty glass, staring at it, rolling it slowly between her hands.

"You promised to help me out of these clothes, remember?" Ramie teased.

Emma glanced at her, but didn't meet her eyes. "I'm sorry, but I'm tired. Do you mind?"

"Of course not." Ramie placed a hand on Emma's forehead. "You feel a little warm. Maybe you're coming down with something." She stood and held her hand out. "Let's get you to bed so you can get some rest." She wiggled her fingers, waiting for Emma to take her hand. When she did, Emma's felt cool and clammy against her skin.

Emma undressed and climbed into bed, wrapping herself in the covers. It wasn't long afterward that Ramie joined her and slid against Emma's back. She slipped her arm over Emma's waist to snuggle against her. "Are you warm enough, darling?" she asked.

"Yes," Emma mumbled. After a few moments, she quietly asked, "Do you remember when I told you I had been in love once?"

"Uh-huh," Ramie answered, shifting her body slightly.

"I was twenty-four. She was barely twenty-one. She was my sister's best friend, but, honestly, I didn't notice her for years. Then, quite unexpectedly, there she was. I couldn't get her out of my mind. It wasn't long before we were spending all our time together. I fell in love for the first time in my life, but like most dreams, it ended."

"What happened?" Ramie asked, running her hand up Emma's side.

"Her father found out we were...involved and two women together, that way, simply wasn't acceptable," Emma said.

"That was a long time ago, sweetheart," Ramie muttered.

"I thought if I loved her enough she would stay, but she didn't. She wasn't prepared to handle the pressure from her family."

"Then she couldn't have loved you as much as you loved her."

"Two women together in the early seventies was scandalous. My father kicked me out of his house after I admitted I was in love with her. I never saw him alive again and my sister still refuses to speak to me. You don't understand how others will look at you, the pressure being with me will cause you. I've been there and I can't ask you to risk the same things for me."

"Except I'm not afraid and I won't leave you," Ramie said gently.

"The woman you met tonight, Frances Westmoreland, is the woman I was in love with," Emma admitted.

Ramie was quiet for a few minutes before finally forcing Emma to turn over and look at her.

"You look amazingly like her," Emma blurted out. "I noticed the resemblance ten years ago and every moment since you returned. I'm sorry." Tears trickled from her eyes as she spoke.

"But you do know I'm not her?"

"Of course I do. I'm not delusional," Emma huffed.

"And neither am I." Ramie scooted closer to Emma. "So now we know we're both sane," she said, running a finger down Emma's chest.

"I just told you that you remind me of my former lover. Why aren't you upset?"

Ramie shrugged. "I suppose because she *was* your lover. Seeing her again tonight after so many years must have been a shock. She's very attractive, but I'm not her."

"I'm sorry I ruined our evening," Emma said with a sniff.

"There will be other evenings, darling. Now go to sleep," Ramie said. She yawned and rolled over.

Emma snuggled against her and whispered, "I love you."

Ramie took Emma's hand and drew it around her. "Love you, too." Within minutes both women were sleeping.

EMMA WALKED TOWARD her office after class. It was near the beginning of the spring semester. She glanced into open offices and waved to a few of her colleagues. She turned the corner and stopped suddenly. She considered leaving, but Frances Westmoreland, who was sitting in a chair outside Emma's office, glanced up from the book in her hand and smiled.

Emma unlocked her office and turned to face Frances. "Can I help you, Mrs. Westmoreland?"

"If you can spare a minute or two, Emma, I'd like to speak to you," Frances said.

"Of course." Emma opened her office door and held it to allow Frances to enter. "Make yourself comfortable. I can heat some water if you'd like some tea."

"No, thanks. Did you have a good Christmas?"

"It was fine," Emma answered as she hung her suit jacket on the back of her chair and sat. "And you?"

Frances laughed. "We spent the holidays with my parents. What do you think? It was God-awful and none of us could get away fast enough."

"How are your parents?"

"They're as dreary and predictable as ever, but now that they're growing older, I feel an obligation to visit them periodically. The curse of the eldest daughter, I suppose."

At that point conversation failed both women. Frances looked around the office at the diplomas and awards hanging behind Emma's desk. Emma knew she should say something, but her mind was blank. Frances was as lovely as ever, only in a more mature way.

Frances stared at a painting on the wall next to Emma's desk, a faint smile on her face. "I did love you, you know," she said softly. "Unfortunately, I wasn't strong or brave enough to fight for us...for you."

"I couldn't give you what you wanted most. I understood that," Emma said through gritted teeth remembering the last beautiful spring day she saw Frances. The day her heart cracked and shattered.

"I know I hurt you, Emma, and hope that one day you'll be able to forgive me." Frances shrugged and smiled weakly. "That's really why I'm here today."

"As long as you're happy, that's all that matters," Emma said.

Frances turned to look at Emma. "I am. Philip is a good husband and father. He's been very patient and gentle. He's always known I loved someone before him, but we've rarely discussed it. He has no idea who the other person was."

Emma stared at her entwined fingers, realizing she had been squeezing them together so tightly her knuckles were white. She made a conscious effort to relax her hands and leaned back in her chair. "I loved you and won't apologize for that," she choked out. "What do you expect me to say, Fran?"

Frances dropped her gaze to the floor. She took a deep breath before speaking again. "Tell me you're happy, Emma. Coming here seemed like the right thing to do an hour ago, but it was obviously a mistake." Frances picked up her book and purse, then stood to reach for the doorknob.

"Wait," Emma said. She got up and moved around her desk. She stopped in front of Frances and brought her hands up to lightly grip Frances' upper arms. "There's nothing to forgive, Fran. You made the only decision you could, and although it took me a while, I finally know what love is." Emma pulled Frances into a soft embrace. "You will always have a special place in my heart."

Frances wrapped her arms firmly around Emma's body and held her. "Thank you, Emma," she whispered.

Chapter Nineteen

EMMA RUMMAGED around in her shoulder purse to fish out the keys as she climbed the stairs to her office in Donlevy Hall. The damn things always seemed to fall to the bottom of her purse no matter what she did. She stopped at the top of the stairs and felt around until she pulled them out triumphantly. She and Ramie just returned from a relaxing week at her cabin for spring break. She couldn't stop a smile, remembering the child-like excitement on Ramie's face when she caught her first fish. The excitement was followed quickly by disgust at the idea of touching the slick, wiggling creature to remove the hook from its mouth. The weather was warming and held the promise of another beautiful summer. On her first day back, she had an appointment with a graduate student to discuss his qualifications to act as her assistant during the following fall semester.

She almost ran into Howard as she hurried around the corner leading to the faculty offices. She reached out and grabbed his arm to stop her momentum.

"Ohmygod, Howard! I am so sorry."

"Have you heard yet?" he asked, looking flustered.

"Heard what?"

"Franklin is dead."

"I'm sorry?" she asked as if she hadn't heard him correctly.

"Franklin and his wife were driving home last night. An oncoming vehicle took a curve too wide and hit them head on. Franklin didn't make it."

"And Mrs. Douglas?"

"Critical."

A WEEK AFTER Franklin Douglas' funeral, Emma sat in her office marking her students' latest attempts to impress her with their writing ability...unsuccessfully. The only semi-good news she'd heard in the past couple of weeks was that Martha Douglas would survive her injuries, but would be paralyzed below the waist. The English Department was trudging along like a boat without a rudder until Franklin's replacement was named, The phone on her desk rang and she felt for it as she continued to read.

"Emma Rothenberg," she answered absently, circling another

mistake on a student's paper.

"Dr. Rothenberg, this is Dean Campbell's secretary. Are you available for a brief meeting this afternoon at two?"

"I have a class at three."

"I don't believe it will last long."

"May I ask what it concerns?"

"He didn't tell me."

"I'll be there at two then," Emma said before placing the receiver on its cradle and resuming her grading.

Emma left Donlevy Hall and walked the relatively short distance to the Administration Building that housed the Office of the Dean of Arts and Sciences. It was a newer building and she was grateful there was an elevator in the main lobby. She stepped inside and pressed the button for the fourth floor. She walked into the reception area and nodded at the young woman behind the main desk.

"Dr. Rothenberg?" the secretary asked.

"Yes. I'm a few minutes early."

"Let me check to see if Dean Campbell can see you now."

The woman left for a minute and then opened the office door, holding it as Emma entered.

"Good to see you again, Emma," Dean Campbell said as he stood from his desk and walked around it to greet her with a warm two-handed handshake.

Emma had only spoken to the Dean a few times at university functions since he replaced Stanton Carver, but found him to be a friendly, out-going man with a rather serious streak when it came to running the College of Arts and Sciences. He was relatively young with a slight paunch that indicated a healthy appetite and little time for exercise.

He leaned against his desk and ran a hand through his thinning hair. "Please have a seat, Emma," he said with a smile although his forehead was creased into a frown. She had never met anyone who could smile and frown at the same time, but met his gaze as she sat.

"I've heard a few rumors concerning you, Emma," he began.

"I don't pay much attention to rumors, Dean Campbell," she said, wondering which rumors he was referring to. She leaned back and crossed her legs, preferring to see where this conversation would go before she made any further comments.

"Not long after I assumed this office from Dean Carver I was approached by a group of students allegedly representing the student body as a whole. They seemed particularly upset about the grades students were receiving in a number of classes. One of those was yours."

"Every student entering my classes, from the beginning level through the graduate level, is made aware of my grading policy and my expectations before a word of subject-matter is introduced. I feel certain there are many complaints from students at the lower levels. However, this is a university, not the fifth or sixth year of high school. Freshmen enter believing what they were expected to learn in high school has no relevance here and as a result are ill-prepared for the rigors that should be demanded at this level. Their mothers and fathers can no longer save them with their checkbooks. What they've heard about university is that there are four years of keg parties to look forward to before they stumble out with a diploma in hand. It is insulting that any of this university's professors, all extremely knowledgeable individuals, would be expected to dumb down their curriculum to mollycoddle spoiled children. I resent it and refuse to do it. I will never apologize for demanding excellence from my students."

Dean Campbell smiled. "That's another rumor I've heard about you, Dr. Rothenberg, that you're quite tenacious concerning your subject area as well as unafraid to voice your opinions."

"I love the written word and love studying it. Part of my job is imparting not only knowledge, but an appreciation for written works. I simply expect students in my courses to be able to translate what they learn into a coherent explanation."

Campbell nodded. "I agree and wouldn't expect you, or any professor, to change how they teach or grade. Students must learn to adapt to realities outside the bubble they have grown up in." He pushed away from the desk and crossed his arms over his chest. "How is Ramie?" he asked. Dr. Campbell and Ramie had met briefly a number of times in the past year and been involved in several discussions concerning art.

"She's fine, as far as I know. Why do you ask?"

Campbell shrugged. "Curiosity. I hate to lose her, but her time as our artist-in-residence will be ending in May. Do you know her plans afterwards?"

"I assume she will return to her previous position in Vermont," Emma said. "She really hasn't said, but that would be my guess."

Dr. Campbell shook his head and muttered, "A shame about Franklin. He was a good man."

"Yes, he was and a fine department chair. I visited his wife in the hospital not long ago and am pleased she will recover."

He sat behind his desk again and laid his arms on the top, lacing his fingers together and taking a deep breath. He finally looked at Emma and said, "I will need to appoint a replacement for Franklin. Would you be interested in assuming that position, Dr. Rothenberg?"

Emma didn't know what to say and sat blinking at Campbell for a few moments. She opened her mouth to speak, but closed it again. "I'm in the midst of teaching a unit, Dean Campbell. Would I be keeping my classes?"

"Only until we find a replacement for your position. Perhaps a month. Certainly not beyond this semester."

"There are others within the department with more experience who might be better suited. Appointing me may not be a popular choice, considering the current dynamics in the English Department."

"Actually, three of the most senior professors within the department came to me a few days ago and recommended you for the position. A couple are looking at retirement soon and believe you will provide consistent leadership, as well as continuity, for many more years." He pushed himself up from the desk again. "Please consider it and let me know your decision. If you decide to turn the offer down, I will be forced to look elsewhere, perhaps outside the university."

"Thank you, Dean Campbell," Emma said as she rose and glanced at her wristwatch. "I have a class to prepare for."

She felt sweaty and was sure her face had paled as she nodded at the secretary on her way out of the office. The cold, fresh air struck her when she stepped outside and walked toward Donlevy Hall. She stopped halfway there and sat down heavily on a bench next to the sidewalk. Of all the things Dean Campbell could have talked to her about, appointing her to replace Franklin Douglas as the department chair hadn't been a topic she'd considered. The goal of virtually every professor was to eventually become a department head, but she had never seriously thought about it. What would it mean to her relationship with Ramie? The department chair was expected to host social events throughout each term. It would mean opening her private life to a greater extent and to closer scrutiny than she considered desirable or acceptable.

EMMA PLOPPED INTO the chair behind her office desk after her final class and took a deep breath. She picked up the receiver to her phone and punched in a number, then waited, trying to calm her nerves.

"Sunderlund," a familiar voice answered after the third ring.

"Hello darling," Emma said.

"Emma. Is something wrong, sweetie? You don't usually call

unless you're on the way home," Ramie laughed.

Emma sighed. "Nothing's wrong. I just missed you."

"That's sweet, baby, and sounds very promising." Ramie laughed. "In fact, if you come home soon I might consider ripping your clothes off and having my way with you. Doesn't that sound decadent and yummy?"

"Ramie?"

"Yeah."

"I love you."

Ramie laughed again and the sound of it warmed Emma's soul. "Good to know, Em. I'd hate to think I've been wasting my energy on someone who doesn't appreciate my myriad of talents."

"I definitely do."

An hour later Emma pushed the front door to her house open. As soon as she removed her jacket, she smiled as she saw Ramie come toward her. Emma grabbed her and shoved her against the door, covering her mouth in a deep, probing kiss while her hands found their way to Ramie's full breasts.

"I hope you haven't made any plans for the weekend," Emma said in a low voice as she kissed and lightly bit around Ramie's neck, lingering at the tender area beneath her ear. "I don't plan to let you out of bed any time soon."

"Promises, promises," Ramie groaned, pressing her body closer against Emma's.

"I have an overwhelming need to touch you and have you touch me," Emma said, sucking Ramie's ear lobe into her mouth. "And you're mine for the whole weekend."

"I'll do anything you want, my love, but wouldn't we be more comfortable upstairs?"

"OH GOD! THAT was just too damn good, baby," Ramie said as she collapsed against Emma's shoulder. "You truly are a beast, Em. The way you take me is indescribable. I love it so much." Ramie pushed herself on to her elbows and smiled. "I'll need nourishment before round two though. Stay where you are. I'll be right back, okay?"

"Okay," Emma answered as she stroked along the side of Ramie's face.

Ramie made her way off the bed and sashayed naked out of the room, returning several minutes later with a tray laden with fruit and cheese, a bottle of wine tucked under her arm. She picked up a plump strawberry and dipped it in chocolate, then held it out to Emma.

"I've been offered the department chairmanship," Emma said after swallowing.

Ramie barely avoided dumping the entire tray onto the bed as she threw her arms around Emma and hugged her, following it with a passionate kiss that left Emma breathless. "Congratulations, darling!"

"I haven't accepted the position yet. I told Dean Campbell I needed to think about it, but have to let him know when I return on Monday," Emma explained.

"What are you waiting for? We both know you want it and are the right person for the job."

"I don't want to do anything that might change our relationship. The department chairmanship would demand a great deal of my time and I am finally beginning to enjoy my life for the first time in years." She leaned over to nuzzle her mouth on Ramie's neck. "It wouldn't be fair to you if we were forced to sneak around anymore than we already do."

Ramie frowned and scooted away. "Then maybe we shouldn't see one another any longer."

"That cannot be what you want," Emma said, moving closer and lowering her lips to drop a kiss on Ramie's shoulder. "I'll call Campbell and turn down the position. It's not worth losing you. I've waited too long. I love you."

Ramie's voice shook when she spoke again. "Great. Then I'll have to spend the rest of my life knowing you hate me because you gave up your dream job because of *me*. No, thank you!"

She slid off the bed and stormed into the bathroom, tears streaming down her face. She slammed the door behind her.

Emma crawled out of bed and went to the bathroom door. When she tried to turn the knob it was locked. She leaned her forehead against it. "Please, Ramie. Open the door."

"No! Go away and leave me alone!"

"I'll leave if that's what you want, but not as long as you're in there," Emma said.

"Then it's going to be a fucking long night for you!"

The entire situation was absurd. Campbell's offer made Emma feel validated professionally and she could barely wait to share the good news with Ramie. She had always considered herself rather sedate until Ramie touched her and demanded everything hidden inside. The second she saw Ramie coming toward her that afternoon she felt like a caged animal that had been set free. Was she willing to lose that feeling for a job? After a lifetime of calm, safe, little flings that she knew wouldn't develop into anything and only satisfied the needs of her body but not her soul, she had finally found a woman she wanted in her life forever. She was sure she'd never find another relationship like it in spite of the huge difference in their ages. She felt young again when Ramie was with her.

She would accept Dean Campbell's offer and keep Ramie with her. Having Ramie remain by her side was worth any risk. Now was the time to face her fears. She flopped down on the bed to wait for Ramie's stomach to coax her out of the bathroom. She was sound asleep when she was awakened by Ramie's body snuggling back against her for warmth. Emma kissed the top of her head and grabbed a cover to pull over them.

"Let's not do that again," Ramie muttered sleepily. "I'm exhausted."

"Me, too, baby," Emma whispered and tightened her arm around her.

"We need new reading material for the bathroom," Ramie yawned. "I was forced to read some crap article about the discovery of ancient medieval texts."

Emma smiled and placed a second kiss on the top of her lover's head. "Actually, I thought that was a rather fascinating article," she whispered. "Move in with me."

"Can we discuss it in the morning?" Ramie muttered.

"Of course," Emma answered with a smile as she drew Ramie closer.

EMMA AWAKENED SATURDAY morning to find Ramie sitting cross-legged next to her and staring at her intently.

"Is something wrong?" Emma asked as she stretched lazily and yawned before rubbing her face.

Ramie shook her head.

"Are you still mad at me?"

"No. I just like watching you sleep," Ramie replied. "Did you ask me to move in with you last night or was that a dream?"

Emma sat up and re-arranged the bedcovers. "I did ask, but you told me we would discuss it today. Would you rather wait until after breakfast?"

"Why would you ask me that?"

"About breakfast?"

"No. About moving in with you."

"It's time, don't you think? I love you beyond reason and now that your artist-in-residence status is ending soon, I want you with me all the time."

"But what about your promotion to department chair? It's your dream."

"I plan to accept Dean Campbell's offer," Emma said,

bringing her hand up to cup Ramie's face. "It is my professional dream, but you are my personal dream. I'm tired of hiding who I am and am prepared to deal with any problems that may arise." She stroked Ramie's cheek lightly with her thumb. "Please say yes, darling."

And Ramie did say yes, rather enthusiastically. The remainder of the weekend they made plans for the future. Ramie's position as artist-in-residence would expire at the end of the spring term and she decided to pursue her career as a full-time sculptress rather than returning to Vermont to teach. With the help of the contacts she made while at Overland, she hoped to obtain a few commissions. Their lives were finally settling into a calm existence, filled with the intimacy Emma had dreamed of as a young woman.

Chapter Twenty

DUST SETTLED IN Emma's hair as she carried her tools out of the old shed and stacked them near the house in early April. It had only taken a few hours for the footer for the new shed addition to be dug out and filled with cement. Four men began nailing studs together which would be set onto bolts embedded in the cement while one cut a line through the original shed slab to be used for the new PVC water line. Once the three walls were set, they promised the remainder of the addition would only take another day or two to sheetrock, tape, and float. It was a simple eight-by-ten-foot addition with a sloped roofline.

After dropping off the final armful of tools, Emma stepped into the now vacant shed. "What do you think?" she asked. They had spent the previous weekend packing and moving Ramie's extra tools and sculpting materials out of the Fine Arts Building. Now Ramie was busily dusting and sweeping the floor and shelves. There was still a nip in the air and Emma rubbed her cold hands together before burying them in the front pouch of her sweatshirt.

"It will be beautiful when it's finished and a dream to work in," Ramie said.

Emma wrapped her arms around Ramie and hugged her, kissing the top of her head. "I thought we could find a small air conditioning and heating unit and have it installed. You would be comfortable all year round then."

"It doesn't get that hot in here, Em."

"But you'll freeze to death in the winter."

"I can get a space heater."

"Whatever you want, but I made the offer. I'm going to get some tea. You want anything?"

Ramie picked up a cup and drank the remaining chilly coffee before handing Emma the cup. "I wouldn't mind a refill. Thank you, baby."

Emma stepped outside in time to see a flatbed truck backing up her driveway. Everything she'd ordered from the building supply center had already been delivered. A relatively large, tarp-wrapped item was lashed to eyebolts screwed into the wooden truck bed. Ramie stepped behind Emma and rested her hands on her shoulders for a moment.

"What's that?" Emma asked.

"Your gift," Ramie said, planting a light kiss near Emma's ear. "Where do you want it?"

"I don't understand," Emma said

Ramie moved in front of Emma and smiled. "It's *Untouchable,*" she said. She leaned closer and ran a finger down the center of Emma's work shirt with a lecherous grin. "But not anymore." With a laugh at the look on Emma's face, Ramie backed away a few steps before turning and skipping toward the truck. When it stopped, Ramie climbed into the bed and untied the ropes holding the covered item in place, revealing the statue. It gleamed in the sunlight as Emma climbed up to join Ramie. She reached out and tentatively stroked the statue.

"It's stunning in the sunlight," Emma said with awe in her voice as she ran her hand over the form and smiled broadly. "I'd almost forgotten how magnificent she is."

"Careful about how you touch her or I might get jealous," Ramie warned. "It's you. Every time I touched it while I was working on it, I imagined I was touching you. She belongs here."

Emma looked down at Ramie. "You'll have to show me later how you imagined touching me."

"I already have, but will be more than willing to give you a repeat performance tonight, darling."

Three men piled out of the truck and made their way to the back. Ramie glanced down at them. "The stones around the base can be set in the workroom," she said. Then she looked back up at Emma. "Where do you want your statue placed?" Ramie tapped a polished stone. "This is the base for it."

Emma prepared her tea and refilled Ramie's cup while the men wrestled with the stones, putting them where Ramie directed. The statue was the last item to be unloaded. Emma took a few unused paving stones and placed them near the center of the back garden. Satisfied with the location, she watched as the base was set to cover the stones and then the statue unloaded by a hoist and swung off the truck to rest on the base. She admired it from several angles before nodding her satisfaction with its placement. Then she brought a chair outside and sat sipping her tea and enjoying the gleaming marble. Ramie joined her and sat on her lap to drink her coffee.

"I'm trying to decide what kind of plants would look best around her," Emma said. "We'll have to make a trip to the garden center."

"Tomorrow," Ramie nodded. "But they should be colorful and perennial, I think."

"So do I. Maybe small around the base and then layered into something larger," Emma said. She rubbed her hand slowly up and down Ramie's back, smiling as she remembered the feel of Ramie's warm, soft skin beneath her fingertips. "I don't deserve anything so wonderful, but thank you."

Ramie turned to look at Emma. "I love you so much, Em. I hope I never disappoint you."

"Nothing you do could possibly disappoint me."

Ramie ducked her head to find Emma's lips and kissed her deeply. It was a kiss that promised much.

EMMA PUSHED HER fingers through the rich soil of her backyard garden. The sun shining down created a shadow from *Untouchable* that seemed to flow across the garden. While Emma couldn't say she loved pulling weeds, she did love the feel and smell of the warm, musky dirt on her hands. She spotted an earthworm slithering into the soil near her hand and flicked a little dirt back to watch the pinkish-blue body gleam in the sunlight as it effortlessly burrowed deeper. She stood and stepped awkwardly on the handle of a garden trowel, causing her to lose her balance. She reached out and braced her hand on the statue, inadvertently landing on a hard white breast.

"Playing with yourself again, darling?" Ramie quipped with a grin as she carried a cup of coffee toward the workshop.

"You could offer to help, you know," Emma grumbled.

Ramie stared at Emma as she fought to avoid stepping on her newly planted flowers. "I helped you last night, but obviously it wasn't enough." Ramie lowered her eyes slightly and snarled, "You're an insatiable beast, Emma Rothenberg."

Emma finally managed to shove her body away from the statue to stand firmly on the grass. "What wonderful thing are you creating now, sweetie?" She wiped her hands over the sides of her old jeans to remove excess dirt.

"I haven't decided yet." Ramie wiggled her eyebrows and grinned. "Wanna inspire me?"

Emma laughed. "And you call me insatiable."

"I'm young and my muse requires continuous stimulation." Ramie saw the fleeting look on Emma's face and covered her mouth. "I'm sorry, darling. I didn't mean..."

"I know what you meant. It's all right. Have you already had breakfast?"

Ramie nodded. "I made some toast. I left two slices with jam on the counter for you."

"Thanks."

By mid-afternoon, Emma decided to use the peace and quiet of the weekend to complete work on an article she was writing for a literary quarterly and had already put off far too long. She showered and changed into more comfortable clothing. She smiled at the difference between her clothing and Ramie's. She ran a hand down the well-washed fabric of Ramie's favorite blouse. It smelled like her lover and brought a smile to her lips. She never believed she would find someone who made her so consistently happy until she met a woman twenty years her junior. A woman who loved her with youthful abandon and made Emma feel younger as well. She hadn't allowed herself to feel this way since...well, in a very long time.

Their lives had settled into a comfortable and familiar rhythm. Emma was surprised at the ease that surrounded their relationship. Could it really be this easy, she wondered. Ramie seemed much more mature than most thirty-one-year-old women. Ramie was loving and considerate, never interfering with Emma's work other than to gently remind her it was getting late and she should get some sleep. It wasn't a demand or plea for sexual gratification. While they enjoyed what Emma believed was a normal, satisfying private life, nothing about it was demanding. They fell asleep touching one another each night, awoke each morning and prepared for work. They chatted about how their work was going over dinner each evening. Their routines were so...normal. Every day, Ramie told Emma she loved her. Emma had proclaimed her undying love for another woman once and meant it, but had still been abandoned. Her love hadn't been enough then and she prayed that her love this time would not leave her life in shambles again.

Emma returned to her work and was adding the final touches to her paper when her thoughts were distracted by the front doorbell. She set her pen down and stood up. A pertinent thought came to mind and she circled a phrase before walking the short distance between her office and the front room, glancing around at the tidy furniture. She opened the door and found an older couple standing on the front porch. Before Emma could say anything, the woman asked, "Is Laramie Sunderlund here?"

The couple looked vaguely familiar, but Emma couldn't place them. "Yes, she is. And you are?"

"Her parents," the woman said tightly. "And who are you?"

"Uh, Emma Rothenberg. This is my house."

The women frowned. "Could we speak to our daughter?"

"Of course," Emma answered, trying to keep her voice steady. She vaguely remembered catching a brief glimpse of two people over ten years earlier entering the hospital recovery room as she was leaving. "She's in her workshop. I'll get her. Please, come in and have a seat." Emma pushed the screen open and waited for the couple to enter before excusing herself.

She headed outside, unsure of how she felt about the unannounced appearance of her lover's parents. Ramie had flown to Vermont for Thanksgiving and a week at Christmas. Both times she asked Emma to accompany her, but Emma had begged off, claiming she had work she needed to complete. In truth, she hadn't wanted to face what would, no doubt, be an awkward meeting. She faced hostile parents once in her life and lost that battle. She wasn't prepared to repeat that. Now they were standing in her living room.

Emma opened the door of the workshop, now messier than it was a few months before. Ramie was examining a stone slab on the table in front of her, running her hands over it, her ubiquitous headphones covering her ears, and her body swaying slightly to whatever beat she was listening to as she marked lines on the slab. Emma thought the scene was adorable and hated to interrupt it. Finally, she stepped behind Ramie and slid her arms around her waist, savoring the feel of Ramie's body against hers. No matter how much she tried to ignore it, Ramie's warmth aroused her. Ramie pulled her headphones down around her neck as she pivoted in Emma's arms and pushed onto her tiptoes to kiss her. "Hello, darling," she said. "I've been waiting for that."

"Your parents are here," Emma said.

"What?"

"Your parents are here," Emma repeated calmly. "Were you expecting them?"

"No." Ramie frowned as she took Emma's hand. She removed her headphones, unclipped the Walkman attached to her waist, and tossed them on the workbench before they walked back toward the house. As she always did, Emma glanced at *Untouchable*. Its beauty never failed to take her breath away. She reached around Ramie to open the back door and followed her inside. "Do you want me to leave you alone to talk?" she whispered.

"No. I want you with me, honey."

Ramie strode into the front room and hugged her parents warmly, but Emma saw them looking at her. Emma asked, "Would either of you care for tea or coffee? Ramie?"

"Coffee would be wonderful, darling. Mom? Dad?" After subtle nods from the couple, Ramie said, "Coffee all around. Let's have a seat, shall we?" Ramie perched on one corner of the couch and drew her feet up beneath her while Emma was grateful to retreat into the kitchen to attend to a task she could accomplish without being pulled into what would undoubtedly be a strained conversation. When she returned, she set a tray holding their cups, along with sugar and creamer, on the coffee table and joined Ramie on the couch. Ramie took a sip and said, "It's wonderful, Em. Thank you." Then she turned her attention to her mother and father. They both looked a little stiff and uncomfortable. "Mom, Dad," she started, smiling at Emma. "This is Dr. Emma Rothenberg and this is her home." Ramie shifted her eyes to her parents. "To what do we owe this rather impromptu visit?"

"We haven't heard from you in a while and, since next week is your birthday, we decided to drive down and surprise you," Mrs. Sunderlund said. "When we didn't find you at home, we drove to the art department. Dr. Joyner suggested we might find you here. Obviously she was correct."

"I wish you had called first. We would have planned something," Ramie said.

"I did call, but you apparently were unavailable," Mrs. Sunderlund replied. As she sipped her coffee, her eyes drifted over Emma. "Barry called before we left. He's trying to get a jump on next fall's schedule before the summer break and needs to know when you'll return. You need to contact him soon."

Ramie glanced at Emma and answered the question she saw in her eyes. "Barry Fredrickson, the chairman of the art department at Vermont."

Emma saw the look in Amie Sunderlund's blue eyes. If looks could kill, Emma would almost assuredly be a corpse. She didn't know what to say.

"You only took a temporary leave of absence," Amie continued. "He assumes you will be returning for the fall semester."

"I know what he expects, Mother, but my time here won't be over for a few more weeks," Ramie said. "Barry knows that." She glanced at Emma. "But I've decided to remain here. I won't be returning to Vermont."

"What?" Mrs. Sunderlund said, jerking her head up as a shocked look ran across her face.

"Emma's—" Ramie began.

"I've asked Ramie to share my home and she's accepted," Emma interrupted.

"It's the right decision," Ramie answered. She reached out and took Emma's hand.

"How old are you, Dr. Rothenberg?" Ramie's mother asked abruptly.

"Fifty-two," Emma admitted.

"Our daughter isn't even thirty-one yet. She's practically a child!"

"Age is irrelevant, Mother," Ramie said.

"We have never interfered with how you chose to live your life or with your personal decisions, but..." Mrs. Sunderlund began as she looked at Ramie.

"If you're planning to start now, then save your breath, Mother. I'm considering what's right for me as far as the future is concerned."

"Your position here will be over in less than a month," Mrs. Sunderlund said. She shot a withering glance at Emma.

"I'm aware of that," Ramie said.

"What are you planning to do then, Ramie? Let your *lover* support you?"

"Mother! That's incredibly insulting, even for you," Ramie said.

"How long have you...uh...been together?" Mr. Sunderlund asked.

Ramie smiled at her father. "Since early in November, I think."

"Why didn't you tell us you were living with someone when you were home at Thanksgiving or Christmas?" Mrs. Sunderlund asked, shaking her head. "Or, were you ashamed because she's twice you age?"

"I'm not ashamed of anything! I don't need your permission for anything I do! No matter what you think, I know what's best for me!"

"Don't get excited, Ramie," Mr. Sunderlund said calmly. He looked at Emma. "Our daughter is a grown woman, accustomed to making her own decisions without consulting us."

"But living with a woman *her* age!" Mrs. Sunderlund said, pointing at Emma.

After several awkward, silent moments, Emma cleared her throat and leaned forward to rest her elbows on her knees. "I admit I never envisioned living with a woman as young...or as lovely as your daughter. No one was more shocked than I that she was interested in pursuing a relationship with me. I hope to treasure her for as long as she will allow it. She has filled a place in my life that I allowed to remain neglected for too long and I am grateful for that." Emma stood and said, "I have never been in this situation before and am slightly uncertain what is expected of me, but we have a guest room if you wish to stay here during your visit. Now if you'll excuse me, I need to get dinner started."

RAMIE SMILED AS Emma left the room. "Do either of you have any further questions, comments, or insults you'd care to toss out?"

Larry finished his coffee and shrugged. "It seems obvious to me Dr. Rothenberg cares for you, Ramie. Although she isn't what we anticipated, I'm sure we'll find a way to adjust."

Amie folded her arms over her chest and leaned back with a frown. Larry nudged her arm and said, "I seem to remember your parents not being that fond of me either, honey."

"My father was ready to grab his shotgun and blow your brains out, especially after I told him I was pregnant," Amie said. She looked at Ramie and added, "I haven't heard her say she loves you yet, Ramie."

"She tells me every day," Ramie said defensively. "Do I need to record it for you?"

"Have you considered that she may simply be using you?"

"For what? There's very little I can offer her. She's not a dirty old man who's trying to prove his virility, for God's sake. I've considered everything I need to. I love her and know she loves me. What more could I possibly ask for?"

"What does she do? Teach?"

"She's actually the new head of the English Department."

"She's obviously not an idiot then," Amie retorted. "She has to know you'll come to your senses eventually and find someone more suitable. Until then, I suppose I'll have to learn to respect your decision. But that doesn't mean I have to like it."

EMMA BEGAN PEELING potatoes over the sink. Her hands were shaking and she clenched them into fists. A light touch on her back startled her. "Are you all right, darling?"

"I'll be fine," Emma mumbled. "Are they staying?"

"Yes, but will leave if their being here upsets you."

"I made the offer, Ramie. I'll let you show them to the guest room and get them settled while I finish dinner."

"Look at me, Emma," Ramie said softly.

Emma glanced over her shoulder.

"Really look at me," Ramie pressed.

Emma took a deep breath and turned to face Ramie.

"They know I wouldn't be here, with you, if I didn't want to be. Please don't ever doubt that I love you, Em." She stroked Emma's cheek.

"They look at me like I'm a child molester," Emma said. "I'm sorry, sweetheart. I simply wasn't prepared. You should have mentioned you were living here."

"I won't officially be living here until the end of the semester. I'll show them the guest room while you finish cooking."

Emma knew she shouldn't feel so insecure. "How long will they be staying?"

"Until my birthday, if that's all right."

"It's fine."

Much later that night, after a still somewhat uncomfortable conversation over dinner, Emma left the bathroom adjoining the master bedroom. Ramie smiled and turned the cover back, revealing an enticing, naked body. "You *cannot* be serious," Emma whispered. "Your parents are sleeping right below us."

"I won't change how I behave because they're here, Emma. Now remove that ridiculous nightgown and come to bed. You look like Mother Hubbard, for God's sake."

As Emma settled beside Ramie, she felt her warm body shaking with laughter. "What?" she asked.

"I've never seen you so inhibited," Ramie snorted.

"I'm not accustomed to having my lover's parents in my house...our house."

"Your lover. Umm, I like the sound of that," Ramie sighed as she rolled into Emma's arms and began tracing lazy patterns on her abdomen with a fingertip. "Touch me, darling."

"Please, Ramie. Don't make this any more difficult than it already is."

"What's wrong, baby?" Ramie teased as she felt Emma's body react to her touches.

"Now you're just being a brat," Emma huffed.

Ramie scooted up slightly and found Emma's lips. "And since I am a brat, I'm used to getting what I want," she said against Emma's lips. "So give up and make love to me the way only you can." Her tongue teased Emma's mouth until her lips parted allowing Ramie to slip inside as her hand skimmed over Emma's body.

Emma groaned as her hand found its way into silken blonde tresses. When Ramie finally pulled her mouth away. Emma panted, "God. You don't play fair." She pushed Ramie onto her back and lowered her mouth to her lover's breast, encircling the already tight, erect nipple.

"Neither...do you," Ramie hissed as her body rose to meet Emma's.

Emma surrendered herself to the pleasure she felt. They swallowed one another's cries until both were exhausted. Ramie rested her head on Emma's shoulder and softly stroked her body until sleep claimed them.

WHEN EMMA AWAKENED the next morning, Ramie was

still sound asleep, her curly hair splayed around her head. Emma couldn't look at her peaceful face without smiling. This was how life was supposed to be and she felt a happiness she hadn't known for too many years. She owed it all to the woman beside her. She quietly slipped from beneath the bed covers and quickly dressed before making her way downstairs. When she entered the kitchen, she found Larry Sunderlund standing in front of the kitchen window drinking a cup of coffee.

"Good morning, Dr. Rothenberg," he said cheerfully.

Emma took a cup from the cupboard and filled it, offering him a refill. "Emma, please," she said as she topped off his cup.

"You have a lovely place here. I was just admiring your garden."

"Ramie helped me with it. Would you like to see her studio?"

He nodded and Emma led him into the back yard. "I liked this house because while the front yard is small and easy to maintain, the back is quite spacious. And it's close enough to the university that I can walk to work most days."

"That's a beautiful statue," he commented as he stared at *Untouchable*. "It's one of Ramie's, isn't it?"

Emma smiled. "Yes. Ramie gave it to me as a gift even though I offered to pay her handsomely for it."

"She worked on it while she was recuperating from her…her assault. Do her hands still bother her?" he asked.

Emma smiled, remembering how deftly Ramie's hands had moved over her body the night before. "They don't seem to, Mr. Sunderlund," she answered.

"Larry."

"This is where Ramie creates her work now, Larry," Emma said as she opened the workshop door and stepped inside. "You'll have to excuse the temporary mess, but we've only recently moved her tools and materials here from the university."

"She still has quite a bit in her loft at home," Larry said. "Hope she can get everything in here." Larry walked in and looked around. "What's she working on now?"

"I'm not sure what she's calling it yet."

"I think I'll entitle it Woodland Wonderland," Ramie said from behind them. She crossed the room and set her coffee cup on her worktable before slipping her arm around Emma's waist. "You should have awakened me, honey," she said as Emma leaned down to kiss her forehead.

Ramie looked at her father. "Has Mother recovered from her snit yet?"

"She will, but she'll always worry about you, you know," Larry answered. "I think you're in good hands with Emma, but your mother may be harder to convince."

"She'll be okay." Ramie glanced up at Emma. "Maybe we can go to Vermont over the summer break."

"Perhaps," Emma said. "Your father told me you still have some things up there we'll need to move."

"Maybe after lunch when everyone is wide awake, we can show you where I've spent the last year working. Then perhaps I can talk you into helping me move my things here from my current residence."

"At least it will give me something to do," Larry laughed.

"I noticed a few weeds coming up in the garden," Ramie said, patting Emma's stomach. "I'll fix breakfast and let you attack them."

"You're cooking?" Emma asked.

"I know *how* to cook, sweetie. I just prefer not to unless it's an emergency," Ramie smirked. "Besides, you'd be amazed what I can whip up in a popcorn popper, if necessary."

Emma opened the addition to Ramie's studio and walked in to find her gardening tools. When she stepped out she was surprised to find Amie Sunderlund waiting for her, arms folded over her chest. She swallowed hard and took a deep breath. "What can I do for you, Mrs. Sunderlund?" she asked, envisioning another semi-confrontation. Truthfully, if she had a daughter as alluring as Ramie, she might feel the same way.

"Ramie suggested you might need some assistance," Amie said. "But I think she may be hoping you and I can reach some sort of...accord."

"Is that what you want as well?"

Amie cocked her head to one side. "Frankly, I wish my daughter had never met you. But she has always been strong-willed. I should have expected something like this. Where did you meet?"

Emma dropped a foam kneepad in front of the garden and knelt on it. "She was a student in one of my classes the year she was...uh...hurt." She couldn't force herself to look at Amie, but decided to tell the woman everything she knew. "She was an enchanting young woman and a capable student in a class she had no genuine interest in. One of the men who attacked her was my former assistant. I overheard them having a heated argument not long before the attack."

"But you didn't warn her," Amie said through gritted teeth.

"I never dreamed the situation would go as far as it did. If I'd known, I would have done *anything* to protect her from that pain and suffering." Emma felt a tear fall onto her cheek and quickly wiped it away. "I'm so sorry."

"You're the woman who claimed to be Ramie's aunt at the hospital, aren't you?" Amie asked.

"The hospital wouldn't allow anyone other than a family member in and she was so afraid. I couldn't leave her there alone and frightened. She was only a child."

"She still is," Amie said as she dropped to her knees next to Emma and ran her hands through the dirt in the garden. She grasped a handful and raised it to her nose. "I love the earthy smell of the soil. It holds the promise of life. Thank you for watching over Ramie until we arrived. I know now why she came back to Overland. She wasn't happy after we brought her home, but she seems content now and apparently, you're the reason. But if you *ever* hurt her, I *swear* you'll regret it."

Chapter Twenty-one

EMMA'S EYES FLUTTERED open and she stretched in an attempt to wake up. She and Ramie spent a few days in Vermont packing the sculpting materials Ramie had stored at her parents' home and arrived back in Ohio late the day before. Exhausted, they fell asleep early and Emma had slept like the dead. When she reached across the bed, she was a little surprised to find herself alone. She rolled out of the bed, pulling her terrycloth robe over her shoulders. The sun was shining brightly in the early fall sky. She groaned remembering the stacks of paperwork on her desk still awaiting her attention before the new semester began, as well as a series of budgetary meetings on her calendar.

She made her way downstairs and into the kitchen. Ramie had made a pot of coffee and was probably in her workshop, as usual. Walking carefully out the back door, Emma made her way to Ramie's refuge. Ramie turned slightly and smiled when she saw Emma. When Emma stopped behind her, Ramie set her tools on the worktable and turned. She grabbed the edges of Emma's robe and pulled her into a hungry morning kiss. While Emma tried to find a stable place to set her coffee down, Ramie's cool hands wandered into Emma's robe to touch the warm skin inside, making Emma jump slightly.

"You're up early," Emma muttered against Ramie's lips. "I thought you would sleep in after yesterday's long drive. You should have gotten me up."

Ramie's hands slid over Emma's butt cheeks and kneaded them, drawing Emma closer. "You were sleeping so soundly I didn't want to disturb you," Ramie said as she nibbled along Emma's upper chest. "I love watching you sleep."

"Well, I'm awake now," Emma said, her hands tangling in Ramie's curly hair. "You have very strong hands, you know."

Ramie withdrew her hands, holding them up and wiggling her fingers. "These old things?" she asked with a smile.

Emma took Ramie's hands and brought them to her mouth, lavishing each with kisses before releasing them. Ramie turned back around and picked up Emma's cup for a drink. "Have you given any more thought to the departmental fall get-together?" Ramie asked nonchalantly.

"No," Emma replied. "But obviously you have."

"It's an annual event, you know. I thought we could erect a

few canopy tents and hold it outdoors this year while the weather is still warm."

"I was considering a brunch or something. It's the simplest thing to do. I can have it catered. A sort of come and go affair."

"Still afraid people will look at us like we're freaks?" Ramie asked.

"Anyone with two eyes and a brain has to know we are...uh...you know," Emma said uncomfortably.

"What? That we're lovers?" Ramie covered her mouth and her eyes widened in horror. "You mean those two nice women actually...sleep together...in the same bed!" She laughed as Emma glared at her. "Actually, I thought we should host something here and I can be your hostess."

"When were you planning to find the time, Ramie? Between your work and my schedule, I think my idea is easier."

Ramie covered Emma's hand with her own. "I'll find a few people to help me. Let me do this, Em. I know a few frat boys who might be willing to act as security if you're afraid of an English Department riot," she teased.

"If you insist, then all right," Emma huffed. "Your mother did warn me that you were occasionally stubborn."

"Oh, really?" Ramie asked with a laugh. "And what else did she tell you?"

"Not much. She wanted me to promise I'd never hurt you." Emma shrugged. "I hope I won't, but I couldn't promise not to. Neither can you."

"Why? Are you still waiting for me to leave you?"

Emma shook her head. "Perhaps. But for now you make me incredibly happy." She smiled. "And I like being happy very much."

"I promise to make you even happier later." Ramie waggled her eyebrows suggestively.

"I'm sure you will, darling," Emma laughed.

Their discussion was interrupted by the ringing of the phone in the studio. Emma released Ramie and said, "I'll get it."

"If it's your secret girlfriend, tell her you'll be too tired to see her later because I already have plans to wear your ass out," Ramie quipped as she picked up Emma's coffee cup and took a sip.

Emma looked over her shoulder and smiled. "She already knows that."

Ramie choked on her drink as Emma laughed before answering the phone. "It's Sylvia," she said, handing the receiver to Ramie.

Emma finished her coffee and carried it into the house, where she stacked dishes from the night before in the sink. She had just squirted dishwashing liquid into the water when she felt Ramie's body press against her back.

"Mmm. I love the way you feel, baby," Ramie moaned.

"What did Sylvia want, besides her usual attempts at phone seduction?" Emma asked.

"She wants me to drop by her office Friday afternoon. There's some evaluation paperwork she needs me to sign before she can submit her final report about my stay last year." She slid her hands up to Emma's shoulders and began massaging them.

"Oooh, you keep doing that and I might fall asleep right here," Emma hummed.

"That's okay. I know how to wake you up," Ramie giggled as she tickled Emma's sides.

Emma spun around quickly and grabbed Ramie's wrists. "Be careful or you might awaken the beast," she growled.

Ramie smiled. "God, I hope so."

Emma pulled her closer against her body and lowered her mouth to Ramie's ear. "You're the only one who has ever coaxed the beast out," she whispered.

"I'm so ready for you, baby," Ramie groaned, as she tried to free her hands.

But Emma held them firmly. Her eyes darkened as growing desire coursed through her body. Her thigh pressed firmly into Ramie's crotch. Ramie rode Emma's thigh, pressing harder with each stroke of her hips. "Please, baby," Ramie whimpered as her body moved urgently against Emma's. "Let me touch you!"

Emma's eyes looked hazy and slightly unfocused, but she continued to hold Ramie as she lowered her lips to cover her tight nipple through her thin t-shirt, eliciting a tortured gasp. Ramie bucked hard against her and threw her head back. Emma released her to place one hand on Ramie's back to press her breast closer as her other hand worked into the elastic waist of her loose cotton lounging pants and over the slick folds that greeted her. She slipped into Ramie's center and felt her fingers being drawn in by the constricting muscles. "Come for me, baby," she managed as she lightly bit the distended nipple. Ramie's body stiffened as her orgasm raced through her while Emma continued to stroke her gently until she collapsed in her lover's arms.

"Ohmygod," Ramie panted, trying to catch her breath. "That had to be the beast *and* her sister."

"Our very own *menage à trois*," Emma murmured against Ramie's ear. "Now I need to get dressed for work."

"What?" Ramie asked, her eyes still slightly unfocused.

Emma chuckled before kissing her lightly. "I'd love to stay

and play, but I have a meeting with Dean Campbell in about an hour."

"That's so not fair, Emma," Ramie pouted.

"Well, would you rather I left you unsatisfied?" Emma asked with a smile.

"You never leave me unsatisfied, darling. Try to come home on time tonight."

"I will," Emma promised, stepping back and leaving Ramie standing alone in the kitchen.

RAMIE TURNED THE doorknob of her studio and walked inside. She picked up her headphones and slipped them over her ears before turning the volume on her Walkman up. She stared at the wooden crates the movers delivered from Vermont, standing against the far wall. Today she would unpack them and reorganize her workspace. She rolled a triangular platform in front of the first crate and locked the wheels in place before wrestling one edge of the crate onto the platform. She slid the crate slowly onto the platform and unlocked the wheels, rolling it toward her workbench. She picked up a small crowbar and began prying the lid of the crate off. The contents were heavily wrapped in a pliable foam material to protect each item.

She reached up to grab the rope to an overhead hoist and tied it around the largest item. Satisfied it was secured, she moved to a second rope wrapped around a heavy cleat attached to a wall beam, placed a foot against the wall, and began pulling to remove the heavy item. Within minutes she lowered it onto the workbench and wound the rope back around the cleat. She found a carton cutter and cut through the protective foam to reveal a slab of pink marble. She ran her hand over the face of the slab and took a deep breath. Eventually this, along with others, would be stored in a studio closet for future use.

The idea of her every dream coming true brought a smile to her lips as she pulled a bandanna from her back pocket to wipe the sweat from her face.

A flash of blinding pain, partially deflected by her headphones, ran across the back of her head. She fell to her knees and fought the sudden nausea attacking her body. The headphones were ripped off and a hand under her chin pulled her head back roughly before she heard a voice rumble into her ear.

"You don't know how much I'm planning to enjoy this," a deep voice hissed. "I can't promise the same for you though."

Fingers slid around her throat and began squeezing. Ramie was too disoriented to fight back and her eyelids fluttered as she struggled to breathe. She managed to raise a hand to the fingers relentlessly tightening around her neck as darkness began stealing her sight. Ramie opened her mouth, but no sound left her lips as she felt her body slip into the blackness of the unknown.

Chapter Twenty-two

EMMA LEANED BACK in one of the leather chairs that surrounded the large walnut conference table in a room near Dean Campbell's office. She had stopped listening to the budget discussion for the College of Arts and Sciences programs several minutes earlier. Her only concern was the English Department. While interesting topics, she cared very little about anthropology, history, or political science. She doodled aimlessly on the legal pad in front of her.

She smiled to herself remembering how Ramie's body had felt as it responded to her touch that morning. It had been incredibly hot and pliant beneath her fingertips. She never thought anything could be more meaningful to her than her chosen profession. But she'd been wrong. Ramie was more important than anything. She frowned slightly and re-arranged her body into a more comfortable position. But how long would her relationship with Ramie last, the creature in her mind called doubt asked. She shook her head to drive it away.

A second legal pad slid in front of her. "Whatcha thinkin' about?" Sylvia Joyner had written.

Emma drew a zero and moved the pad back.

"Is that a zero or something incredibly dirty...and hot?" Sylvia quickly penned.

"Shut up!" Emma wrote back.

"That's cute," came the reply.

"What is?"

"You're blushing! I'm jealous!"

Before she could reply again, Emma was called upon to give her monthly report and her justifications for unexpected budget requests. As she opened a folder in front of her, she caught the smirk on Sylvia's face out of the corner of her eye and cleared her throat before beginning.

RAMIE GROANED AND blinked to cleared her vision. She wasn't sure what had happened as she tried to roll over. Her head throbbed, her fingers tingled, and her brain felt like it was wrapped in gauze. She vaguely remembered not being able to breathe. Her throat hurt when she attempted to swallow. She heard a steady, metallic, clinking sound and twisted her head, looking for its source. Still blinking to clear her vision, her eyes swept over the crates she'd started unpacking and her workbench before stopping at a pair of jean-clad legs standing at her feet. Her gaze traveled quickly up his body to his face. A neatly trimmed beard and moustache covered his lower face and as he gazed down at her his lips curled into a smile that didn't extend to his eyes, which blazed with hatred.

She tried to sit up, but then saw that her wrists were bound tightly by a thin zip tie. The stiff plastic threatened to cut into her skin. Almost any movement caused pain. The man squatted next to her and took the end of the plastic strip, pulling it a few notches tighter. The pain was excruciating as she tried to position her hands to alleviate the pressure biting into her skin.

"I can make it tighter," he said nonchalantly. "But you wouldn't like it."

"What do you want?" Ramie ground out as she fought against the pain.

"Nothing. I'm simply killing time, entertaining myself, until Emma comes home to join us. Then I can entertain myself with both of you. Won't that be fun? I know it will be for me."

"W...who are you?" Ramie asked through gritted teeth.

He stood and took something off the workbench before squatting down again. He tapped two of her chisels together and her eyes widened.

"These shut you up the last time," he said gruffly. "Think they'll work again?" He laughed as she forced her hands into fists despite the pain.

Ramie wiggled her body in an attempt to get away from him. Travis Whitman! He had hurt her once before, but she couldn't allow it to happen again. God only knew what he might do to Emma. Her hands were numb. They were red and swollen, making the strip binding them together even tighter. If she did nothing, she could lose the use of her hands. Not to mention her life.

"You don't need to hurt Emma. She's done nothing to you," Ramie said as calmly as possible.

"She had me fired! Because of you!"

"Because I told her what you wanted," she lied.

"I knew it! You just couldn't keep your fucking mouth shut."

A hard slap across her face stung, but before she could recover he jammed the chisel under the zip tie and twisted it. He forced a rag into her mouth to muffle her scream. It obstructed her ability to breathe and she choked on it as she flailed her legs to push away from him. Tears from the pain of the zip tie cutting into her wrists filled her eyes as she kicked at him, her lungs burning, desperate to take a breath.

The studio door burst open and a loud, angry scream broke the air as Ramie saw Emma charge in and swing an object like a baseball bat at Travis. It struck him solidly along the side of the head. He fell back. Emma raised the object again and slammed it down across his forehead.

Blood ran in rivulets along the side of his head and he didn't move.

Emma dropped to her knees and jerked the rag from Ramie's mouth. A second later Ramie coughed and gasped for a breath as she attempted to speak.

"M...my h...hands," she rasped.

"Son of a bitch." Emma grabbed a pair of wire-cutters from the workbench. She carefully examined the object now buried in Ramie's wrists. She slid the tip of the wire-cutters under the zip tie and cut through it, releasing the pressure. Ramie curled her arms up against her chest and groaned as circulation flooded into her numb fingers.

Ramie heard a noise and her eyes widened. "Behind—" she started, but Travis grabbed Emma's shirt before she could turn around. Emma swung an arm and her elbow struck his nose before he could duck. He released her and fell against the workbench before stumbling to the ground. The marble slab Ramie had unpacked earlier teetered slowly back and forth before it began to settle again.

Ramie, still cradling her hands against her chest, used her legs to move her body around and drew them up. She looked at Emma and said, "Move!" Then she kicked the workbench. The slab rocked precariously and she kicked the workbench again. She watched as the slab tumbled over the edge and onto Travis Whitman with a sickening crunch of bone as it crushed his skull.

Ramie felt herself being gently gathered into Emma's arms. "Hang on, baby, while I call 9-1-1," Emma said as she cradled Ramie against her chest and pulled her cell from the pocket of her suit. Ramie shivered at the sight of blood crawling across the studio floor.

Chapter Twenty-three

EMMA PULLED INTO her driveway and turned off the ignition. She glanced across the front seat to where Ramie was dozing. She reached over to brush thick strands of blonde curls away from Ramie's face and smiled at the blessedly peaceful softness of her features. Ramie's hands, no longer swollen, rested limply on her thighs. The sight of the white bandages encircling her wrists, made Emma's heart clench remembering the plastic that had cut into her skin. Although there was still some pain, Ramie was able to move her fingers and draw her hands into fists before she was released from the hospital. It took two days for the swelling to diminish, but according to her doctor, Ramie hadn't suffered any permanent damage as a result of Whitman's attack.

Emma opened the car door and quietly shut it, looking around the back yard. She walked to Ramie's studio and took a deep breath as she opened the door. After Whitman's body was removed, she contacted a company in Columbus that specialized in cleaning crime scenes. They worked around the clock to remove any hint of what happened inside the small building. She closed the studio door and walked back to her car, opening the passenger side door. She leaned in and placed a soft kiss on Ramie's forehead. Ramie's eyes snapped open, but relaxed when she saw Emma's face.

"We're home, baby," Emma said with a smile. She held a hand out. "Let me help you." Careful not to touch Ramie's wrists, she took her elbow and guided her out of the vehicle. She placed an arm around Ramie's waist, walking slowly toward the house. Ramie leaned against Emma as she unlocked the back door.

"Why do I feel so damn tired and weak?" Ramie asked.

"It's the painkillers, I think. The doctor wants you to rest."

"Well, turning me into a zombie probably isn't what he had in mind," Ramie muttered, her speech slurring slightly.

"Let me get you into bed, then I'll bring in your things."

A lop-sided smile cut across Ramie's mouth. "You'll do anything to get me in your bed, won't you?" she giggled.

"I prefer my women conscious," Emma answered, struggling to get Ramie up the stairs.

"You're no fun," Ramie whined.

Emma stopped at the top of the stairs to catch her breath, then led Ramie into the bedroom. Ramie sat on the edge of the bed, playing with Emma's hair when she knelt down to remove Ramie's shoes.

"Kiss me, Emma," she said softly.

"After you've slept off the painkiller," Emma said, looking up.

"I killed a man," Ramie muttered. She blinked hard. "Why don't I feel sorry about that?"

"It was self-defense, sweetie. You saved me. You saved us both." Emma stroked the side of Ramie's face.

Ramie shook her head. "I wanted him to die. I wanted him to die for what he did to me. All I could think about was the pain he caused. He had to pay for that!" Her voice got louder with each statement.

Emma stood and pulled Ramie against her, unsure what she could say. She had seen the aftermath of both attacks and understood the simmering anger Ramie was holding inside. She couldn't say she was upset about the death of Travis Whitman, even though it may have been a tragedy. But it was one he'd brought on himself.

"Lie back, sweetheart," Emma said. "You'll feel better after a nap. Then I'll fix you some real food."

"Stay with me. Just until I fall asleep. Please," Ramie pleaded.

"Of course." Emma climbed over Ramie. Then she snugged her body against her, slipping an arm over Ramie's waist. Almost unconsciously she began the same routine she did most nights, running her fingers lightly over Ramie's hips, down her thighs, and back up over the swell of her buttocks before beginning the process again. Her eyelids grew heavy as she inhaled the fresh citrus scent of Ramie's shampoo. Ramie's steady, deep breaths gradually lulled Emma to sleep.

Fingers moving across Emma's forehead awakened her. When she looked up, Ramie was staring down at her, the only light in the room coming from the half-moon hanging high in the night sky.

"Feeling better?" Emma asked, her voice raspy from sleep.

"A little," Ramie mumbled. Her eyes shimmered with a distant look in the moonlight.

"Welcome home," Emma whispered as her hand slipped into Ramie's curly hair, drawing her into a soft kiss. But the passion Emma usually felt in Ramie's lips was missing.

"I'm sorry," Ramie said when Emma brought the brief kiss to an end. She rolled over, her back to Emma.

She's leaving me, Emma thought as she stared into the darkness above her. *Because I couldn't protect her.* Tears of loss trickled slowly down her temple and into her hairline. She always thought Ramie would leave one day, but she hadn't expected it this soon. She had even begun to think her happiness could last forever. She should have listened to the inner voice that cautioned her.

For that moment all she wanted was a final chance to feel the warmth of Ramie's body against hers, breathe in the scents that were uniquely hers. Then there were the memories of Ramie's hands on her body, the feel of her mouth, the caresses that made her lose her mind with desire, and the pleasure she'd never known before. The constant invitation she found in Ramie's deep blue eyes when she thought Emma wasn't looking. Despite all of that, she wouldn't beg her not to leave, not to walk away and leave Emma's life in shambles again.

After that night, Emma worked later hours than usual and was exhausted by the time she dragged herself home. Many nights Ramie wasn't home waiting for her. There were no more intimate moments between them, no more lingering looks, or affectionate touches, but neither was willing to discuss it.

Finally, after nearly two weeks of long, silent evenings, filled with nothing more than small, inconsequential comments, Emma set her fork down on her plate and looked at Ramie. "Are you going to tell me what's wrong?" she asked. "This nothingness between us is driving me crazy."

"Sorry," Ramie muttered.

"Saying you're sorry isn't good enough, Ramie. Talk to me, for God's sake."

"I can't right now."

"Why?"

"I need time to think."

"About what? Us?"

"Of course not! How can you ask me that?"

Emma began holding up one finger at a time. "You barely speak to me. You haven't touched me in weeks. You refuse to let me touch you. You don't answer when I call. You're gone when I come home. Do I need to continue?"

"No," Ramie said.

Emma shifted her gaze to the table, afraid to ask the next question, but needing to. "Is there…someone else?"

"No."

Emma shoved her chair back and stood. She placed her dishes in the sink and strode out of the kitchen, leaving Ramie alone. She went into her home office, lit a cigarette, and poured a stiff drink. She inhaled deeply and quickly swallowed her drink, hoping to drown the hurt and anger she was feeling. Her hands shook as she poured a second drink. She always knew Ramie would leave her, but wasn't prepared when the day came. She heard a light tap on the office door frame, but ignored it, too filled with her own thoughts.

"I'm sorry," Ramie said quietly from behind Emma.

"You've already said that," Emma managed, crushing out her cigarette.

"I don't know what to do."

Emma set her glass down and forced herself to move closer to Ramie. "I know you're not happy, but I don't know what I've done."

When Ramie looked up at Emma, the blue of her eyes was swimming in tears. "You...you haven't done anything. I...I killed a man," she stammered as tears fell to her cheeks.

Unable to stop herself, Emma tried to take Ramie into her arms to comfort her. "It was self-defense. You did what you had to do to survive, Ramie."

Ramie pushed Emma away. "But I'm *glad* he's dead. I'm glad! I wanted to kill him. I can't just go on like nothing's happened. You can't understand how it feels, knowing I'm a murderer."

"You're not!" Emma insisted. "He caused his own death. Do you seriously think he would have stopped until he killed you? Killed both of us?"

"I need to go away and be alone to sort everything out. Get my mind straight again."

"You're leaving me?"

"Yes. I think it's the best thing. I've lost myself and need to find me again." Ramie reached out toward Emma, but Emma pulled back.

Emma's voice was hard when she said, "You're right. You should leave."

Ramie turned to walk out of the office, pausing for a moment before disappearing from view. Emma didn't follow her.

THE DEPARTMENTAL GET-TOGETHER was scheduled for a Friday evening and even though her heart wasn't in it, Emma took the day off to get everything set up. The only thing missing was Ramie. Fortunately, Ramie had already made arrangements to have the tents set up and discussed the final arrangements with the caterer. Howard and the Westmorelands volunteered to come early to complete the decorating and place signs directing guests into the back yard. As Emma was carrying a tray of hors d'oeuvers from the kitchen she saw Frances Westmoreland standing beside her garden, sipping a glass of punch.

"How is it?" Emma asked. "Not too strong?"

"No," Frances said with a smile. "It's perfect, but I wouldn't have more than a couple of glasses." She nodded toward the garden. "I see you still have a green thumb. Your flowers are beautiful."

"Thank you. They smell wonderful through the windows at night."

"That's you, isn't it?" Frances asked, looking at *Untouchable*.

Emma blushed. "No one knows that," she said.

"I'd recognize you anywhere, Emma." She laughed at the look on Emma's embarrassed face. "Did Ramie sculpt it?"

"Yes. During her rehab when she was injured several years ago. I'd appreciate it if no one else knew."

"My lips are sealed," Frances said with a smile. "Where is Ramie?"

"She left. Whitman's death upset her," Emma said. "I should get these canapés where they belong before everyone arrives."

An hour later Emma's back yard was bustling with English professors and their spouses or significant others. Emma mixed with various groups, listening to their discussions and complaints while trying to maintain her composure. She knew she was becoming irritable and sought someplace away from her guests to settle herself. Sylvia joined her, carrying a glass of punch. She smiled as she leaned against the back wall of Emma's house.

"Nice party," Sylvia commented.

"I suppose," Emma said with a shrug. "But I'll be glad when they all decide to wander home. I have a headache from being forced to smile so much."

"A little punch will solve that. A lot of punch will make you forget you ever had a headache. I think someone added a little extra to it."

"God! They're as bad as a group of frat boys," Emma snorted. "Well, I suppose I should resume my mingling to see what they're bitching about now."

"Where's Ramie? I haven't seen her all evening," Sylvia commented.

Emma hesitated before answering. "She's gone," she finally said, unable to look at Sylvia.

"When will she be back? I have a client interested in offering her a commission. It could be quite lucrative."

"Truthfully, she won't be back." Emma reached out and took Sylvia's drink, downing it in two swallows. "I could make a guess, but at the moment, I'm not even sure where she is."

"What are you saying, Emma?"

When Emma looked at Sylvia, her eyes hard and filled with undisguised hurt. "She left me, goddammit," Emma hissed. "I need another glass of that damn punch."

Sylvia grabbed Emma by the arm, stopping her from leaving. "And you let her go? Just like that?"

"It was her decision."

"Did you fight for her?"

"I risked my career, my professional reputation, the respect of my colleagues, everything for her. I can't force anyone to stay with me, Sylvia. It has to be their choice."

"But they never choose you."

"No," Emma said, biting back her pain.

"Ramie did."

EMMA LOCATED HER rental vehicle, unlocked the driver side door, and slid behind the steering wheel. She took time to adjust the mirrors before turning the key in the ignition and lowering the window to let fresh air in and allow the slightly stale odor inside to escape. Emma unfolded a map of the area to check which road she needed to take from the airport. She was in Burlington a few months earlier, but would be driving in an unfamiliar direction this trip. Satisfied she could locate her destination without getting lost, she slung an arm over the front seat, looked behind her, and backed out of the rental slot.

The relatively short drive was amazing. Emma enjoyed watching the trees in Ohio change color each year, but the view of vibrant red, gold, and orange leaves along the road to Ramie's parents' home was magnificent. She slowed and pulled to the side of the highway overlooking a gentle valley not far from her turn-off to scan what Ramie had talked about so many times. Emma could easily see why she loved it so much. The breeze rustling the leaves in the trees around her was cool, bringing a vague hint of the winter to follow within a month or two. Emma signaled and glanced over her shoulder before pulling back onto the highway.

The Sunderlund home hadn't changed much since Emma had spent a tense and uncomfortable week there in June packing the last of Ramie's sculpting materials for shipping to Ohio. If this trip didn't turn out the way Emma hoped, she would be shipping them back to Vermont soon. She parked and stepped out of her car, taking a moment to straighten her clothes and calm her nerves. She wasn't sure Ramie was here, but couldn't think of anywhere else she might have gone. This was where she felt safest.

Emma should have called before flying to Vermont. She had

picked up the phone a dozen times, but hung up before she finished dialing. Ramie needed time away, time alone, away from Emma. She was willing to give Ramie the time she needed although she didn't believe Ramie would return to her. She was too deeply wounded, but Emma had to know Ramie was all right. She had to look into those deep blue eyes one more time and she couldn't do that over the phone. Emma took a deep breath before making her way onto the front porch and knocking on the door. She stepped back and waited. When the door finally opened, the smile on Amie Sunderlund's face disappeared.

"Mrs. Sunderlund." Emma said flatly. "Is Ramie here?"

"No. She went out." Amie's words were clipped as she began to push the door closed.

Emma reached out and stopped it with her hand. "Do you know when she'll return? I need to speak to her," she asked.

"She needs for you to leave her alone now that she's finally coming to her senses. Please leave."

"Who is it, Amie?" Larry Sunderlund asked as he entered the living room. He smiled when he saw Emma standing at the front door. "Emma! It's good to see you again." He looked at his wife. "Well, don't just stand there, Amie. Invite our guest in."

"Dr. Rothenberg was just leaving," Amie said.

"Ridiculous! Not before Ramie gets home," he chuckled.

Amie started for the kitchen as Emma stepped inside. "Thank you, Larry," she said.

"You're welcome here anytime, Emma. Would you like something to drink or eat?" he asked. "We just finished lunch."

"No, thanks. I stopped for something before I came here," Emma said. "I really came up to speak to Ramie. Do you know where she might be or when she will be back? I'm prepared to wait as long as I need to."

Larry frowned. "I'm not sure. She leaves, saying she needs time to think, and comes home when she's ready. I'm worried about her, Emma. She doesn't draw or sculpt anymore."

"Please tell me where she might go. I have to talk to her," Emma insisted.

WITH A LIST of places Ramie could have gone to clutched in her hand, Emma hurried to her rental vehicle. She studied her map and drove back toward the main highway to begin her search. She remembered a small, rocky beach on the shore of Lake Champlain where Ramie had taken her in June. Ramie called it her thinking place. A place she went to work out a problem with a piece she was sculpting.

Emma parked the car and stepped out onto the gravel. The chilly wind off the lake ruffled her hair as she gazed out at ripples of water washing onto the shore. She smiled when her eyes stopped at a huddled figure sitting next to a boulder, blonde curls whipping around her head in the wind. Ramie's arms were wrapped around her legs, which were drawn up to her chest.

Emma leaned back into the car and pulled her jacket from the back seat before carefully making her way down the rocky slope to where Ramie sat gazing over the lake. Ramie flinched when Emma draped her jacket over Ramie's shoulders, but drew it more closely around her body. She pressed her face into the lining before turning to watch Emma lower herself onto the sandy spot beside her. Emma brought her legs up and wrapped her arms around them, matching Ramie's position.

"I'm sorry," Emma said, looking out over the water.

"You didn't do anything," Ramie replied.

"I didn't understand how much you were hurting. I only knew how much I was. I miss you, Ramie. I need you in my life. I'm tired of giving up and won't let you give up either."

"I haven't given up."

"You left me," Emma muttered. "You're letting Travis Whitman win."

"What?"

"You left me."

"I didn't want to stay and hurt you."

"But you did and I was angry." Emma turned to look at Ramie. "Everyone I've ever cared about has left me. Frances because she was young and afraid. My father because he was ashamed of who I was. My sister because I was afraid to let her know who I was. Millie because she was afraid to lose the security her marriage provided. I wasn't brave enough to fight to hold on to any of them. I was a coward, but I won't let a worthless piece of shit like Whitman steal that from me again. He died because of his own actions and took you with him. I love you, Ramie, and will do anything I have to in order to convince you to stay with me. I'm tired of letting fear rule my life."

While Emma spoke, tears trickled down Ramie's cheeks as she continued staring straight ahead. Her hair tousled wildly around her head and Emma brought a hand up in an attempt to tame it. Ramie tilted her head slightly, pressing it against Emma's touch.

"Turn around," Emma said. When Ramie didn't move, she added, "Please."

Ramie swiveled away and Emma placed legs along either side of Ramie's body. "Close your eyes and take deep breaths,"

Emma said in a much lower voice. She placed her hands on Ramie's shoulders and squeezed lightly. She moved one hand up to Ramie's neck, continuing to rub and squeeze. "Too hard?" she asked.

"No," Ramie replied as she dropped her head forward.

Gradually Emma worked her way across Ramie's shoulders and down her arms. Ramie closed her eyes as she began to relax. "I love touching you."

"I was hurting and in a bad place," Ramie said. "I didn't want to take you there with me. I needed to be alone, but didn't mean to hurt you."

"Do you still...love me?" Emma asked haltingly, removing her hands.

Ramie turned to face Emma, searching her face before curling her lips into the smile Emma was used to seeing. She touched Emma's cheek and drew her closer to capture her lips in a deep, hungry kiss. "I'm not afraid, Emma. This time you win," she whispered, hugging Emma tightly. "Take me home," she said.

Emma pressed against Ramie, feeling the heat from Ramie's body warming the deepest, coldest parts of hers. She felt whole again for the first time.

More Brenda Adcock titles:

In the Midnight Hour

What happens when you wake up to find the woman of your dreams in your bed? All-night radio hostess Desdemona, Queen of the Night draws her listening audience with her sultry, seductive voice, the only thing of value she possesses. During the day she becomes an insecure, unattractive woman named Marsha Barrett, living in a world with too many mirrors. She is comfortable with her obscurity until she meets Colleen Walters, a tall, attractive woman hired to expand her listening audience by selling Desdemona to new markets. When she wakes up in bed with Colleen after a night at a club, Marsha is terrified. A woman like Colleen would never go to bed with a woman like Marsha. She might dream about such a thing, but in the harsh reality of daylight, it would never happen. Beauty is only drawn to beauty and Marsha refuses to believe beauty could ever be drawn to anyone who looks like her. Just as she begins to believe happiness may be possible, the past returns determined to destroy them.

ISBN: 978-1-61929-188-1
eISBN: 978-1-61929-187-4

The Chameleon

Six years ago Detective Christine Shaw left her happy life and a good job in Texas to follow her libido to New York City. She's still a cop, but her stewardess girlfriend has flown the coop and Chris hasn't been able to fill the void. Everything in her life begins to change when she and her partner are assigned to a high profile case.

The murder of Broadway star Elaine Barrie propels Chris into a whole new world. A fan of the murdered actress since she was a teenager, Chris isn't prepared for the secrets she uncovers during their investigation, including her attraction to the daughter of her number one suspect.

Was the victim any of the personalities witnesses describe, or was the real person a chameleon, satisfying the expectations of each person she met?

ISBN 978-1-61929-102-7
eISBN: 978-1-61929-103-4

The Game of Denial

Joan Carmichael, a successful New York businesswoman, lost the love of her life ten years earlier. Alone, she raised their four children, always cherishing her deep love for her wife. Her memories of their life together come back even stronger as one of their daughters prepares to marry. Joan and her four adult kids fly to Virginia to meet the groom's family and attend the ceremony at the small horse farm owned by the mother of the fiancé.

Evelyn "Evey" Chase, also a widow, has secrets in her past, and her memories of her dead husband aren't pleasant. She's concerned about meeting her future daughter-in-law's family, certain that she and her three kids will have little in common with the wealthy New Yorkers. Besides, the thought of two women in a relationship bringing up a family together makes her uncomfortable, even though her daughter-in-law assures her that lesbianism is not hereditary or catching.

When the two women meet they are drawn to one another in a way neither anticipated, and the game of denial begins. Evey fights her attraction and doesn't realize the effect she has on Joan. Joan tries to shake off her feelings, seeing them as a betrayal to the memory of her wife. Besides, isn't Evey Chase straight? After Evey and Joan share an intimate moment at the wedding reception, they are both emotionally terrified and Joan flees. Will Joan overcome the feeling of betraying her former mate and stop denying her desire to be happy again? Can Evey finally face her past in order to accept the love of another woman and the desire to live the life she had once dreamed of?

ISBN: 978-1-61929-130-0
eISBN: 978-1-61929-131-7

The Sea Hawk

Dr. Julia Blanchard, a marine archaeologist, and her team of divers have spent almost eighteen months excavating the remains of a ship found a few miles off the coast of Georgia. Although they learn quite a bit about the nineteenth century sailing vessel, they have found nothing that would reveal the identity of the ship they have nicknamed "The Georgia Peach."

Her rescue at sea leads her on an unexpected journey into the true identity of the Peach and the captain and crew who called it their home. Her travels take her to the island of Martinique, the eastern Caribbean islands, the Louisiana German Coast and New Orleans at the close of the War of 1812.

How had the Peach come to rest in the waters off the Georgia coast? What had become of her alluring and enigmatic captain, Simone Moreau? Can love conquer everything, even time?

ISBN 978-1-935053-10-1

Available in print and eBook formats

Pipeline

What do you do when the mistakes you made in the past come back to slap you in the face with a vengeance? Joanna Carlisle, a fifty-seven year old photojournalist, has only begun to adjust to retirement on her small ranch outside Kerrville, Texas, when she finds herself unwillingly sucked into an investigation of illegal aliens being smuggled into the United States to fill the ranks of cheap labor needed to increase corporate profits.

An unexpected visit by her former lover, Cate Hammond, and the attempted murder of their son, forces Jo to finally face what she had given up. Although she hasn't seen Cate or their son for fifteen years, she finds that the feelings she had for Cate had only been dormant, but had never died. No matter how much she fights her attraction to Cate, Jo cannot help but wonder whether she had made the right decision when she chose career and independence over love.

ISBN 978-1-932300-64-2

Available in print and eBook formats

Reiko's Garden

Hatred...like love...knows no boundaries.

How much impact can one person have on a life?

When sixty-five-year old Callie Owen returns to her rural childhood home in Eastern Tennessee to attend the funeral of a woman she hasn't seen in twenty years, she's forced to face the fears, heartache, and turbulent events that scarred both her body and her mind. Drawing strength from Jean, her partner of thirty years, and from their two grown children, Callie stays in the valley longer than she had anticipated and relives the years that changed her life forever.

In 1949, Japanese war bride Reiko Sanders came to Frost Valley, Tennessee with her soldier husband and infant son. Callie Owen was an inquisitive ten-year-old whose curiosity about the stranger drove her to disobey her father for just one peek at the woman who had become the subject of so much speculation. Despite Callie's fears, she soon finds that the exotic-looking woman is kind and caring, and the two forge a tentative, but secret friendship.

When Callie and her five brothers and sisters were left orphaned, Reiko provided emotional support to Callie. The bond between them continued to grow stronger until Callie left Frost Valley as a teenager, emotionally and physically scarred, vowing never to return and never to forgive.

It's not until Callie goes "home" that she allows herself to remember how Reiko influenced her life. Once and for all, can she face the terrible events of her past? Or will they come back to destroy all that she loves?

ISBN 978-1-932300-77-2

Available in print and eBook formats

Redress of Grievances

Harriett Markham is a defense attorney in Austin, Texas, who lost everything eleven years earlier. She had been an associate with a Dallas firm and involved in an affair with a senior partner, Alexis Dunne. Harriett represented a rape/murder client named Jared Wilkes and got the charges dismissed on a technicality. When Wilkes committed a rape and murder after his release, Harriett was devastated. She resigned and moved to Austin, leaving everything behind, including her lover.

Despite lingering feelings for Alexis, Harriet becomes involved with a sex-offense investigator, Jessie Rains, a woman struggling with secrets of her own. Harriet thinks she might finally be happy, but then Alexis re-enters her life. She refers a case of multiple homicide allegedly committed by Sharon Taggart, a woman with no motive for the crimes. Harriett is creeped out by the brutal murders, but reluctantly agrees to handle the defense.

As Harriett's team prepares for trial, disturbing information comes to light. Sharon denies any involvement in the crimes, but the evidence against her seems overwhelming. Harriett is plunged into a case rife with twisty psychological motives, questionable sanity, and a client with a complex and disturbing life. Is she guilty or not? And will Harriet's legal defense bring about justice—or another Wilkes case?

Recipient of a 2008 award from the Golden Crown Literary Society, the premiere organization for the support and nourishment of quality lesbian literature. *Redress of Grievances* won in the category of Lesbian Mystery.

ISBN 978-1-932300-86-4

Available in print and eBook formats

Tunnel Vision

Royce Brodie, a 50-year-old homicide detective in the quiet town of Cedar Springs, a bedroom community 30 miles from Austin, Texas, has spent the last seven years coming to grips with the incident that took the life of her partner and narrowly missed taking her own. The peace and quiet she had been enjoying is shattered by two seemingly unrelated murders in the same week: the first, a John Doe, and the second, a janitor at the local university.

As Brodie and her partner, Curtis Nicholls, begin their investigation, the assignment of a new trainee disrupts Brodie's life. Not only is Maggie Weston Brodie's former lover, but her father had been Brodie's commander at the Austin Police Department and nearly destroyed her career.

As the three detectives try to piece together the scattered evidence to solve the two murders, they become convinced the two murders are related. The discovery of a similar murder committed five years earlier at a small university in upstate New York creates a sense of urgency as they realize they are chasing a serial killer.

The already difficult case becomes even more so when a third victim is found. But the case becomes personal for Brodie when Maggie becomes the killer's next target. Unless Brodie finds a way to save Maggie, she could face losing everything a second time.

ISBN 978-1-935053-19-4-

Available in print and eBook formats

Soiled Dove

In 1872, sixteen-year-old Loretta Digby fled her home in Indiana to escape an abusive step-father. Rescued from the streets of St. Joseph, Missouri by brothel owner Jack Coulter, she turns to the only work available. By twenty she became a much sought after prostitute catering to St. Jo's most influential men and dreaming of the day she can leave her past behind and start her life anew. Working with teacher, Hettie Tobias, who is traveling west for a teaching position in Trinidad, Colorado, Loretta and Amelia leave their former lives behind.

In the foothills of the Sangre de Cristo Mountains outside Trinidad, Clare McIlhenney has been struggling for years to make her father's dream of owning a cattle ranch in the west come true. Working with a few ranch hands and her foreman, Ino Valdez, Clare has slowly built the ranch over the last twenty years while overcoming everything that should have stopped her.

In the spring of 1876 Loretta and her friends arrive in the dusty Colorado town. Her first meeting with Clare McIlhenney is less than inspiring. When Clare is injured, over her strenuous objections, Ino hires Loretta as a temporary cook and housekeeper for the ranch. Over the next few months, Clare struggles with her unwanted attraction to the much younger woman, unable to forget the events of her past that led to the deaths of everyone she had been close to. Determined to never lose anyone else, Clare closed off her emotions and became a distant and disliked stranger to everyone around her.

Will Loretta be able to keep her past a secret and find a new life? Will Clare open herself up to loss yet again and put her own prejudices behind her? In a story of the struggles in a harsh and unforgiving time will the two women find peace at last?

Recipient of a 2011 award from the Golden Crown Literary Society, the premiere organization for the support and nourishment of quality lesbian literature. *Soiled Dove* won in the category of Historical Romance.

ISBN 978-1-935053-35-4

Available in print and eBook formats

The Other Mrs. Champion

Sarah Champion, 55, of Massachusetts, was leading the perfect life with Kelley, her partner and wife of twenty-five years. That is, until Kelley was struck down by an unexpected stroke away from home. But Sarah discovers she hadn't known her partner and lover as well as she thought.

Accompanied by Kelley's long-time friend and attorney, Sarah and her children rush to Vancouver, British Columbia to say their goodbyes, only to discover another woman, Pauline, keeping a vigil over Kelley in the hospital. Confronted by the fact that her wife also has a Canadian wife, Sarah struggles to find answers to resolve her emotional and personal turmoil.

Alone and lonely, Sarah turns to the only other person who knew Kelley as well as she did—Pauline Champion. Will the two women be able to forge a friendship despite their simmering animosity? Will their growing attraction eventually become Kelley's final gift to the women she loved?

ISBN 978-1-935053-46-0
eISBN: 978-1-61929-032-7

Picking Up the Pieces

Athon Dailey hasn't had many breaks in her life other than the ones she made for herself by living up to her reputation as a tough girl until she meets Lauren Shelton, a new girl at school in Duvalle, Texas. Tamed by Lauren's affection, Athon begins to believe there could be a brighter future. When Lauren's parents discover the growing relationship they send her away, making sure the two girls never have contact, leaving Athon alone and abandoned.

Twenty years later the two women meet again. Athon has established a successful military career as a helicopter pilot while Lauren has returned to Duvalle to teach. It doesn't take long for them to rekindle their feelings for one another and they finally get the chance to rebuild their teenage dreams. Permanent happiness is within their grasp when Athon's unit is deployed.

Athon comes home in a coma, diagnosed with a traumatic brain injury. She awakens to find Lauren by her side to welcome her home. When Athon chooses to retire and return to Texas, neither realizes the twists and turns the journey home will take. The Athon Dailey who returned to Lauren is not the woman she remembers. In order for their relationship to survive, Lauren begins her search for the woman she loves. Will Athon finally find her way back to Lauren and the dream they both once had? Does Lauren have the courage to live with a woman who is now a stranger?

ISBN 978-1-61929-120-1
eISBN: 978-1-61929-121-8

About the Author

Originally from the Appalachian region of Eastern Tennessee, Brenda now lives in Central Texas, near Austin. She began writing in junior high school where she wrote an admittedly hokey western serial to entertain her friends. Completing her graduate studies in Eastern European history in 1971, she worked as a graphic artist, a public relations specialist for the military and a display advertising specialist until she finally had to admit that her mother might have been right and earned her teaching certification. Amazingly, she retired from teaching world history and political science in December of 2013 after thirty years. Brenda and her partner of nineteen years, Cheryl, are the parents of four occasionally grown children, as well as five grandchildren, soon to be six. Rounding out their home is a laid back blonde cat named Tudie and a three-year old Puggle named Peanut, who snores like a freight train. She may be contacted at adcockb10@yahoo.com and welcomes all comments.

OTHER YELLOW ROSE PUBLICATIONS

Brenda Adcock	Soiled Dove	978-1-935053-35-4
Brenda Adcock	The Sea Hawk	978-1-935053-10-1
Brenda Adcock	The Other Mrs. Champion	978-1-935053-46-0
Brenda Adcock	Picking Up the Pieces	978-1-61929-120-1
Brenda Adcock	The Game of Denial	978-1-61929-130-0
Brenda Adcock	In the Midnight Hour	978-1-61929-188-1
Janet Albert	Twenty-four Days	978-1-935053-16-3
Janet Albert	A Table for Two	978-1-935053-27-9
Janet Albert	Casa Parisi	978-1-61929-015-0
Georgia Beers	Thy Neighbor's Wife	1-932300-15-5
Georgia Beers	Turning the Page	978-1-932300-71-0
Rrrose Carbinela	Romance:Mild to Wild	978-1-61929-200-0
Rrrose Carbinela	Time For Love	978-1-61929-216-9
Carrie Carr	Destiny's Bridge	1-932300-11-2
Carrie Carr	Faith's Crossing	1-932300-12-0
Carrie Carr	Hope's Path	1-932300-40-6
Carrie Carr	Love's Journey	978-1-932300-65-9
Carrie Carr	Strength of the Heart	978-1-932300-81-9
Carrie Carr	The Way Things Should Be	978-1-932300-39-0
Carrie Carr	To Hold Forever	978-1-932300-21-5
Carrie Carr	Trust Our Tomorrows	978-1-61929-011-2
Carrie Carr	Piperton	978-1-935053-20-0
Carrie Carr	Something to Be Thankful For	1-932300-04-X
Carrie Carr	Diving Into the Turn	978-1-932300-54-3
Carrie Carr	Heart's Resolve	978-1-61929-051-8
Carrie Carr	Beyond Always	978-1-61929-160-7
J M Carr	Hard Lessons	978-1-61929-162-1
Sharon G. Clark	A Majestic Affair	978-1-61929-178-2
Tonie Chacon	Struck! A Titanic Love Story	978-1-61929-226-0
Sky Croft	Amazonia	978-1-61929-066-2
Sky Croft	Amazonia: An Impossible Choice	978-1-61929-180-5
Sky Croft	Mountain Rescue: The Ascent	978-1-61929-098-3
Sky Croft	Mountain Rescue: On the Edge	978-1-61929-206-2
Cronin and Foster	Blue Collar Lesbian Erotica	978-1-935053-01-9
Cronin and Foster	Women in Uniform	978-1-935053-31-6
Cronin and Foster	Women in Sports	978-1-61929-278-9
Pat Cronin	Souls' Rescue	978-1-935053-30-9
A. L. Duncan	The Gardener of Aria Manor	978-1-61929-158-4
A.L. Duncan	Secrets of Angels	978-1-61929-228-4
Verda Foster	The Gift	978-1-61929-029-7
Verda Foster	The Chosen	978-1-61929-027-3
Verda Foster	These Dreams	978-1-61929-025-9
Anna Furtado	The Heart's Desire	1-932300-32-5
Anna Furtado	The Heart's Strength	978-1-932300-93-2
Anna Furtado	The Heart's Longing	978-1-935053-26-2
Pauline George	Jess	978-1-61929-138-6

Pauline George	199 Steps To Love	978-1-61929-214-7
Melissa Good	Eye of the Storm	1-932300-13-9
Melissa Good	Hurricane Watch	978-1-935053-00-2
Melissa Good	Moving Target	978-1-61929-150-8
Melissa Good	Red Sky At Morning	978-1-932300-80-2
Melissa Good	Storm Surge: Book One	978-1-935053-28-6
Melissa Good	Storm Surge: Book Two	978-1-935053-39-2
Melissa Good	Stormy Waters	978-1-61929-082-2
Melissa Good	Thicker Than Water	1-932300-24-4
Melissa Good	Terrors of the High Seas	1-932300-45-7
Melissa Good	Tropical Storm	978-1-932300-60-4
Melissa Good	Tropical Convergence	978-1-935053-18-7
Melissa Good	Winds of Change Book One	978-1-61929-194-2
Melissa Good	Winds of Change Book Two	978-1-61929-232-1
Regina A. Hanel	Love Another Day	978-1-935053-44-6
Regina A. Hanel	WhiteDragon	978-1-61929-142-3
Regina A. Hanel	A Deeper Blue	978-1-61929-258-1
Jeanine Hoffman	Lights & Sirens	978-1-61929-114-0
Jeanine Hoffman	Strength in Numbers	978-1-61929-108-9
Jeanine Hoffman	Back Swing	978-1-61929-136-2
Maya Indigal	Until Soon	978-1-932300-31-4
Jennifer Jackson	It's Elementary	978-1-61929-084-6
Jennifer Jackson	It's Elementary, Too	978-1-61929-218-5
K. E. Lane	And, Playing the Role of Herself	978-1-932300-72-7
Helen Macpherson	Love's Redemption	978-1-935053-04-0
Kate McLachlan	Christmas Crush	978-1-61929-195-9
J. Y Morgan	Learning To Trust	978-1-932300-59-8
J. Y. Morgan	Download	978-1-932300-88-8
A. K. Naten	Turning Tides	978-1-932300-47-5
Lynne Norris	One Promise	978-1-932300-92-5
Paula Offutt	Butch Girls Can Fix Anything	978-1-932300-74-1
Surtees and Dunne	True Colours	978-1-932300-52-9
Surtees and Dunne	Many Roads to Travel	978-1-932300-55-0
Patty Schramm	Finding Gracie's Glory	978-1-61929-237-6
Vicki Stevenson	Family Affairs	978-1-932300-97-0
Vicki Stevenson	Family Values	978-1-932300-89-5
Vicki Stevenson	Family Ties	978-1-935053-03-3
Vicki Stevenson	Certain Personal Matters	978-1-935053-06-4
Vicki Stevenson	Callie's Dilemma	978-1-61929-003-7

VISIT US ONLINE AT
www.regalcrest.biz

At the Regal Crest Website You'll Find

- The latest news about forthcoming titles and new releases
- Our complete backlist of romance, mystery, thriller and adventure titles
- Information about your favorite authors
- Current bestsellers
- Media tearsheets to print and take with you when you shop
- Which books are also available as eBooks.

Regal Crest print titles are available from all progressive booksellers including numerous sources online. Our distributors are Bella Distribution and Ingram.

CPSIA information can be obtained
at www.ICGtesting.com
Printed in the USA
LVHW080127160520
655580LV00003B/449

9 781619 292109